A NEW CONSCIOUSNESS IS SPRINGING UP ACROSS AMERICA

This is the extraordinary story of one man's journey across America, viewing the continent and its people in light of the recent spiritual renaissance, and exploring the role of the channelers as vanguards of this New Age. In a remarkable spiritual odyssey into America's physical as well as spiritual landscape, Mark Cotta Vaz chronicles the real-life psychic breakthroughs taking place across the country. He discovers that tapping the wisdom of the channelers can uncover timeless and essential truths.

Are we heading for the glorious "Age of Aquarius," or the apocalyptic end of the world foretold by ancient prophecies? Can contact be made with forces from the "other side"? These and other far-reaching questions are explored in this remarkable, profoundly important account of one man's search for meaning and for . . .

SPIRIT IN THE LAND

A moving tale of the modern soul— and man's search for himself

W9-BYN-588

⊘ SIGNET (0451)

HIDDEN POWERS OF THE MIND

☐ **THE SPIRIT IN THE LAND Beyond Time and Space with America's Channelers by Mark Cotta Vaz.** One man's fabulous journey—in quest of life's meaning ... Does the body and consciousness survive death? Are the channelers true vanguards of the New Age? Are we, as the psychics say, "Millenium Bound?" The answers are here in this remarkable account of the far-reaching spiritual awakening now sweeping the country. (157176—$3.95)

☐ **TRANSCENDENTAL MEDITATION: THE SCIENCE OF BEING AND ART OF LIVING by Maharishi Mahesh Yogi.** Overcome the crises of modern life through meditation. This classic work, a source of profound knowledge and inspiration, tells how to achieve greater satisfaction, increased energy, reduced stress and sharper mental clarity in all spheres of life. (153863—$4.95)

☐ **THE POWER OF ALPHA THINKING: Miracle of the Wind by Jess Stearn.** Through his own experiences and the documented accounts of others, Jess Stearn describes the technique used to control alpha brain waves. Introduction by Dr. John Balos, Medical Director, Mental Health Unit, Glendale Adventist Hospital. (141911—$3.95)

Price slightly higher in Canada

Buy them at your local bookstore or use this convenient coupon for ordering.

NEW AMERICAN LIBRARY
P.O. Box 999, Bergenfield, New Jersey 07621

Please send me the books I have checked above. I am enclosing $_____
(please add $1.00 to this order to cover postage and handling). Send check or money order—no cash or C.O.D.'s. Prices and numbers are subject to change without notice.

Name_____

Address_____

City _____ State _____ Zip Code _____
Allow 4-6 weeks for delivery.
This offer is subject to withdrawal without notice.

SPIRIT IN THE LAND

BEYOND TIME AND SPACE
WITH AMERICA'S CHANNELERS

BY

MARK COTTA VAZ

A SIGNET BOOK

NEW AMERICAN LIBRARY

NAL BOOKS ARE AVAILABLE AT QUANTITY DISCOUNTS WHEN USED TO PROMOTE PRODUCTS OR SERVICES. FOR INFORMATION PLEASE WRITE TO PREMIUM MARKETING DIVISION, NEW AMERICAN LIBRARY, 1633 BROADWAY, NEW YORK, NEW YORK 10019.

Copyright © 1988 by Mark Cotta Vaz

All rights reserved.

SIGNET TRADEMARK REG. U.S. PAT. OFF. AND FOREIGN COUNTRIES REGISTERED TRADEMARK—MARCA REGISTRADA HECHO EN CHICAGO, U.S.A.

SIGNET, SIGNET CLASSIC, MENTOR, ONYX, PLUME, MERIDIAN and NAL BOOKS are published by NAL PENGUIN INC., 1633 Broadway, New York, New York 10019.

First Printing, December, 1988

1 2 3 4 5 6 7 8 9

PRINTED IN THE UNITED STATES OF AMERICA

Dedication

With love and admiration to my Mother and Father and my brothers and sisters: Katherine, Maria, Patrick, Peter, and Teresa.

Thanks and Acknowledgments

I'm thankful for the chance to have encountered the Spirit in the Land during the course of this project . . . Special thanks to John Silbersack, Senior Editor at New American Library, for giving me the opportunity to write this book, and for all his help and encouragement along the way . . . A hug and a high-five to my sister Katherine, herself a fine writer and editor, who showed me the ropes and told me how to climb them . . . My appreciation to Jon King, editor at *Sierra* magazine, for showing me how to master the details of writing with grace and style—and to Bill McKeown for his sage advice related to this project . . . My gratitude will also never dim for computer masters David Modjeska, Charles Jackson, and Kevin Ergil. All three in their own unselfish and unique ways helped me PC this book to final manuscript form . . . My appreciation also extends to Kirsten Olson at JFK University for her assistance—likewise to Tom and Linda Hidas for a research tip or two along the way . . . Thanks to my aunt Anne Dudley, without whom the Southwest leg of my research would not have been possible . . . My gratitude to Jan and Ted Robles for arranging an amazing Florida itinerary for me . . . I'm also thankful for the lifelong friendship and support of Patrick McCallum—if not blood brothers, we are brothers of the spirit . . . A special love wish to my late grandmother, Grace Sullivan, for her gifts of kindness . . . An eternal offering of love and appreciation to my parents for raising their kids with knowledge, wisdom, discipline, and joy (and to Clementina Vaz for being our familial avatar of fun) . . . My best wishes to Dr. Raymond Pomerleau, whose fascination with life is contagious and whose advice over the years has been an incomparable resource . . . A deep bow and acknowledgment to Choy-Li-Fut Kung Fu Grandmaster Doc-Fai Wong, my sifu and an inspiration to all his students. He taught us that gentleness is the true measure of strength . . . And my respect and appreciation to all the good folks herein who allowed me to record their encounters, visions, and dreams of the Spirit in the Land.

—Mark Vaz
San Francisco, 1988

Contents

Introduction

Part I

Contact

Part II

Channeling Zones

Part III

Down to Earth

Part IV

Millennium Bound

Introduction

For ages humankind has looked to the stars and wondered if other beings existed in the universe. Petroglyphs and legends offer the tantalizing possibility that contact with entities alien to our planet has occurred in the past.

But the view of our place in the vastness of space has changed considerably since those earlier eras and even recent centuries, when Earth was considered the center of creation.

Modern astronomical calculations knock those old creation theories off the exalted pedestal where they were once enshrined. The possibility of our making physical contact with outer space life seems remote considering the distance between cosmic neighborhoods.

Earth is one of nine planets circling our sun, and that sun is one of 250 billion other stars that make up our Milky Way galaxy. To get from one end of the galaxy to the other would take 100,000 light-years—a distance of 6 trillion miles a year. There are estimated to be hundreds of billions of other galaxies with about a million light-years separating each. And in this universe there is said to be 10 billion trillion times more empty space than stellar matter.

It has taken earthbound science thousands of years to travel some 240,000 miles to our moon.

Yet we still hope to somehow bridge the incredible distances between us and Them. We turn our tracking stations to the stars, hoping to catch some snippet of interstellar chatter. We shoot space probes out of our atmosphere on lonely journeys out of our solar system in hopes that the craft might catch the attention of some alien space voyager.

Humankind has also looked within as well as without.

Many a dreamer has wondered if the body and consciousness survives death, and what dimensions of time and space might exist in the proverbial Other Side. In this area, too, we have been frustrated: No final answer has been provided to that final question.

This desire to know our place in the universe and to make contact with forces outside ourselves may account for the phenomenon known as channeling.

Seemingly overnight Americans are claiming to be channels by which disembodied entities are communicating with us across time and space. These human channels are not maniac crazies or clerical mystics, but include housewives, psychologists, and insurance adjusters.

The idea of human beings accessing spiritual entities or realms, though, is an ancient tradition in virtually all cultures. Channels have been recognized variously through time and place as mediums, seers, or oracles.

Socrates believed that a revelation produced during a fit of madness was a divine gift. God was said to possess the ancient oracles, using their vocal cords to speak through.

Alexander the Great believed in the power of oracles. The Macedonian-born king revered his kingdom's sacred oracle of Delphi, as well as oracles in distant lands. During Alexander's long march toward the unknown reaches of Asia, and before his most pivotal battle, he sought advice from the oracle at Egypt's Temple of Ammon. When he emerged from the temple he had "received the answer which his heart desired."[1]

Cultures in our own time, including the Taoist practitioners of China, the voodoo priests of Haiti, and tribal peoples from Africa to Australia believe in some form of communion with spiritual forces.

The Tibetan people believe that a spirit minister and protector of religion known as Dorje Drakden descends from the "inconceivable mansion" at the heart of "illimitable space" to enter the host body of the state oracle during official ceremonies. To accompaniment of music, prayers, and under the watchful eyes of the Dalai Lama and his government officials, the oracle's body is said to undergo physical changes as the trance state deepens. When the host body is completely possessed, the Dalai Lama shares a silver cup of tea with the entity and can then whisper secret questions in the protector's ear and receive the whispered answers.[2]

Channeling in America is part of a homegrown spiritual movement dubbed the "New Age," ostensibly an effort to reconnect with lost spiritual values. Actress Shirley MacLaine has been touted for proclaiming the worth of channeling and other New Age pursuits in best-selling books. One of her books *Out on a Limb*, was made into a successful ABC-TV miniseries. The film also featured an actual trance channeling session.

But the great media machine that popularized channeling coast-to-coast has also provocatively zeroed in on the Gucci-clad truth seekers and celebrity gurus of the New Age. There is no denying that channeling makes for great copy and bizarre visuals. Thanks to many local and national television programs, viewers have had the opportunity to watch channels close their eyes and, after a few shudders and twitches marking their descent into a trance state, allegedly allow an otherworldly entity to manipulate their body and vocal cords to speak to the material world. There is also a banal quality to this mysticism-by-media, particularly the sight of talk-show hosts gently interrupting the channeling of otherworldly pronouncements for a very commercial break.

"Awash in our media zeitgeist we can use some divine intervention,'' opines in a 1987 *Playboy* article on channeling. ''But this being late-Eighties America, we need it repackaged—postmodernized—preferably in telegenic bytes by blow-dried shamans.''[3]

There's even been the use of channeling to contact dead celebrities, notably the late rock 'n' roll king, Elvis Presley. For those with a need to know, Elvis the Pelvis is ''not in body yet. . . . He is working on the Other Side for the benefit of the planet without the temptations of the flesh,'' a psychic reported during an exclusive channeling session for *USA Today*, August 12, 1987. Incidentally, the King had some intriguing past lives, including ancient Roman gigs as a gladiator killed by a lion in the ring and as a high official who abused his power, says the psychic.

Psychic prognostications have become an annual exercise in the pages of the nation's tabloids. Some of the predictions for 1987 that didn't pan out: A French magazine did not publish nude photos of Ayatollah Khomeini; *Wheel of Fortune* TV star Vanna White did not become governor of Puerto Rico; and at last look millions of New Yorkers were not being chased from the boroughs by armies of giant man-eating worms.

Such psychic pratfalls have given the critics and debunkers of channeling and other psychic phenomena the kind of field day not seen since master magician Harry Houdini cleaned house on fraudulent spiritualistic mediums in the 1920s. James Randi, a psychic debunker with a long-standing offer of $10,000 for anyone able to provide a provable display of supernatural powers, claims a genuine desire to meet a mystic, but doubts he'll ever be introduced. ''It's like sitting next to a chimney for thirty-five years waiting for a fat man in a red suit to appear,'' he told *Discover* magazine. ''At the end you can't say you've proven Santa Claus doesn't exist. But you can say, 'Based on my experience, I don't expect him to show up next year.' ''[4]

''I'm aware that the culture regards channeling as strange or occult,'' admits Dr. Jose Stevens, a licensed family counselor and psychologist from California who has worked with channels. "Very fundamentalist religions particularly feel channeling is the devil's work. But many people have this ability. It's just dormant. We as a society are very primitive in our ideas of what human beings can do."

The media hypes and critical snipes aside, the practice of channeling in the U.S. is growing—some estimates count one thousand practicing channels in the Los Angeles area alone. More than a need to connect with beings from Beyond is behind the phenomenon, say the true believers. They say that channeling is one of the heralding activities ushering in the Age of Aquarius, the prophesied millennium of peace and prosperity. Channels are seen as the vanguards for this coming New Age.

The New Age is said to have already begun on August 16, 1987, the date of the so-called Harmonic Convergence. Newspapers from *USA Today* to *The Wall Street Journal* did front-page pieces on the event, which was hailed as the Woodstock of the 1980s. The Convergence reportedly marked the end of a cycle of the ancient Mayan calendar and the fulfillment of ancient prohpecies. A major planetary event, pure and simple, said the New Agers. The Convergence would be marked by UFO landings, signs in the heavens, and other amazing sights.

"In 3113 B.C., the earth and sun entered a 'galactic beam' which we will leave in A.D. 2012," *USA Today* said, faithfully reporting the New Age belief. "We will hit a shift point and enter a new vibrational phase which will prepare us to leave the beam."

According to the faithful, this transition would result in global destruction unless a minimum of 144,000 people gathered in sacred spots around the planet "to resonate" the good vibrations in. On the appointed day there was a lot of hugging and mantra humming at U.S. gatherings from Mount Shasta to Central Park's Strawberry Fields. But estimates counted a mere 20,000 resonators assembled at the publicized sacred sites around the globe, considerably less than the 144,000 required for averting disaster. (Thousands more did celebrate the event at personal power places. I myself admit to sending off good vibes on the appointed day with my brother Patrick from the bleacher section of Boston's famed Fenway Park during a Red Sox game. Patrick felt it was an appropriate Convergence spot since Fenway and baseball was both sacred site and ceremony to the locals.) But despite the low turnout, the weekend passed without any apocalyptic conflagrations. Skyscrapers didn't topple and rising coastal tides didn't overwhelm seaboard cities as feared. Neither was there an outbreak of mass telepathy, a shift into the fourth dimension, or even the hoped-for flying saucer landings.

The media largely shrugged off the event as just another periodic but harmless outbreak of spiritual craziness. But there are many who attest that wondrous things did happen during the Harmonic Convergence. Some reported to me that they saw whirling lights in the sky, while others felt themselves attuned to higher spiritual frequencies.

Many psychics and channels report that we have indeed crossed the threshold to the New Age, and we will ultimately be receivers of more light energy. They say the vibratory rates of our bodies must increase to handle the spiritual speed-up now underway. We are, the psychics say, millennium-bound.

Is channeling helping to pave the way to this New Age by tapping the wisdom of spirit beings, or entities from other dimensions? Or is it a trick of the subconscious by residents of a lonely planet in the low-rent district of the Milky Way galaxy hungry for a transcendent divinity?

We will profile herein the often bizarre beings and messages coming through. Channeling controversies as well as traditions will also earn a look. This will be a journey into America's physical and psychic landscape as we seek out manifestations of the spirit in the land. As noted earlier, the accessing of otherworldly realms by paranormal means has been evidenced throughout history and culture. America is no exception. The psychic people we now call channels answered to the title "mediums" during America's Spiritualism era of the late nineteenth and early twentieth centuries.

Before embarking on our journey we should define terms, specifically what our definition of "channeling" will be.

JZ Knight, who channels Ramtha, a being from ancient Lemuria, draws a clear distinction between a medium and a channel. "Channeling is a very rare phenomenon," Knight told me. "Some of the prophets in the Bible were absolute, true channels. The spirit of God literally took them over and they would speak as the mouthpiece." Knight claims to "move aside" so that Ramtha can use her body as an instrument. She says that in such a state the full force of the energy is animating her body. When Ramtha leaves and Knight's consciousness returns, she has no recollection of the proceedings.

Some channels do not like to be possessed by an outside entity and prefer to be conscious, if meditatively detached, during a channeling session. Entities are said to manifest to a conscious channel as voices only they can hear, or as mental pictures only they experience. Such spectral communications must then be interpreted by the channel.

To simplify matters, we will define channeling as the entire range of trance or conscious communication with spirits and other disembodied entities. We will also consider the phenomenon of direct accessing of information from spiritual sources through intuition, precognition, and extrasensory perception as a form of channeling. (There is a theory that all the knowledge of the universe exits in a spiritual state called the Akashic Records, or in what Carl Jung termed the "superconscious." It is believed that during moments of intuition or precognition we directly tap into this infinite information resource. This is also believed to be the source used by spirit entities when the clients of channels ask for information on past lives or future events.)

We'll also take a tremulous look at the evil spirits and demons who allegedly prey on us mere mortals. We'll also visit the variety of channeling zones, including the dream state.

Then there is the matter of the entities themselves. Channels reveal a whole mystic pantheon of beings. This includes our personal spirit guides, the spirits of people who have died and passed on, entities that have never incarnated on earth, even beings who reside on other planets and dimensions.

We'll look at some of the information coming in from these disembodied sources, and come to some earthshaking conclusions regarding our prospects for either a glorious New Age of peace or the apocalyptic end of the world foretold by ancient prophecies.

As for myself, I confess no convivial relationship with whatever beings might reside in the void. But I have had enough brushes with paranormal phenomena to convince me that the universe is more than a grinding, clockwork machine animated by random accidents.

As a kid I grew up in a big backyard in a small town in the San Francisco Bay area. Having trees to climb, good solid earth to run on and dig into, animals to play with, and the fruits and flowers of an abundant garden to enjoy helped forge an affinity with the invisible, elemental things.

Growing up Portuguese/Irish and Catholic, I heard the stories (some related many years later) of relatives from the old country who could foretell the future, or heal through the power of God. We were also taught that God and His angels had been appearing to the good of heart throughout history. My dad always kept us aware of the need to honor the spirits of the ancestors in prayer as well as memory.

During holidays Mom stressed the spiritual, not the commercial, aspect of the holy day observance. So, for example, the day after we folded away the angel wings or the demon masks worn during Halloween trick-or-treat we would honor the saints in heaven during the feast of All Saints Day. And the day after that we would pray for the souls in purgatory during All Soul's Day.

Channeling speaks to the ageless desire to learn the place of humanity in this immeasurable universe. It is staggering news if, as psychics and mystics claim, channels have always existed whereby humankind can gain entrance to the limitless truth of spiritual dimensions.

If channeling is real, and we are now in contact with sentient beings from other dimensions, it means we are not alone in the universe. It means that although time and space may imprison our mortal bodies, our spirit and consciousness can also travel to the ends of the universe.

It's time to break on through to the Other Side. It's time to make contact.

—————— Part I ——————

Contact

1

Entities

One of the first channels I ever met was a soft-spoken young man named Richard Ryal. He had been referred to me by psychologist Jose Stevens. (I was to discover that a grapevine crisscrossed the country connecting channels, psychics, and mystics with each other. A meeting with one channeler would invariably produce new leads, names, or phone numbers of another individual who was a conduit to entities residing beyond time and space.) Ryal lived in the Marin County town of Mill Valley, just a short trip across the Golden Gate Bridge from my home in San Francisco. I called up Ryal to arrange an interview. He told me he had just returned from the "relentless and almost hopeless frontier wilderness" of Alaska, where he had been teaching an Anchorage channeling group the "energy-activation" process of opening inner consciousness to gain access to the spiritual realms.

His talk of accessing the infinite power of spiritual realms and the chance that he would be taking me one step Beyond for an encounter with spectral forces had me hooked. We set an interview date, Ryal promising that I would be able to converse with Diya, the mysterious entity that channeled through him.

As is the wont of many such channeled entities, Diya also manifested to other host channels. I would later meet Kathryn Ridall, who learned to channel Diya through Richard Ryal's energy-activation process. When talking of the entity Kathryn ascribed maleness to the overwhelming force of energy she told me would come into her whenever she channeled at will.

"Diya has compared himself to an enormous computer," said Ridall, who holds a Ph.D. in psychology from the Institute of Integral Studies in San Francisco. "Once, Diya told me, 'Imagine sitting in a drive-in movie theater surrounded by thousands and thousands of screens all being viewed simultaneously—that is my reality.'"

Richard Ryal's apprenticeship with the spirits began in 1976 during a summer stay in the woods of central Massachusetts. During solitary walks he had sensed invisible, intelligent presences around him. Ryal recognized the presences as spirit entities and developed the ability to contact and communicate with them at will.

Throughout that experience he had also sensed a powerful spirit that, while staying in the background, pervaded his awareness by sheer force of power. Ryal began to train himself to reach out and communicate with this powerful entity. By 1982 Ryal successfully made contact and began channeling at will the being known as Diya.

When I met Richard Ryal he made it clear to me that he was seeking not only contact, but a merging of consciousness with Diya. Ryal sheepishly admitted that the melding had its disadvantages: His phone had been disconnected because he'd forgotten to pay the bill, one of a number of difficulties he was experiencing with "linear reality." I asked him what would happen if he actually completed his anticipated merging with the entity.

"Everything," he calmly replied during our talk in his living room. "More and more it happens. I experience a significant amount of that merging now. I found out it's possible to generate these states out of natural, pure life-force energy. I resonate energy with Diya. I experience all the cells of my body vibrating at a new state. From there I try to move with Diya to the area of greatest breakthrough to see what can be transformed. When we understand that we can move from points of conscious energy, we can move from ego-center to merging consciousness.''

"It sounds like you're giving yourself up," I observed as Ryal began setting up his tape machine to record the channeling that was about to begin.

"It won't change what I am." He shrugged. "I'll just meet and merge consciousness on Diya's level. You see, most people relate with guides as we're here and they're out there. Diya's point is we're all in this together as part of personal and planetary transformation.''

Soon Ryal was ready to channel. Like many channels he claimed he could achieve that state at will. He turned on the tape recorder to preserve the session, closed his eyes, and began to relax into a light trance state. Before he went under, he told me Diya would enter into him and use his vocal cords to communicate with me.

After a few moments Ryal began channeling:

"Welcome. I am Diya, and I ask you to join me in honoring the spirit that brings us together. Understand that each individual must keep personal integrity while opening up more and more to the consciousness of the group mind. The next area of human evolution will center in the back of the brain where it interlocks with the spinal column. This is the doorway to the group mind, the primary telepathic gate at this time.

"Be aware that there are beings who are not incarnate on your planet that you have a direct relationship with. We can communicate with you and you can communicate with us. But under the law of relationships, if guides work with you, it's reciprocal—you are working with guides.''

"Why don't you manifest yourself to all humans so they can believe you exist?" I asked.

"There are forms of life superior, as well as inferior, to yours, if you must use a scale of measurement," the soft, slow Diya voice assured me. "The universe is so full of life. There has been, and will continue to be, contact. But human beings are fearful of contact. One does not exactly feel invited to such a place of hostility.''

"How are you merging with Richard?'' I asked, looking at Richard seated across from me.

"With Richard we work primarily on the area of simultaneous communication. We attune our consciousness to a harmonious vibration, like two musical notes played together with a specific harmony. I have never incarnated, and it is not my intent to incarnate, on your planet. Yet part of my work with your planet includes a certain level of relationship with the human species. Therefore, I'm using Richard, and a few others, to familiarize themselves with qualities of consciousness on other planes so that they can open up the capacities of others to these dimensions.''

"What is the nature of those planes where you take Richard?''

"Where I take him are typically areas of reality where I worked with him a great deal before he incarnated in his present identity. Richard inhabits energy bodies on these different realities. Events arise as expansions in the environment, and the environment is the mind in which he is experiencing them. Even now as I talk through him there is a part of him that is extended into these realities. It is easier for me to enter through his consciousness [at those points] to speak To you. Here the environment seems to move through you and you seem to move through the environment. We generate evolutions in these states to let him know he is part of the energy consciousness that permeates the entire universe.

"His ego must be broken down in different ways, so his work is not an expression of his point of view but of the possibilities everyone can experience from their own points of view.''

"Won't that make it difficult for him to live on this Earth plane?''

"Yes. But the difficulties are not permanent. It is

part of the challenge—the nature by which your planet is known to us.

"Beings in every level are struggling to develop. That's why it's absolutely crucial to keep your sense of integrity. Many beings would offer themselves as guides who have neither the wisdom or the compassion to help you, but are drawn to you simply by fascination, or a desire for physical experience not available to them.

"Don't be impressed by guides. If you can put it to use, then it's good, but you're not here to be my disciple. All beings must take responsibility for their actions. Just because a being is spiritual energy doesn't guarantee anything at all about them. It doesn't necessarily even make them interesting. Compassion must be the primary focus, the realization that we're all manifestations of the same spirit. You're incarnated so that you can be fulfilled.

"The transformation of many planets, many species, and planes of reality are being coordinated with yours. That is why I'm speaking to you. We're all part of this. Find your significance and sense of purpose, but you must have integrity; do not just seek the romance of multidimensional experience. Be open to all that is possible, for when you honor yourself you honor the entire universe."

With that, the Diya voice faded and Richard Ryal blearily opened his eyes.

One group attempting to collect and organize channeled information is the Michael Foundation. The foundation's headquarters are located in a quiet residential neighborhood in Orinda, California. In the converted house are stored hundreds of taped-recorded communications from the entity known as Michael—or transmissions, as the channeled material is referred to at the foundation.

Through the transmissions the entity has revealed itself to be an energy composed of 1,050 individual essences that had once been incarnated on earth. The

Michael Teachings claim the entity prefers to work with small groups during pivotal periods in human and planetary evolution. Michael says it has taught groups in pre-fall Rome to telepathically channel visual information.

Modern-day contact by Michael was made through ouija board sessions in the 1960s, arriving just in time for the New Age shift in planetary consciousness.

Michael adherents use the Chinese word *Tao* to describe an infinite god being interested in "being things." In the Michael cosmology, the Tao, seeking to know itself, removes a part of its infinite whole and sends it out through the levels of existence. When that part lands at the farthest point, it has reached the place of total forgetting—Earth. Here, on a planet of separation and fragmentation, the Tao must discover its nature and begin the journey back to the original whole.

"It's a very rich, colorful game," comments psychologist Dr. Jose Stevens. "The Earth is very much like an amusement park with a lot of rides, choices, extremes of pleasure and pain. To play the game of Earth you need a body. To get the richest and most varied experience it's impossible to use one body and one lifetime, so one has to incarnate.

"Channeling is a way for us who incarnate in physical form to communicate with beings who are a little closer to remembering they are the Tao."

According to the Michael teachings, each earthly incarnation leads to a maturing of the individual soul. When masses of maturing souls incarnate on the planet simultaneously there is the opportunity for major shifts in individual and planetary consciousness. Such a shift, from the me-first attitude of "baby" and "infant" souls to a "mature-soul cycle" is coming, according to Michael students.

Mark Thomas, a news director for a San Francisco Bay area radio station, has been a conscious channel of the Michael entity since 1984. Thomas was attracted to channeling by a lifetime interest in the paranormal. With practice he began to control the exhausting sensation of "amazing amounts of outside energy ripping through" his body. When I met him, I asked him to channel for me.

Thomas smiled, sat erect against his straight-back chair, rubbed his eyes, closed them, and prepared to bring through the entity known as Michael. He was silent, his head drooping slightly forward. Abruptly he snapped back to attention, his eyes open and glazed over.

"Good evening," he said, in a slow, measured intonation of his normal voice. To another observer in the room it might have seemed as if the conversation had barely missed a beat.

"Earth has been a kind of experiment," Thomas began, allegedly translating the direct messages from Michael that were coming into his head. "A lot of things are being discovered and observed here. One is what happens on a planet seeded with people who are basically in their history very warlike and who, at some point, have experiences of other beings to give them a sense of Oneness.

"There was a discussion made that they [Earth beings] have a more individual consciousness, a feeling of being separate from others around them."

"Who made this decision?" I asked.

"It was a decision by the caretakers of that race of people on Earth. Long, long ago humans were seeded on this planet. Other people brought them here, worked with them for a time, and then left. But humans are not guinea pigs. Our perception of life is integrated wholeness."

"Can you describe what it's like where you are?"

"It's a place where you create out of your consciousness whatever it is that you need. But [like you] we're trying to get a larger conception of what it's all about. There are beings on planes above us. All seek the harmony. Each person has a memory of that harmony. We seek that merging, too."

The Michael voice mentioned a coming global soul

shift, but allowed for the existence at all times of "infinite parallel possibilities" and dimensions. The voice described a parallel earth that had too many paranoid baby-soul fingers on the triggers of cataclysmic weapons. On October 22, 1985, that parallel earth devastated itself in an apocalyptic war, the Michael voice claimed.

The voice, ready to depart, predicted that channeling would become a significant form of communication within the next half century. But extraordinary forms of communication were evidently not without earthly precedent.

"There used to be the experience on your planet of mass dreaming," the voice recalled. "A race of people dreamed, and all contributed parts, to a single dream. In that dreaming state they worked through and processed feelings they had. Dreams are about meeting people. In Atlantis there was some of this, and at other points of human development. In the mature-soul cycle it'll happen more. You are still learning and growing. You are held in this universe in love and life. More balance is coming."

The voice stopped. Mark Thomas rubbed his eyes.

"Sometimes I wish my mouth could move as fast as the information coming in." He smiled. "I get pictures in my head, a rush of images. I'm visually oriented so the information comes in that way.

"You know, when you asked Michael what it was like where they exist, I got a feeling for the first time of what it really is like!"

He let that settle in and reflected further.

"They have a sense of humor watching us, like parents watching a baby stumble at it's learning to walk."

"When you communicate with spirits, it's something you feel, you feel the energy," observes Sun Bear, a medicine man of the Bear tribe of Washington state. "You feel the power and you're able to communicate with it because it's one with you and you're a part of it. It's an intelligent exchange.

''But I'm not beating down the doors of heaven every day trying to have instant communication with the Great Spirit. I go along for days when I'm just eating and sleeping and living and alive and that's fine, too. And then when I need something powerful to happen, that's what I'm going to be praying for.''

Then there are those who feel channeling can provide an unprecedented information source to assist us in our more scientific pursuits.

''All knowledge is out there: past, present, future, and all possibility,'' observes Dr. William Kautz, director of the Center for Applied Intuition. ''To learn how to tap into it is a process of learning how to say yes instead of no, of getting rid of fears instead of repressing them, of being open and vulnerable, just letting life energy flow through you without blocking it. It's one of the most powerful things that can happen to you.''

Psychics maintain that everyone is born with a spiritual nature, but we too often suppress these natural abilities.

Others are born with psychic abilities and spiritual insights too powerful to ignore.

June Bowermaster, a medium from Cassadaga, Florida, gave her first lecture on reincarnation at the age of five. (Her German-Lutheran mother wasn't thrilled, but her Scot-Irish-Indian father was more supportive.) Among her psychic abilities as a young girl was a talent for reading a person's emotional state by the color of their aura. ''All of a sudden it dawned on me that not everybody was seeing what I was seeing,'' June says. ''So I learned to shut up.''

Patricia Diegel, a psychic working in Sedona, Arizona, remembers a strong precognitive streak as a young girl. In the course of doing one of her household chores she discovered that instead of struggling to carry the five-gallon pails of fresh milk from the barn to her house, she could simply levitate the buckets. An incredulous neighbor witnessed the feat one day and complained to Patricia's mother. After a good scolding she stopped levitating things.

Chris Griscom, director of the Light Institute, a New Age center in New Mexico, speaks for most psychic prodigies when she admits: "People who grow up having insights that other people don't have—it's rough. It was not pleasant. It wasn't great and magical in terms of the outside world. It was great and magical for the inside of me. But then I had to stuff it.

"People saw me as odd. Rocks used to speak and there were entities all over the place, and I used to get out of my body to fly all over.

"One time, when I was nine years old, I told a friend, 'I'm going to visit you tonight when you're sleeping.' I was showing off a bit. And I did. I just went out of my body to his bedroom and stood at the bed. The kid woke up and of course he was scared. He didn't want to play with me anymore. I didn't know. It was normal to me."

Gay Luce, who now conducts workshops in the ancient mystery-school traditions, also kept her transcendent light under wraps for a while. But an inner satisfaction that there was an entire dimension of reality behind "the plane of ordinary life" gave her comfort. "I'd experience the light level going up a thousandfold and all of a sudden I'd be put into what I guess is *samadhi* [a state of advanced enlightenment]," she recalls. "I'd feel like I was flowing out into everything and everything was flowing into me. I was in bliss just walking the dog down a busy street in New York City. I'd just want to stop wherever I was and appreciate it, not move for an hour or so. People thought that was a little strange. It was like falling in love with the sky or the earth."

There are three channels in particular who have been very public, and sometimes controversial, figures in the New Age movement: Jach Pursel, who channels an entity known as Lazaris; Kevin Ryerson, who welcomes Spirit; and JZ Knight, who hosts Ramtha. All three conduct personal consultations in which clients can ask the entities for insight and guidance on their past lives, present path, and future prospects. The three also present their own programs, seminars, and weekend retreats. When they speak at large New Age gatherings, they draw thousands. All three claim to move aside while in trance, allowing the entity to animate their body and use their vocal cords.

Let's consider each of them and the entities they host. . . .

Before Jach Pursel began channeling Lazaris he was a successful insurance adjuster. His first encounter with the entity was at a Ramada Inn in Bloomington, Illinois. Pursel was trying to unwind in his hotel room after a long day of business meetings. He had never had the discipline for meditation, although he had made some fitful attempts at practicing regularly. But that fateful night he was so tired he thought a contemplative state would be an ideal way to relax.

As he concentrated on his breathing he felt himself drifting deeper and deeper into an inner realm he had never dreamed of. "All of a sudden, vivid imagery began," Pursel would later explain in a 1987 interview. "It was early evening. Dense forest, somewhat dark. I was walking along a path and came to a brook, very aware of stones, the water bouncing over them, the sounds. I scooped up the water and splashed it over my face. I turned around and saw a log cabin with a thatched roof nestled in the trees, smoke coming out of the chimney, a bright light on inside, the door slightly ajar. I walked up the steps, opened the door, and went in. A man dressed in white robes was standing next to a counter; behind him was a blackboard and to the side a fire lit in a fireplace. I asked him his name and he said, 'Lazaris.' Then he started talking about all kinds of things."[1]

The entity revealed in later sessions that it was actually a being of limitless intelligence and consciousness that had never manifested in physical form. The entity also channeled exclusively through Pursel (duly noted on Lazaris products and promotional material).

In 1976 Jach and his wife Peny decided to forgo the promising insurance career and devote more time to channeling. Jach was already booking trance-channeling sessions for small groups and individuals. In a few years Lazaris was channeling for people from all over the world (the bulk of Pursel's appointments are conducted through telephone-channeling sessions). There would also be a sizable Lazaris following in the film industry, including actor Michael York and television star Sharon Gless.

Concept Synergy, a California-based company, was formed to handle the tapes, videos, and other business generated by the accumulating Lazaris teachings. (Videos of several hours in length deal with such channeled teachings as "Personal Power & Beyond," "The Secret of Manifesting What You Want," and "The Future: How to Create It." Audio tapes provide meditations to help one over the rough spots in spiritual growth and include "Happiness/Peace" and "Handling Menstruation.")

But Jach/Lazaris didn't make a national media splash until a 1986 channeling session on the Merv Griffin TV show. It was the inauguration of celebrity mysticism when Merv pointed out, "Many of our top stars are now consulting not Jach but the entity." And then, on national television, Jach shut his eyes and Lazaris came in. . . .

Lazaris workshop tours have covered the country. In 1987–88 alone, Pursel channeled the entity to packed houses in Los Angeles, San Francisco, Seattle, Denver, Chicago, Kansas City, Atlanta, New Orleans, Philadelphia, and other cities.

Lazaris followers are true believers, confident that their disembodied entity of choice has a line on an absolute truth not found in other channels. As an outsider I noticed an evident distrust of other channeled information. In a Concept Synergy information release describing a run of tapes known as the Goddess Series, it's noted: "As the New Age emerges, so the Goddess steps forth from the fog of our prejudice and arrogance. There will be many who will twist and misrepresent this phenomenon. *Many will prey upon our spiritual hunger* to once again know the Goddess. Lazaris will complete this series so that each of us can honestly develop our personal relationship with the Goddess. *Without the societal pollution that would otherwise be there.*" [Emphasis added.]

During a weekend workshop I attended in San Francisco it became clear why Lazaris inspired such a loyal following. Unlike other channels there is an unusual personalizing of the material. The Lazaris teaching not only recognizes individual divinity, but stresses the unlimited potential of group energy. It is an amazing union of narcissism and altruism.

Over and over the voice of the entity speaking through a tranced-out Pursel applauded the assembled for being the "map makers, the visionaries" of the New Age. "You're involved in changing the future . . . there are no prerequisites to growth. When you're ready, you're ready. You're all here for you," Lazaris said.

Lazaris even promised to "come sit with you, be with you" during meditative sessions known as "blendings."

During a blending the lights dim and Pursel/Lazaris, seated on a simple stage, asks everyone to close their eyes. A tape of synthesized New Age music accompanies Lazaris's gentle exhortations to feel the energy being channeled out to everyone. And then Lazaris starts calling out first names, giving bits of advice and encouragement to [presumably] specific people in the audience. ("John, learn to love yourself more. Mary, learn to slow down and go easy. . . .") Then Lazaris calls for all to open their eyes, the music stops, and the lights come on.

The Lazaris teachings are the perfect salve for any lonely-planet blues. According to the entity, each person has the power of free will and the ability to create his or her own reality. There exists an "all that is," a God/Goddess force that loves you and wants you to grow through love and laughter and not through sorrow or pain. In the Lazaris view, Earth is not the low-rent district of the universe. Here, humans are highly evolved spiritual beings with the capacity for infinite love.

At the conclusion of a weekend seminar the audience, one by one walks up to the stage where Pursel/Lazaris sits. It is the opportunity for a momentary embrace between an individual and Pursel's Lazaris-animated form. Perhaps a short, whispered conversation will be exchanged before Pursel/Lazaris reaches into a basket draped with blue velvet, and pulls out and presents a crystal personally charged for the supplicant.

When they turn away, the crystals clutched close to their hearts, many wear smiles of bliss and shed tears of joy.

When Ramtha of Lemuria last strode upon the Earth plane, he conquered three quarters of the known world on a march lasting sixty-three years. But the great warrior would maintain that the greatest conquest he ever made was of himself. At the end of his days, once he had learned to love himself and embrace life, he was taken up by a great wind into Forever, in full view of his people.

The warrior wouldn't return to earth until 1977, 35,000 years later. It was then that Ramtha, all nine feet of him, appeared in the kitchen doorway of JZ Knight.

Knight, the former Tacoma, Washington, housewife and cable-TV executive, claims the ancient warrior appeared to her eyes alone in such unlikely venues as the Safeway supermarket frozen-food section.

Since then, Knight has been channeling the entity. Knight is a petite, pretty blonde, but when she goes into her meditation, moves aside, and allows Ramtha in, she moves like a wrestler stalking an opponent.

When Knight/Ramtha is seated, the entity delivers the talk in a booming baritone.

But when the Ram (as Ramtha is affectionately called) comes in, where exactly does Knight move aside to?

"I go to a light force, I go into that space," Knight told me. "When I pray I get aligned with myself, very peaceful. And it's like a flash and you're traveling down a—I want to say tunnel because you have the sense that there are sides to it, but you don't see any sides, and there's this whistling or ringing sound and you just go to it and the closer you get to it the more you want to be there. It's like an all-loving, magnetic presence.

"It isn't even a trance. I haven't even found the proper term [to describe it]. It's like you're gone. You die.

"And then I'll wake up and it's five hours later. There's just no memory there.

"The energy of Ramtha is an overlay of light. He utilizes the body to where you get absolute clarity and purity of the individual. You get the full thrust of the personified entity."

She admits that the first six months with Ramtha were terrifying. Being jerked out of her consciousness into a light-force tunnel so her body could be used by an ancient warrior spirit was traumatic. "But as I came to understand it, I realized I'd died a thousand deaths," Knight says. "As a result of this, I'm not afraid to die. I understand what it is, what that feels like, the crossing-over of that."

It's been an admittedly tumultuous decade for JZ and the Ram. There was the gossipy publicity given the extravagant luxury of her $1.5-million mansion in Yelm, Washington. A serious scandal ensued when it was reported that the Ram had directed some of his wealthier followers to purchase valuable Arabian horses from Knight's own stables.

There were allegations that Knight was a hoax. Some critics said she had once been a pure channel, but the entity had long since vacated the premises and JZ was playacting.

There was some controversy in Ramtha circles regarding the entity's prediction of catastrophic Earth changes. Ramtha was reportedly telling his followers across the country to pull up stakes and move to the Northwest to escape the coming tribulations. Hundreds have made the move to Ramtha-designated safe areas. Some can afford it, such as the millionaire Wyoming restaurateur who sold his chain of hamburger places to finance a move to rural northern California. There he is building a pyramid-shaped house to presumably wait out the coming disasters in comfort and spiritual equanimity.

Others felt the Earth-change talk was a contradiction of Ramtha's basic message of personal sovereignty and acknowledgment of God within. For many such Ramtha students it was a time of crisis and soul-searching. "When Ramtha said I had to move to the Northwest and butcher my cattle and live off the land—come on, man, I was raised in the suburbs!" Kathleen, a San Francisco Ramtha student, exclaimed to me. She felt the basic message had been subverted by the fear and paranoia surrounding the Earth-change talk. Just the year before she had told me her life had been changed by the Ramtha teachings. Now she was planning on giving away her Ramtha books and tapes. They no longer held any interest for her. "It just seemed like things changed," Kathleen said. "It's like I used to have this great friend named Ramtha. And now—it's like an old boyfriend. Did I just grow out of it? I don't think it's that simple."

I talked with Knight when she and Jeff, her third husband, arrived in San Francisco one night. The following morning JZ was a guest on a popular local TV talk show. I was invited to meet with her the night before in their hotel suite. In their suite Jeff, a professional trainer and breeder of Arabian show horses, was stretched out on the double bed, the TV turned on to a Monday night football game that held his interest.

JZ sat at a little table in front of a picture-perfect window view of San Francisco's skyline. Ramtha, unfortunately, did not drop by.

"Ramtha's first teaching was 'Behold the God the Father and Mother within you,' " she explained. "Ramtha created the term, 'You are creators of your own reality.' Now it's sort of a password of New Age people.

"You create your own reality. The world is how you perceive it. You have choices. You can either be tolerant or intolerant. You can have reverence or irreverence. You can find joy or seek sadness.

"Bringing that teaching home is we have the option to change. That's why the point is we're divine. Like Jesus said, 'What is within me is within you.' Ramtha brought that home to people."

I asked Knight why she and the Ram were such public figures. Clearly the booming trade in Ramtha seminars, books, videos, workshops, special events, and her own personal fame marked a long road from her Tacoma housewife days. But had it been a fair exchange considering the battering she had taken in the press?

"I'm very reluctant [about being in the media]. I've never advertised Ramtha Dialogues, never called up a television show and said, 'Hey, I've got this really spiffy entity I'd like to bring on the show.' I've never done any of that. I don't want to do TV shows. I did my book tour because that was in the contract when I wrote my autobiography." (Her book, *A State of Mind,* was published in 1987 by Warner Books.)

"Ramtha's message is not for small groups," Knight said. "It's for everyone who wants to hear. I think it's without borders. For ten years there was word of mouth about this teacher. Here was a tremendously powerful, loving teacher who had the power to move mountains, who was affecting people's lives and bringing them back to a sense of order of God within them. And that knowledge, in ten years, has spread everywhere, and people made the choice of whether to come or not."

Knight says she has channeled the entity for enthusiastic gatherings of Australian aborigines. Ramtha tapes are also said to play in Buddhist monasteries in Japan, and bootleg Ramtha tapes and videos are popular in the Soviet Union.

But it is in the United States where the Ramtha teachings are serving the greatest need.

According to Knight, "Mystical Americans are coming out of the closet." There is a growing necessity to understand psychic experiences and "not see it in superstitious idiocy," she says. "Traditional science, the media, even religion can't answer these experiences, or ridicules the mystical American as a fool or occultist. So into that vacuum of need comes channeling."

The Ramtha message is that all a person needs to experience spiritual truth is to simply recognize God within. You don't need gurus, or followers, crystals, prayer mats, meditation, or years of spiritual training. But despite Knight's satisfaction with the propagation of the Ramtha message, ten years in the New Age limelight has convinced her to ease off her hectic channeling pace.

"It's hard to love the human race, only because you see so much pain and sorrow, and you endeavor to help someone and they're suspicious of you or hate you if you help them. It still hurts me in a sense to see how hard people can be on people.

"Ramtha said he would be teaching his last teaching through May of 1988. And [Ramtha] will continue to do this, but not as intently as the past ten years."

I asked about the Earth-change controversy, and Knight explained that the Ram was merely telling people that if they made the choice to live on an active earthquake fault, they might have to accept the consequences of a quake. I explained that Ramtha appeared to be predicting disaster across the board, regardless of the area. I never satisfactorily resolved that question with Knight.

I mentioned to her my friend Kathleen's dissatisfac-

tion with the being she had once felt was a friend.
"When a person says Ramtha changed their life, that's
a great statement." Knight smiled. "If her relationship with Ramtha is dimming on the rose, it should.
Because what is important is that life which should be
changed. That's why there isn't a guru or followers.
The message is for the person."

As I prepared to leave, the sound of sirens wailing
in the streets below rose up like the heralds of strange
angels. JZ Knight's final words to me were:

"The message is this: It's within you. And all you
have to do is ask."

It was a quizzical moment for the New Age movement when actress Shirley MacLaine, along with the
producer and director of the ABC-TV miniseries ad-
aptation of her best-selling *Out on a Limb,* had an
important pre-shoot talk with spirit beings.

The book had featured her first encounter with channel Kevin Ryerson. During a session at MacLaine's
Malibu beach house Ryerson had tranced out and
brought in John, a scholar of the Essenes who had
lived at the time of Christ, and Tom McPherson, whose
last earthly tenure was with the Shakespearean crowd
of the old Globe Theatre.

For that authentic touch, it was decided that Ryerson
would play himself, actually going into trance and
channeling his spirit entities on camera. If the spirits
were to appear, their permission would have to be secured.

So MacLaine and her producer and director sat
across from Ryerson, watching as he closed his eyes,
made a few shuddering movements of his body, and
began to channel through the voices of John and Mc-
Pherson. The entities, satisfied that the purpose of the
film was a good one, agreed to participate.

Ryerson would later recollect with a smile the fascinating questions that came up during the filming.
Should screen credits be given to disembodied enti-

ties? Did spirits appearing in a film have to fulfill union obligations and join the Screen Actor's Guild?

John and McPherson are only two of a host of disembodied entities Ryerson collectively calls "Spirit." Others include Obadiah, a Haitian herbalist who lived one hundred fifty years ago; Anton Re, a Nubian man hailing from ancient Egypt; and Japu, a Buddhist monk who resided in the Indus Valley during his last earthly incarnation thousands of years ago.

Of all the high-profile channels, Ryerson appears the most intrigued with the possibilities of using channeling to obtain information and insights useful to society. He has done extensive work with Dr. William Kautz's Center for Applied Intuition, where channeled information is used to develop new inquiries into history, science, business, and medicine. A significant inspiration for Ryerson has been Edgar Cayce, whom he considers one of the greatest information resources of this or any other century.

"The hard sciences try to sweep psychic phenomena under the rug, but there's been too much proven paranormal research," Ryerson says. "Take biofeedback, where you're taught to get voluntary control of heartbeat, blood flow, and other supposedly involuntary actions of the body. We send astronauts to the moon using biofeedback—but Indian yogis have been using it for thousands of years!

"Basically, in dealing with spirit communications, you are being asked to entertain one simple thought: The human personality, the human consciousness, can survive independent of the physical body. Telepathic, near-death, and out-of-the-body experiences provide strong evidence for this."

Ryerson's childhood was full of interest in the psychic. At the age of twenty-two he joined a meditation group based on the teachings of Edgar Cayce. During one deep meditation he experienced a "spontaneous channeling state."

During that first trance the entity John began speaking through. A member of the meditation group had a tape recorder handy and recorded nearly twenty minutes of discourse as the entity introduced himself, described the historical time period of his last incarnation, and provided some past-life information for a few of the assembled. Ryerson did not remember a word of it when he came back to his normal consciousness.

"The guides and teachers who speak through me are primarily energy, and I act not unlike a human telephone or receiver," he says. "Through me people can attune to frequencies or energy beings called Tom Mc-Pherson, Obadiah, and John, who can then divulge to them information, based on their particular inquiry, that will help them facilitate their own life goals.

"These beings aren't limited, as we are, to the five physical senses. They are able to see us in terms of the energy we put out, energy that carries information much as a radio does. They can see these sources of information, whether they're from past lives or from events in this lifetime, and they even have the ability to slide up the time line to predict events before they happen. Again, we are limited to the narrow window of our five physical senses, whereas they have an extrasensory perception that allows them to see our lives in a broader spiritual context."

I had a personal consultation with Ryerson/Spirit in 1986. It was my first encounter with a channeled entity. Janet Murai, a friend of mine, had raved about her visits to Ryerson and I became intrigued. "When I went into my appointment with Kevin, I had no idea of what to expect," she had told me. "It was raining outside on a very noisy street when I went into his office. But inside the channeling room I knew what God was. I lost touch of where I was, of the street sounds, of time."

When the time for my appointment came, I met Ryerson at his "office," actually his San Francisco apartment. We sat in the channeling room Janet had described to me. The walls were painted in soft colors. There were two chairs, a table, and a case with a clock and a tape-recording machine. We sat in straight-back chairs facing each other. Ryerson popped in a tape to record the session and put the machine on PAUSE. He then explained that what I was about to experience was not a nine-to-five reality but an adventure.

He turned on the tape recorder, said good-bye, and closed his eyes. His body began the shuddering fit that preceded the entrance of the entities. Just before the spirits came through, I felt the meditative silence of the room. The ticking of a clock filled the moment before Ryerson opened his mouth to speak with a spir-it's tongue. . . .

For three days after the session I experienced a kind of blissful, light-headed feeling. It was a sense of floating through things, but alert and turned on. Whatever the energy was, it wore off after the third day, like a businessman's holiday tan. It was strange after such a one-on-one conversation with Spirit to see Ryerson on TV movies, or reading about him in national magazines.

The aura of celebrity attendant to channels such as Pursel, Knight, and Ryerson was often uncomfortable to them. Ryerson once described how he was sometimes recognized and approached in public with an awed reverence by clients who confused him with the spiritual entities.

I saw Ryerson again in 1987 at a New Age Expo in San Francisco, but this time it was from afar. Since the airing of *Out on a Limb,* Ryerson had been a hot ticket on the New Age circuit. We waited for the auditorium doors to open in a line that curled like a mandala around the lobby of the convention center.

Author George Leonard, who had just finished making a presentation in an adjacent room, walked up to me and asked what the line was all about. I told him we were waiting to get in to see channel Kevin Ryerson. Leonard shook his head. He muttered words to the effect that a channeling circus wasn't what the New Age was all about. Everyone can do it themselves, he said, and walked off. The doors opened and we went in.

The space inside the amphitheater was a combination airplane hangar, soundstage, and assembly hall for the conducting of some Orwellian Big Brother vision. Thousands of folding chairs were lined up in neat rows. The chairs all faced a giant raised stage adorned with plants and with two comfortable chairs center stage. Banks of powerful lights illuminated the stage, which was flanked on either side by giant video screens to project the images of Ryerson and television personality Joyce DeWitt who was there to "share my very special friend."

There were some technical difficulties in opening the proceedings, followed by New Agers in the back rows interrupting DeWitt's introduction with shouts of "We can't hear you." By the end of the evening, Ryerson was channeling and Tom McPherson was coming through. His old days with the Globe Theatre crowd served him in good stead as he brought Irish wit and showmanship to the multitudes. It was entertaining.

During the final question-and-answer period someone asked where to go to escape the impending global catastrophies. McPherson cooled his banter and said, in simplicity itself, that people shouldn't run but stand and learn how to love more, to cultivate a compassionate nature.

At the conclusion there was a rush for the exits. It had been a long program. By the time Ryerson had performed the awaited channeling and the final Q & A had been asked and answered it was near midnight.

Some of the high-profile channeling has the feel of spectacle rather than spirituality about it. Channeling may be filling a vacuum of spiritual need, as JZ Knight noted, but it is also a system without a structure, a field without parameters. Unlike other cultural organizations of religious belief, which long ago developed ways to effectively assimilate spiritual truths, there is often an anything-goes atmosphere surrounding many New Age channeling beliefs.

But Americans don't have to journey to Mecca or search for a Hindu savant in India to learn how to effectively access and harness spiritual energy and truth. Native American tribal peoples have been channeling spiritual entities and energy for hundreds of years.

It would do well to remember those tribal spiritual traditions that preceded all others on this continent. Remember back to those days when all could feel, without cynicism or conflict, the spirit in the land. . . .

2

Whispers from the Darkness

The Indian sweat lodge ceremony is an ancient method for contacting the spirit world. To enter the lodge, a human shows respect for the four-legged relations by crawling through the entrance like an animal entering its den. From a fire being tended outside the lodge are brought the sacred stones that have been heated to a red-hot pitch. The rocks are placed in a pit that has been dug in the center of the lodge. When water is poured onto the hot stones, the sizzle and steam fills the small space of the lodge with the heat of purification. And then prayers are offered up to the Great Spirit.

Every act attendant to the main ceremony is considered sacred. In the sweat ceremony, the building of the lodge itself is part of an ongoing prayer to the Great Spirit. The skeletal form of the lodge is constructed from twelve, or sometimes sixteen, white willow trees, representing the bones of the ancestors who have died and gone to live closer to the Great Spirit. The willows are bent into a beehive shape, and the sticks forming a square at the top represent the sacred four directions. A covering of tarp, blankets, or quilts is then laid over the form to complete the lodge. When finished, the entire construct traditionally stands no higher than a man's ribs. In the center of the lodge, a pit is then dug to serve as the altar for the heated rocks.

The dirt scooped out to form the altar is used to

form a pathway leading through the entrance and out
to a little altar mound that sits between the lodge and
the sacred fire. It is along this pathway that the spirits
walk to join those in the lodge.

The gathering of the rocks is another sacred task.
They must be chosen with care. The stones must be
able to withstand the sacred fire without crumbling or
bursting. The sticks for the sacred fire of no end are
stacked in a tepee shape over the stones. Once red-hot
the rocks will come alive as the power of the sun, the
Great Spirit's breath of life.

The leader of the ceremony sits at the inner entrance
to see that the rocks are carefully brought in, that sage
and sweet grass are there to sprinkle on the rocks, that
the sacred pipe is ready. The water is brought in to
pour on the stones, and there will usually be a drum
beaten during the singing and chanting.

When all is ready, the flap serving as a door is pulled
down over the entrance, and the tiny lodge becomes a
world of infinite dimensions. In that potentially claustrophobic, suffocating darkness one encounters their
own fears and ignorance. The water is poured on the
rocks and the steam immediately causes those within
to sweat. The prayers and drums begin calling to the
Great Spirit and all "the relations" of life. Before the
rite is over, the doorway will be opened four times,
completing four rounds in honor of the four directions.
During each round prayers are offered up to the universe, rising up like great winged birds.

Whatever fear is encountered, or manifestation of
spirit, or release of emotions experienced, all the participants will have sweated a little bit of their flesh
upon the Mother Earth, and opened their spiritual nature to the Great Spirit.[1]

In the Native American tradition, the shaman or
medicine man is particularly adept at accessing the
forces of the spirit world through the sweat lodge and
other rituals. ("Medicine man" is a clumsy Anglo
term for this high spiritual calling.)

Some medicine men are close to the thunder beings

who provide the rain and thunder. Some medicine men are great healers and can suck a person's disease out of their flesh or entreat the assistance of spirits to effect a cure. Other medicine people experience powerful visions that can shape their tribe's future course.

Lame Deer, a Lakota Sioux medicine man of the twentieth century, has described an ancient channeling ceremony known as *yuwipi*. A medicine man wrapped like a mummy in a blanket enables spirits to speak through to answer the needs of those who have called the meeting. The ceremony is held in a dark room secured against even a trickle of moonlight.

"And out of this utter darkness comes the roaring of drums, the sounds of prayers, the high-pitched songs," Lame Deer has said. "And among all these sounds your ear catches the voices of the spirits—tiny voices, ghostlike, whispering to you from the darkness."[2]

The vision quest is another powerful native rite. The seeker retreats for days into the rugged crucible of the wilderness, without food or water, praying to the Great Spirit. If of strong heart and pure purpose, the seeker might return from the ordeal with a powerful vision, a special power, or something of equal beauty to add to the great circle of the nation. The visionary experience was, and is, a powerful way Indians have communicated with spiritual beings.

The ghost dance was one of the last great visions the Native Americans were given before their stewardship of the land slipped into the hands of the European settlers. The vision was given to Jack Wilson, a Paiute Indian raised by whites, during an illness he suffered at the height of a solar eclipse in 1890. In his vision he was said to have traveled to the spirit world to communicate with God and the departed. The spirit had promised to come to all the Indian nations to raise the dead, sweep the white intruders from the continent, and return the once vast buffalo herds—which had been decimated by the immigrant expansion and the railroads—to the Great Plains.

The ghost dance was given as the instrument by which the Indians would be delivered from the threat of genocide. It was believed that the ghost shirt, painted with sacred icons and worn during the dancing, would make the wearer impervious to the white man's bullets.

Jack Wilson became known as Wovoka and was hailed by Indians as a true messenger of the Great Spirit. And so Cheyenne and Shoshone, Arapaho and Sioux, and the peoples of other tribes met throughout the territories to dance the ghost dance.

The U.S. cavalry of the reservation outposts saw the full force of the ghost dance. The ceremony was sweeping through the land, with hundreds of Indians gathering to dance, even in the snows. Sitting Bull, one of the ghost dance leaders, was identified as one of the "fomenters of disturbances" and assassinated before daybreak on December 15, 1890.

The Sioux ghost dance leader Big Foot, hearing of the death of Sitting Bull and a U.S. War Department order for his arrest, gathered over three hundred of his people and left his place in the Dakota Badlands to head for what he presumed was the security of the Pine Ridge agency. He hoped that Red Cloud, the powerful leader who resided there, could protect him and his people from the soldiers. Ill from pneumonia, Big Foot led the desperate march from a pony drag. But as they neared Pine Ridge, the army was waiting for them.

On December 28, 1890, Big Foot and his people were captured by the U.S. 7th Cavalry and marched to the nearest cavalry outpost. That night they were directed to make camp in the hollow of a creek near a place known as Wounded Knee Creek.

In the morning the people awoke to find the cavalrymen ready with rifles and Hotchkiss guns encircled above their encampment. The soldiers disarmed the Indians, but the people were unafraid—the power of the ghost dance was in their shirts and in their souls.

And the Hotchkiss guns opened up in explosions of close-range fire.

One twenty-seven-year-old Oglala Sioux who had been awaiting Big Foot's arrival at a camp some fifteen miles from Wounded Knee Creek heard the shooting. The violent sounds confirmed the premonitions of trouble that had disturbed his sleep all during the night. He quickly readied himself, carefully putting on his sacred shirt. The images on the shirt detailed the incredible vision the Great Spirit had given him at the age of nine. The back of the shirt depicted a spotted eagle in full wing. On the left shoulder rose the morning star. Slashing across the shirt breast from the left shoulder was a bright rainbow. Another rainbow encircled the neck. Over the whole shirt were red streaks of lightning. At each shoulder elbow and wrist was an eagle feather.

The young Oglala youth painted his face red. Finally he put one eagle feather in his hair to stand for unity and the Oneness of the Great Spirit.

He saddled up and, armed with only his sacred bow clutched in his right hand, stirred his buckskin to a gallop and rode in the direction of the shooting. He was soon met and joined by twenty other Indians on horseback. They, too, had heard the fearsome noises and had rode out to investigate.

At the top of a ridge the party could see the smoke of gunfire from the terrible battle below them. The young warrior led the small band in a charge to the battlefield, crying for his people to take courage and fight. Holding his sacred bow out in front, they were protected from the bullets fired at them by the white cavalrymen.

But the cause was lost. Despite their ghost dance shirts an estimated three hundred Indians, including Big Foot, died that day at Wounded Knee. When night came, a chilling wind swept the land, a blizzard rolled in after it, and the corpses of the dead were buried in the freezing snow.

Looking back from the "high hill of my old age," Black Elk, that young Oglala Sioux who had charged to the scene with his sacred shirt and bow, remembered that terrible day: "I can still see the butchered women and children lying heaped and scattered all along the crooked gulch as plain as when I saw them with eyes still young. And I can see that something else died there in the bloody mud, and was buried in the blizzard. A people's dream died there. It was a beautiful dream.

"And I, to whom so great a vision was given in my youth—you see me now a pitiful old man who has done nothing, for the nation's hoop is broken and scattered. There is no center any longer, and the sacred tree is dead."[3]

Black Elk spoke those words to John G. Neihardt, who first met him in August 1930. Neihardt was working on a history of the ghost dance period, and had gone to the Pine Ridge Indian reservation to talk to old medicine people about those fateful days. When he met Black Elk he heard about more than the ghost dance. Black Elk also shared the details of the great vision and the healing powers given him by the Great Spirit.

"Of course it was not I who cured," Black Elk told Neihardt. "It was the power from the outer world, and the visions and ceremonies had only made me like a hole through which the power could come to the two-leggeds. If I thought I was doing it myself, the hole would close up and no power could come through."

Before they talked Black Elk had brought out his sacred pipe. To all Indians the pipe is a sacred altar and a gift from the Great Spirit. As he filled the pipe with the bark of a red willow, Black Elk explained the symbology of the pipe.

Four ribbons hanging from the stem represented the four corners of the universe. A black ribbon acknowledged the thunder beings, who lived in the west and brought the rain. A white ribbon stood for the cleansing wind of the north. A red ribbon represented the east, which brought the light and the morning star to shine wisdom into every heart. And a yellow ribbon was for the south, land of summer and growth. The four ribbons were separate, yet one. It was the mystery of Wakan-Tanka, the Great Spirit.

Black Elk was also wearing an eagle feather, just as he had that terrible day at Wounded Knee. He told Neihardt that the eagle feather stood for that mystical unity of the Great Spirit. The eagle feather was also a prayer and the hope that "the thoughts of men should rise as high as eagles do."

Black Elk then offered the pipe to the spirits of the four directions, to Father Sky and Mother Earth, to the Great Spirit.

"Great Spirit, Great Spirit, my Grandfather, all over the earth the faces of living things are all alike," he prayed. "With tenderness have these come up out of the ground. Look upon these faces of children without number and with children in their arms, that they may face the winds and walk the good road to the day of quiet."

And then the two shared the pipe's sacred smoke so that there would be only good between them.[4]

The discovery of gold in California in 1849 was a powerful lure to the settlement of the West. The rambling conquests of the warrior kings of history had been fueled by lesser riches than the millions of dollars worth of precious metal that lay waiting under tons of Sierra rock and shale.

The prospectors who were part of the overland migration to the gold country had journeyed across the barren prairies, climbed the Colorado Rockies, and crossed the Utah desert and the dry desolation of Nevada. And then one final, formidable barrier had to be survived—the Sierra Nevada range. In the Sierras one brief flurry of bad weather could bury a band of settlers in freezing snow. Strange tales came out of the passage of those ageless peaks: sightings of the spirit world and other visions made under the influence of exhaustion and hunger. Small wonder that mysticism prevailed among the survivors of that journey. On the last mountain bluff many an altar of thanksgiving fashioned from sticks and branches was offered to God.

The settling of the West was full of strange encounters with the spirit in the land. There were tales of gunfighters with a mystic touch who could pull lightning out of their holsters, of cursed gold mines haunted by the aimless wanderings of spectral prospectors, of strange creatures and hauntings in the wilderness. And of course there were the preachers and visionaries who followed the miners, settlers, cattle barons, and railroad magnates to the promised land.

There were a few easygoing mystics as well. Consider gold miner Bob Rohane, nicknamed the "Astral Kid" by his fellow gold diggers. Rohane worked a claim in Nevada's Esmeralda County in the first decade of this century—with the help of his spirit guides.

The spirits had reportedly guided the Astral Kid to a spot of almost certain riches. (Years after the site was abandoned by the original miners, a deeply buried vein of rich ore was actually discovered.) But despite the supernatural assist, the claim was no easy pickings for the Kid. His spirit guides forbade him from using wheelbarrows and machinery in the dig. Rohane was forced to remove the earth and rock from his 125-foot tunnel in candle boxes.

The Astral Kid was a friend and legend to his fellow miners. During long winter evenings the Kid entertained the miners with tales of his astral body travels to exotic bawdy spots in Hong Kong and Melbourne. When the Astral Kid finally began to hit a promising vein he received a sudden message from his spirits to leave immediately for Australia. Without hesitation the Astral Kid took off, in body, and was never seen or heard from again.[5]

Many of the religious movements founded by the settlers of the new land not only accepted, but encouraged mystical experiences. In the Shaker communities mystical visions were honored as gifts from the spirit and recorded in the form of beautiful colored drawings. Joseph Smith claimed to have founded the

Mormon religion after Moroni, a celestial messenger of God, appeared to him.

The modern era of spirit-world contact in America, known as Spiritualism, is said to have begun with the spirit-world communications Kate and Margaret Fox experienced in their house in Hydesville, New York. The sisters, aged seven and ten respectively, heard a mysterious rapping and the moving of unseen furniture the night of March 31, 1848. As a game, the sisters devised a code of claps and raps to communicate with the sounds. The Fox family became convinced the children had made contact with an intelligent spirit entity from the Other Side.

Mrs. Fox and her daughters toured America, talking about the Hydesville spirit rapping and the spirit world. The Fox sisters were a sensation. The fanfare prompted people all over the country to come forward with their own strange tales of ghostly visions and unearthly manifestations.

The Fox sisters were ultimately tragic figures. They became the targets of investigators convinced that the spirit sounds at Hydesville were a fraud. University professors advanced such theories as "snapping of the knee joints" to explain the alleged rapping. Margaret Fox, in addition to suffering from alcoholism in her later years, also fell into severe financial trouble. And then in 1888 Margaret revealed that she and her sister were indeed frauds.

Margaret recanted her confession the following year, explaining that her earlier statements had been made under mental duress caused by her financial problems and the frenzied pursuit of spiritualist debunkers.

Although the legitimacy of the controversial Fox sisters can be debated, there is little argument that they ushered in the Spiritualistic movement.

It was also the golden age of seances and mediumistic theatrics. Mediums sought to outdo the Fox sisters' table rapping by producing more elaborate manifestations of spirit-world contact. There were tingling bells, levitating furniture, floating musical instruments allegedly played by spectral hands, and the production of ectoplasm, the viscous white substance said to ooze from the medium's body during trance.

Spiritualism even had its celebrity advocates of the period, notably Sir Arthur Conan Doyle, the creator of Sherlock Holmes. President Lincoln is said to have held seances in the White House. The story goes that the ghost of Daniel Webster came through during one seance, and urged the president to proclaim the emancipation of the slaves.[6]

But spiritualism began to change in the twentieth century. Gone, or nearly abandoned, was the gooey ectoplasm, the levitating trumpets, table rapping, slate markings, and other theatrical trappings of the Victorian era.

Psychics today claim that the spirits no longer need to manifest with such elaborate fanfare. Humanity is more receptive, psychics say, and the spirits can come in more directly now. Whatever the reason, the new era of mediumship would be marked by more direct accessing of information and entities.

One of the giants of a new era was a Kentucky farmer's son born in 1877 named Edgar Cayce.

It was discovered later in Cayce's life that he could fall into a trance and speak at length on a variety of subjects he had no training in or knowledge of. Emerging from the trance, he would have no conscious memory of what had transpired during the reading.

Another important psychic was Jane Roberts, who had never experienced the mystical until September 9, 1963, when "a fantastic avalanche of radical, new ideas burst into my head with tremendous force, as if my skull were some sort of receiving station turned up to unbearable volume." Roberts had just made the acquaintance of the entity known as Seth. The Seth material, which was channeled by Roberts until her death, is considered one of the most significant psychic developments of the century.

But while spiritualism was evolving, there was a constancy in the Native American spiritual tradition.

The mysticism of Indian people seemed to be built on a timeless connection with spiritual forces.

I knew that many people believed that the ancient ways had been forgotten, that what had been timeless was now history. I decided to find out if Indians still had ritual contact with the spirit world. The journey took me to the Indian nations, and beyond.

3

Journey into the Fourth World

"AN INDIAN'S WARNING ON DESPOILING EARTH—OLD PROPHECIES FORETOLD WARS, ATOMIC BOMBS."

That was the headline from an article buried on page seven of the second section of the *San Francisco Examiner* on September 28, 1987.

The article described how Thomas Banyacya, a traditional elder of the Hopi tribe, had been in Sacramento to speak at the closing luncheon of the state's first Indian health fair. During his talk Banyacya attacked the U.S. government for the relocation of fourteen thousand Navajos living in the sacred Four Corners area bounded by Arizona, Utah, Colorado, and New Mexico. Banyacya claimed the move was an effort to clear a path for the unbridled use of the area by uranium, ore, and coal mining interests. To so desecrate the sacred area was to anger "the Earth and the spirits," according to Banyacya.

Banyacya claimed to be the last remaining translator of the two-thousand-year-old "Hopi stone tablets of the future" that he and three other Hopis had translated in 1948. The prophecies foretold "two world wars, electricity, skyscrapers, air and space travel, and the atomic bomb," Banyacya had said. There were additional warnings about the "fire" of nuclear warfare.

I was set to leave the following week for a spirit-in-the-land trek through the Hopi and Navajo nations in Arizona. I was hoping to meet traditional medicine people who could give me a flavor of the survival of Native American spiritual traditions in the modern world. I decided to look up Banyacya during my visit to Hopi territory.

I was also hoping to see Grandfather David, a Hopi elder and legendary channel of spiritual energy. I was cautioned that he was one hundred or one hundred ten years old and in frail health. One channel I talked to concluded I would have trouble even finding him.

I had crossed the Southwest several times, but it had been several years since my last visit, and I was excited about returning to the rugged region. A fascination with that land had begun at an early age when my grandmother, who lived for a time in Arizona, made a gift of Hopi kachina dolls to my brothers, sisters, and me one summer. We still have them. Our dolls are colorfully painted wood carvings of human-like figures with fantastic visages and forms. Some are birdlike or coyote creatures, while others have hidden, masked features, sport spectacular headdresses, or have the look of beings alien to earth.

The kachinas are said to come from the mysterious regions of the spirit world. When on earth they abide in the sacred heights of the San Francisco peaks west of the Hopi nation. Kachinas are the spiritual manifestations of the dead, of minerals, animals, birds, plants, the earth, the clouds, the very cosmos. They are not all-powerful deities, but spiritual messenger forces. Kachinas help the Hopi survive in the arid land they inhabit by bringing rain and ensuring good crops. Kachina dolls are given to Hopi children to familiarize them with the spiritual entities and prepare them for eventual initiation into kachina society.

It is believed that the kachinas manifest themselves on Earth in physical form six months out of the year. When the men impersonate kachina entities during ceremonies they become filled with the spirit of the being they represent.

Author Frank Waters describes the wonderment of sitting in a kiva, the sacred Hopi underground ceremonial chamber, and participating in a kachina ceremony:

> In its conception the Hopis have created a form for the everlasting formless; a living symbol unique in the world for that universal and multifold spirit which embodies all living matter; which speaks to us, as only the spirits can speak, through intuitive perception of our own faith in the one enduring mystery of life. One cannot doubt its veracity when in a kiva we hear the strange falsetto yell announcing a presence above, feel the stamp on the roof demanding admittance, and see coming down the ladder a spirit whose manifested form has never been glimpsed among the figures of this mortal world.[1]

It was a strange world I was heading to. It started from my Aunt Anne's cabin in the resort town of Show Low. From there it would be a straight shot north to the Indian nations by car. Anne was letting me borrow one of her cars for the trek, and she had also arranged for a friend of hers, Leroy "Boone" Curtis, a thirty-five-year-old full-blooded Navajo, to accompany me as a guide.

My aunt, Leroy's Apache wife, and their two kids were there to see us off. Our compact car was filled with clothes, sleeping bags, and a cooler full of food. I took the wheel, Leroy hopped in, and we drove off, fortified by their fond farewell and fistfuls of thick, spicy beef jerky. We settled in for a long drive to our destination in the Hopi nation.

As we crossed the border of Arizona into the land of the Navajos, the sun's warmth seemed to turn up a notch. It was all blue sky above, and in all four directions spread a desolate landscape dotted with boulders and sliced by arroyos, with an occasional butte rising out of the earth. Farther on, great mesas came into sight, hovering over us like the petrified remains of ancient giants.

The hot wind was blowing through the car's open windows as we drove. No other cars were in sight. I was feeling like the legendary King of the Road. Talk came easily at such a pace. Leroy mentioned that although his parents lived off the reservation in the town of Joseph City, he had plenty of friends and relatives throughout Navajo territory and knew well the land we were traveling through.

For years Leroy had been traveling over the area for work, play, and also for the rodeo. He had a few championship belts to his credit earned in both Anglo- and Indian-sponsored contests. It had only been a few years since he had packed away his saddle, chaps, and spurs and entrusted the gear to a friend in Navajo country.

One of Leroy's rodeo stories provided a good example of the resourceful attitude often demanded of the people in the region. He had been hitchhiking to a rodeo competition when he found himself stranded between rides in the desert as a drizzly nightfall descended. He didn't have a jacket, only a blanket, and was carrying his heavy saddle and rodeo gear. He stopped by the side of a lonely road and made a fire. When the wood had burnt down to hot, glowing red embers, he completely covered the embers with dirt, put his blanket over it, and laid down on it. The natural heating unit he had built kept him warm through the cold, wet night.

Leroy's rodeo remembrances wandered to the hand trembler business. Hand tremblers were people who could diagnose a person's ills by going into a trance and allowing spirits to come in. In the trance, the hand trembler's hand and arm would shake over a patient's body to divine the cause of a problem and suggest a cure. A powerful hand trembler could also locate lost items and even foretell the future, he said.

Leroy wanted to find a hand trembler because misfortune had been dogging him for six months. During that time he had lost his job, his car, and his home.

The situation had forced him to live with his wife's family in the Apache reservation near Show Low. He had been drinking too much and the barroom brawls that often accompanied his binges had landed him in jail a few times. In fact, days before I left for Arizona, Aunt Anne had called to tell me that she had bailed Leroy out of jail.

To a Navajo such a string of misfortunes was no accident. Leroy was convinced he was in the grip of a powerful curse. Only a hand trembler would be able to diagnose his problem and recommend a solution.

Leroy pulled out the road map. We were heading north on Route 77 to the Hopi village of Hotevilla, where Grandfather David was reported to live. Farther on, back in the Navajo nation and past the town of Tuba City, lived an old woman hand trembler he knew.

The old woman had performed a powerful healing on him in 1978. That was the last bad time for Leroy, another time of drinking and brawling that had led to a divorce from his first wife. Leroy had been hanging out with the Anglos at the time, and a brief involvement with the Mormon religion had distanced him from the old Navajo ways. But his mother, who always held fast to the traditional prayers of her people, finally convinced Leroy that he needed a taste of Navajo medicine. With his mother and brother-in-law along, Leroy drove out to see the hand trembler.

"So, we see this woman and she started doing hand trembling on me, but I found out she knew more than that," Leroy explained as we drove. "She looked through a crystal. She said she could take out what was buried in me. 'I can see what the people are doing to you,' she told me.

"But she said it would take more money, so we paid her. She then took a plain old sewing needle about three or four inches long. She stuck the needle into my stomach and pried out from the skin some pieces of bone and chips of an old arrowhead. There was no blood or nothing, I couldn't feel anything! It didn't hurt and right away I started feeling relaxed. I felt

pretty good. And then she says, 'There's another thing,
this I really have to do. You don't need to give me any
more money. I'm here to help people. You've given
me enough as it is.' "

The whole group, along with the hand trembler, got
back into his car. Leroy's brother-in-law took the
wheel, and with the old woman giving directions they
drove toward the town of Winslow, over one hundred
miles away. As they drove the woman kept looking
into her crystal, as if she was seeing something that
was helping her navigate. Although the woman
claimed to have never traveled that stretch of road, she
seemed to anticipate every hill and curve.

Finally she asked Leroy's brother-in-law to slow
down. Their mysterious destination was close by.

"And then she says, 'I think this is the spot right
here.' So we pulled over and got out. She brought out
her crystal and a six- or seven-inch spearhead and told
me to follow her.

"So I followed her on top of a little hill. There were
a bunch of rocks on top. She kept looking in those
rocks. I was curious. I wondered what she was looking
for. Then she looks at one rock and calls me up: 'Here!
I want you to look at this.' My mom followed me up,
too.

"I looked at it and there was about a two-inch drawing of a man and a woman, and there was a lightning
bolt going between the man and the woman. And at
that time me and my first wife were separated and in
the process of getting a divorce.

" 'This doesn't look very good,' the old woman
said. And she looked into her crystal and said, 'Look
in here—do you recognize these people?' I looked in
the crystal, and I saw two ladies and a man standing
there. And she said, 'You know who it is!' And then
she says, 'You should have seen me earlier. This exact
spot is where you're supposed to have an accident. It's
supposed to kill you!'

"I always used to travel that road when I went to
college up in Utah. That just blew my mind. The fig-

ures on the rock and all that—how could she know? What brought her there? What told her that? It's weird, man.

"So she erased the figures from the rock. We drove her back to her home and after that I felt so light, I felt like I loved everybody—it felt good to be alive. Before that, I was lost, I didn't know what to do!

"And now the problems are happening again. And you know, you just can't keep putting it off, or procrastinate about things like this. Their medicine (whoever is sending the curse) keeps getting stronger. If you go to see a medicine man you can take them by surprise. A powerful medicine man will reverse a spell on you. The good is always stronger than the bad, if you go about it the right way. That's what my mom's always told me."

We stopped for a little hike in a hilly area off the main road. Old chips and fragments of Indian pottery lay among the rocks. If you're lucky, Leroy said, old arrowheads could be found. Such treasures were always unearthed after a hard rain opened up the soil. The pottery designs imitated the forms and color of canyon strata, the clouds, the sun, and the moon.

As we hiked, I told Leroy that finding him a hand trembler was a major priority of our enterprise.

Back in the car and back on the road Leroy got to talking again. He had something on his mind that was more evil, more dangerous than just the power of one curse. There were the sorcerers themselves, the "bad people." He called them the skin walkers.

Skin walkers used spirit powers in evil ways. They could curse someone by getting bits of that person's clothes, hair, stool, even the dirt from their fingernails, putting it all in a mixture in a bottle, and burying it. Then the power would manifest and "mess with your mind" unless you could locate the evil charm, dig it up, and have a medicine man cure you.

Skin walkers kept their identities secret. If they were ever recognized and confronted, they would die.

Skin walkers often met in desolate caves to call upon

the evil forces for power. They raided graveyards for skull bones—and sometimes flesh—that they would grind into the magic powders for use in their nocturnal incantation sessions.

The skin walker talk added an eerie touch to our drive into the hallucinatory vastness of earth and sky. It felt as if we had crossed borders into a strange new world where sky, earth, and water were alive and listening, watching, waiting to swallow us into the belly of a great mystery.

On our way to Hopi land we made a few stops to locate a hand trembler. Leroy remembered that his sister, who lived nearby, knew of another old woman hand trembler. We made a turn off the main highway and drove down a dirt road. As we neared his sister's house, Leroy pointed out the painted desert, where he had spent many wonderful days riding and roping the wild horses of the canyons.

We drove up and parked in front of her house, a simple frame structure weathered by the hot sun and gritty wind. A few chickens wandered around, pecking at the dust near several old black trucks. Leroy knocked on the door and we walked in.

Leroy's sister and her husband were sitting quietly at their kitchen table. The husband was working with his knife on a leather belt while his sister was mulling over a jigsaw puzzle depicting a pastoral landscape of green hills and forest surrounding a farm house. As she talked in Navajo dialect with her brother, she popped into place a little piece of the river. When they were finished talking we said our good-byes and returned to the car. Leroy shook his head. The old woman was no longer considered a reliable hand trembler. She had forgotten many of her prayers and was compensating with an ornery temper.

We arrived in the four thousand square miles of arid, sunbaked country known as Hopi land by the afternoon. This land was the present culmination of their own, and the world's, journey from creation.

The Hopi creation song tells of the lost time when

the infinite Creator, and the gods and spirits he created, fashioned the universe out of the void. The Earth was made with all its wonderment and abundant life. Lastly, the races of humanity were created and instructed on how to live in harmony with the Creator and the creation they had been given.

But those first people forgot the path their Creator had given them. The first world was destroyed with fire from the sky and the burning lava of erupting volcanoes. But a small band of the chosen faithful were allowed safe passage to the place of the next sacred world.

The sacred ways were again forgotten and that second world was destroyed as the Earth spun off its axis, freezing in the cold of space.

A few chosen had been allowed to journey on to the third world. The sacred path was forgotten yet again, and the Earth was drowned by torrential storms and a rising ocean that flooded the land.

The chosen ones on that plane made round, flat boats of hollow reeds, and drifted through many adventures until they reached the "Place of Emergence," a world of challenge and choice: the fourth world.

And Sotuknang, the great being who had been created by the Creator to build the universe, came to the shore of the new world to talk with the chosen ones. This world was not a beautiful paradise like the others, but full of all manner of challenge and diversity.

"What you choose will determine if this time you can carry out the plan of creation on it or whether it must in time be destroyed, too," Sotuknang said. "Now you will separate and go different ways to claim all the Earth for the Creator. Each group of you will follow your own star until it stops. There you will settle. Now I must go. But you will have help from the proper deities, from your good spirits. Just keep your own doors open and always remember what I have told you."[2]

We are in the time of the fourth world.

By the mid-afternoon we pulled into Hotevilla, the

ancient, sacred village of the Hopi. A hand-lettered sign to one side of the dirt road encircling the village told tourists *not* to take photographs, make tape recordings, disturb anything, or go into the sacred kiva area.

We slowly drove around the circumference of the little village. There was a mid-afternoon stillness. No other cars were around and only a few children were walking around under the hot sun.

I spotted a Hopi man tending a horse. I parked the car. Because of some long-standing disputes between Navajo and Hopi, mostly over land-control issues, Leroy decided to wait in the car. I got out and walked over to the man to ask the whereabouts of Grandfather David and Thomas Banyacya.

At first he was reluctant to tell me, but he finally gave in and mentioned that Banyacya lived down the road a few miles at "the white man's town" of Kykotsmoui. He eyed me suspiciously when I asked about Grandfather David. But he again relented and pointed over some scrub brush, past a water tower with "Hotevilla" written on it, and in the general direction of some white houses.

We drove to the general direction. Leroy again waited in the car. I knocked at the door of the big two-story place. There was no answer. I walked up to an adjacent smaller house and looked through a window. I saw an old man, his back to me, pulling on a blue vest. I had a feeling this was the right place. The front door was open but a screen door was closed. I knocked on the metal edge of the screen.

"Grandfather David?"

There was no response. I opened the screen door and walked in.

The old man was sitting on a chair. Across from him an old woman was sitting on a couch, asleep. I approached him. His long lids were shut over hollow, sunken eye sockets. His face was strong and gentle. His thin arms were gently crossed over his abdomen, each hand on the opposite elbow. He seemed to be nodding off.

"Grandfather David?" I whispered this time.

He cocked his head in my direction and turned his lid-covered eyes toward me.

"Yes?" he replied in a hoarse whisper.

I told him I wanted him to tell me about Hopi spiritual traditions, that his comments would be included in a book. He nodded again and was quiet, as if being drawn deep inside himself.

Then he told me that Thomas Banyacya was knowledgeable about such matters and I should talk with him. I gently pressed for more, telling him I desired his words as well. He paused again, nodding and gently rocking to the slow exhalation of his deep breathing.

I was wondering if he had fallen asleep when he suddenly began talking again. He said that he had to perform a healing ceremony in the kiva later that afternoon. The next day he would be free. I should come back then.

I thanked him and said I would return by mid-morning.

Back in the car I told Leroy about the arrangements. We drove off and decided that first thing in the morning we would drive to Kykotsmoui to look up Banyacya. Then we would come back to Hotevilla to see Grandfather David.

Driving on a lonely stretch of highway before twilight, we spotted a hilly rise just off the road and decided to pull over and make a camp there. From the hill we had a panoramic view of the land spreading out to the four directions. In the distance we could see a canyon. Leroy told me he had often gazed at the canyon while driving this stretch of road to Tuba City. He had never hiked into it, but in his dreams he had explored it.

Lying in our sleeping bags, we silently watched the awesome dance of the spirit in the land, the dance humanity has watched, thrilled, and prayed to ever since the first creation.

The last crimson band of twilight dissolved into night. As that final spark of sunlight was shut away, a shadow of darkness, animated and alive, moved across the land and over us. A gigantic orange harvest moon rose out of the horizon, filling the world below us with sweet lunar illumination. Huddled in our bags, comfortable against the cool night air, Leroy broke the silence to muse about how good it would be to find a hand trembler. But somehow the talk ended up with the skin walkers again.

His parents had taught him that in the old days the skin walkers were message carriers who served good causes. Their songs and prayers gave them the power to travel incredible distances during their nightly missions. For power they usually wore a whole coyote skin over their body, including the hollowed-out coyote head that fitted over their own like a skullcap.

Somewhere in time the skin walkers began using their powers for evil. At his parents' house Leroy sometimes heard the chanting and drumbeat of nearby skin walker gatherings. Despite his desire to run and hide he was inexplicably rooted to the spot, in some mysterious way forced to listen to the skin walker's wail deep into the night.

As we fell asleep, the same eerie twinge that I had experienced during the day's driving returned. Looking out at the moonlit land, I had the feeling of being able to see a coyote-skinned figure leaping over rock and brush with incredible speed.

The next morning we drove out to see Thomas Banyacya. Once in the town of Kykotsmoui it wasn't hard getting directions to the house of the Hopi elder. We both got out of the car and walked up to a brick house where a truck was parked in front. An old Hopi woman was out front doing some yard work when we approached. She was bright and cheery until I mentioned being a reporter who wanted to ask Thomas Banyacya some questions. She said he was home, but was getting ready to leave on errands. She turned and walked into the house. As we stood there, Leroy gave me a doubtful look.

Then Thomas Banyacya came out of the house. His long, gray hair was tied behind his back. He was short, with a little paunch. He came over to us, his eyes squinting in the bright morning glare. I mentioned I wanted to talk with him about Hopi spiritual traditions. He looked down at the ground, a grave expression on his face. I told him that Grandfather David had sent us.

He looked up and off into the distance. He muttered that the elders had made the decision not to discuss their spiritual traditions or prophecies without granting prior approval.

I mentioned the Harmonic Convergence and the general interest in native spiritual traditions. He looked at me and shook his head.

"Harmonic Convergence—that's not us," he said. "We don't have anything to do with that."

He said the sacred traditions and prophecies were being paraded around like a circus show. Eyes averted, he drifted back into his house without a word of goodbye.

Leroy thought the man was being unsociable, but I couldn't blame Banyacya. I only hoped Grandfather David would be more accommodating.

There was more activity at Grandfather David's house this time. A young woman with two children had driven up at the same moment. Leroy waited in the car while I walked up to the house. The woman held the door open for me, and I followed her in.

Inside was the older woman I had seen the day before and a middle-aged woman.

The women went into the other room, talking in their Hopi tongue. Grandfather David was sitting in the same chair I had seen him in the day before. His eyelids were shut and he was once again at one with his breathing.

I called his name and he lifted his head in my direction. I sat on a chair next to him and reintroduced myself. For long moments he was quiet. Then he told me he had to perform a healing ceremony in the kiva. I asked him if we could talk before he had to perform the healing. No answer.

I could sense him dropping deep within himself, deeper than even the day before. I was silent, lulled by the sounds of his soft, rhythmic breathing. On the wall in front of me was a framed black-and-white photograph of Grandfather David standing next to an old wood stove. He looked as if he was in his sixties when the shot was snapped.

Suddenly the middle-aged woman stepped into the room, gesticulating with her arms as if shooing something away.

"You want to talk to him—so talk with him!" With that she disappeared back into the other room.

But Grandfather David made no response to my whispered questions. Maybe he heard me, or maybe my voice was like a distant echo to a hiker descending into a deep canyon. I wondered where he had gone.

Then the younger woman and her children left. The old woman slowly walked into the room, crossing to the other side without a glance at us. She sat in a chair by a window and gazed out.

The middle-aged woman came in and sat in a chair in front of me. I told her I was there to find out about Hopi spiritual traditions. She shook her head wearily and looked at the floor. She said the Hopi had decided not to give away their sacred knowledge anymore. Too many times they had seen their sacred truths trampled or abused.

"Could I see the kiva?" I asked.

"No!" she blurted, looking up immediately, and then staring back down at the floor.

There was silence in the room. Grandfather David seemed to have gone someplace far, far away. The older woman still had her back to us, sitting motionless and gazing out the window. I looked at the photo of Grandfather David.

I made my request once more. She slowly shook her head. The Hopi ways were for Hopi people.

"I'm sorry," she said.

"So am I" was my reply.

I shook her hand, touched Grandfather David on the shoulder, and gently closed the screen door on my way out.

I shrugged as I got back into the car and stuck the car key into the ignition.

"I had a feeling they weren't going to talk to you," Leroy said as we drove down the dusty, bumpy road back to the highway. We were headed back into the Navajo nation to find a hand trembler for Leroy.

Leroy talked about the polar influences that had been tugging at him his whole life. One side was the spiritually charged world of his Navajo heritage, the other the logical, rational white culture. The Indian side won out most of the time. Even when he had joined the Mormons, the day still had come when he told his buddies, "This isn't me," took off his suit and tie, and walked away from it.

"I've been brought up around mostly Anglos and they tell you, 'You don't believe that [spiritual] stuff, do you?' I'd say, 'Nah. That's crazy. That's stupid.' But deep down inside I knew. I'd think, if only these people knew what I know. If only they knew what my mother and other people could see."

I think Leroy found some of the Anglo ways perplexing and totally alien. One bad bit of culture shock was an experience he had with the bureaucracy of an Anglo hospital. It damned near killed him.

It started during an altercation in a store in the town of Holbrook. Leroy and an Indian friend noticed two young Mexicans insulting an older Indian man. Leroy stepped in, telling the two they should have more respect for their elders. That was enough to touch off a fight. Leroy knocked one down with a punch, while the other one began grabbling with him. Then Leroy felt something dig into his abdomen. As the two men ran off, Leroy began to fall and his friend caught him.

A deep knife cut had slit open his belly and his guts were starting to spill out.

Bleeding and dizzy from the pain, he held his guts in while his friend drove him to the emergency entrance at the nearby Anglo hospital. But the doctors refused to operate until Leroy gave the receptionist his Navajo census number. Every Navajo was given a number, which included medical coverage by the Navajo nation for the bearer. The doctors weren't going to operate without the number, and Leroy couldn't remember it.

He was sitting, holding his bleeding guts in, feeling scared and faint as his friend frantically looked through his wallet for the precious census number. Then Leroy remembered—it was on the back of his Social Security card. Once the number was secured, the poised attendants clamped an oxygen mask on him, lifted him onto a stretcher, and wheeled him into surgery.

Leroy shook his head in amazement, remembering how the white doctors would have let him die for want of some numbers.

Later that day we finally tracked down some Navajo medicine for Leroy's troubles. We found the hand trembler.

We were driving past Tuba City when Leroy told me to exit the freeway onto a red dirt road. The medicine woman who had cured him in 1978 lived farther up the freeway, but Leroy, not wanting to take the chance that we would drive to the old woman's place and not find her at home, wanted to follow a hunch. The road we had taken would lead to another youthful haunt where he remembered hand trembler talk.

We drove past a windmill that rose above the redrock desert brush and into an open valley holding a scattering of houses. From memory he directed me to the special house. We parked and got out of the car.

A strong wind was blowing, stirring the reddish dust of the craggy earth and carrying sweet smells across the open land. Other than the wind there was an abiding silence in the valley. To one side of the house was a hogan, the traditional Navajo dwelling built of earth walls and supported by timbers. Leroy smiled at the sight of it.

We knocked at the front door. When there was no answer, we walked around to the back of the house. An older woman was sitting in the shade of a covered corral working on animal skins. Leroy spoke to her in Navajo dialect. After a short conversation he turned to me and explained that the woman had recognized him from his childhood visits to the house. She was a hand trembler herself and would help him. He had told the woman I was a friend of his, and she said I could view the session.

She stood up in the sun. She was a large, gray-haired woman. Her skirt, soiled by hard work, billowed in the wind. She gave us a sweet smile and walked with a slight limp to the house. She told Leroy her hand-trembling fee was usually ten dollars, but because she knew him it would be five dollars. Leroy handed her a wrinkled Lincoln, and we went inside her house.

There was a simple, rustic feel to her house. Navajo blankets were piled high on the table of an adjacent room, dried corn and red peppers hung from a wall, and in the corner by the door was a big wood stove with its stove pipe snaking up through the ceiling.

The hand trembler asked Leroy to bring in a spade of dirt from outside and put it on the stove floor. As Leroy got the dirt I sat against the wall by the stove.

Leroy came in with the red dirt and poured a pile of it on the floor. The woman sat down and patted flat the little mound and smoothed it into a pancake shape. She then brought out a crystal and held it in her right hand. She asked Leroy to sit down by her left side, his palms up and his legs stretched out.

The woman closed her eyes, lowered her head, and began mumbling prayers in her Navajo tongue. Keeping her eyes closed and her head turned away from Leroy, she reached over and touched her crystal to the soles of his feet, his palms, both his shoulders, his back, and the top of his head.

The hand trembler then put her head in her right palm, which still clutched the crystal. She talked in a low, guttural voice as her left hand and arm began moving up and down in the direction of Leroy's body. The trembling hand then began drawing images in the dirt, wiping the image away, and drawing another. Then the trembling hand rose and waved over Leroy's body. The trembling fingers went down to the dirt again, and she drew a box shape and smoothed it over. Leroy stared blankly ahead throughout.

When the woman came out of her trance she turned to gaze at Leroy. She talked softly to him while he nodded.

The consultations over, we got up to leave. We swept up the dirt and dropped it outside, where the wind caught it and blew it away. The woman said a few more words to Leroy and we each shook her hand. She gave us a bright, beautiful smile to see us off.

I was anxious to have Leroy describe in detail what had happened. I asked about the crystal she touched to him.

"It gave me a tingling feeling, like you get from static electricity," he said. "It feels weird. When she started, she was praying to Mother Earth, praying for guidance and asking to visualize what was happening to me. She wanted to find out, to see. She knew everything about me, I didn't have to tell her."

The square she drew in the dirt represented the house where he often stayed when at the White River Apache reservation. In her trance she had seen a man come into the house, go out, circle the property, and say the prayer that put the bad spell on him.

The hand trembler had told him he needed two important ceremonies to reverse the bad magic and get on a path of righteousness. One of the ceremonies was the Shield Prayer, which would provide an immediate protection against a curse. The other ceremony was translated in English as the "Good Way" or the "Sing." It was a very powerful ceremony.

"The Sing takes all night," Leroy said. "It's to help

me with my life, to put my life in perspective. I'm going to have to really believe in the medicine man who's going to perform it. And it helps, it really does. It clears your mind of a lot of things. It brings the family closer together. You as an individual start caring for other people, for your family. You start realizing.

"But I have to find a higher priest. It's like the hand trembler is the first, the next is the person who'll do the Shield Prayer, and then, if you really want to see who's doing it [the curse], if you really want bad things taken out of your house, you have to see a stronger medicine man. These are steps you have to take.''

But it would take some money, or something of value to honor the medicine man for his services, Leroy explained. At the moment he was poor, but he was determined to have the Sing performed for himself, his family, for everybody.

The excited talk and hopeful prospects got him to thinking about picking up the rodeo equipment he had left with his friend. He'd get back in shape by riding and roping wild horses in the desert canyons near his sister's house, and then jump back into the rodeo circuit again.

By nightfall we had crossed into New Mexico. We made camp by a desolate canyon and drifted off to sleep under another full moon. I was awakened in the middle of the night by the sound of a lone drum beating in a distant part of the canyon. The sound of a human voice making an owl call drifted above the steady drumming. Coyotes began wailing a refrain in the distance.

I then heard Leroy asking in a whisper if I was awake. I turned over and looked at him. Under the moonlight he was half out of his sleeping bag, leaning on his right forearm, his eyes locked in the direction of the distant canyon drumbeat. He said he had been hearing the drum all night. At one point he thought he had heard a scream. I burrowed back into my bag. It was chilly that night.

"Well, whoever's beating that drum doesn't know we're here." I shrugged.

"How do you know *they* don't know we're here?" Leroy replied.

A solitary drumbeat in the middle of the night, in the middle of nowhere, had all the earmarks of a skin walker session, according to Leroy. And the sound of the owl hoots! Owls were notorious bringers of bad luck, he said.

Finally we drifted off to sleep again. . . .

At dawn when we awoke, the distant drumming was still going strong. We rolled up our sleeping bags, loaded up the car, and got out of there. Leroy told me he had dreamt he was zipped up in his sleeping bag and was being pulled down into the canyon's yawning chasm by the evil drumming. In his dream he called out to me but I was asleep.

On one of our final nights together Leroy finally supplied the final piece of the puzzle I needed to understand his skin walker obsession. It seems the bad people had been haunting his parents' house in Joseph City for years.

"It's been going on ever since I can remember, ever since I was a little kid," he told me by a campfire that night in the hills outside Santa Fe. "My dad had a bow and arrow that a medicine man made a prayer over so it wouldn't misfire, so he wouldn't freeze up when he saw a skin walker. It was a good bow. He'd always get out in the evenings and walk around the house, come back and say, 'Didn't see no skin walker tonight. But I know they're out there!'

"It's a bad thing, really. It's something you don't want to really talk about. They say when you talk about it at night they're usually around, they can hear you. I hope I never see one.

"Before when I was first married I was always skeptical. But deep down inside I always knew what my mom always taught me about skin walkers, witchery, and sorcery. Deep down inside I believed it. I was Indian."

One night the eerie skin walker chant and drumbeat started up outside his parents' house. The front door had been left open, and from his bed his father could see out beyond the front porch. A short distance away a bonfire was raging, the chanting coming from the darkness beyond the flames.

He reached for the rifle he kept by his bed, remembering the time when some of his family had seen painted faces adorned with coyote skulls looking through an open door and peering in at a window. He got out of bed, cocked the rifle, remembering the time coyote claws had scratched at the door trying to get in, how the family had seen a coyote-clad figure bounding away with incredible speed. There had been enough hauntings. . . .

He aimed the weapon beyond the bonfire in the direction of the chanting and the drumming. He squeezed the trigger. The explosion of the shot was answered by an inhuman shriek.

Rifle in hand, Leroy's dad rushed to the front porch, peering into a violent whirlwind that had come out of nowhere. In a few moments the mysterious wind died, leaving in its wake silence and the dying embers of the fire.

He then saw drops of blood spotting the ground and brush. He followed the bloody trail to a house he knew all too well. He had shot his thirteen-year-old niece, who had secretly been a skin walker. She died in the hospital.

And since that time a good share of bad luck and tragedy had shadowed his family.

"It sounds like your whole family should get the Sing," I said.

"We can't afford it," Leroy said, staring into the campfire. "It takes money."

In Santa Fe I met several people who knew Grandfather David. That image of him sitting in silence, the ancient mysteries locked within his mortal frame, tugged at my thoughts. It was somehow gratifying to

meet people who loved and respected him as a friend
and as a channel for the power of the Great Spirit.

One old friend of Grandfather David's was John Free
Soul, an Indian man who led sacred pipe and sweat
lodge ceremonies in the Santa Fe area. "I used to
travel with Grandfather David," Free Soul told me.
"We'd get in a car and travel two days to do a healing
ceremony. In return they'd give us a sack of potatoes
because that was all they had. And sometimes we'd
have to sell those potatoes for enough gas money to
just get us home. We did it that way to keep it clean,
the way the ancient elders brought it down to us. I'm
a twentieth-century person, but to add to that vision is
to me a spiritual betrayal. Truth is truth in 1000 B.C.,
1000 A.D., or 3000 A.D.

"And it brings a tear to my eye that there's a back-
lash among spiritual leaders and they are reticent to
talk [about spiritual matters]. To share in small groups
is one thing, but to have massive gatherings [is an-
other]. And ceremonies are being charged for."

I was in fact going to attend such a gathering several
weeks later put on by the Bear tribe of Washington
state. I would have to find out for myself whether such
gatherings were violating the ancient truth.

By the time we headed back to Arizona, Leroy was
feeling upbeat again. The hand trembler had given him
a path that would help him counteract the evil curse.
He felt good about the prospects of helping his family
again, even of getting back into the rodeo. But a few
miles farther along our desert wasteland drive Leroy
was feeling apprehensive of going back to the house
where he had been cursed. He had hoped the open
road would never end.

We fell into our own individual reveries. The primal
landscape commanded a respectful silence. The spirit
was alive in this land. Leroy broke the silence by ges-
turing at a landscape of scattered red rocks we were
passing. He knew this stretch of land by heart. There
was a story about the red rocks.

Ages ago two sword-wielding twin brothers had heroically sliced up an evil giant. Mortally wounded, the giant had staggered across the land, spilling his life-blood. It had congealed and formed the fossil blood scattered on each side of the strip of highway we were riding into the infinite horizon. . . .

4

The Grandfathers Speak

It was exciting news in New Age circles when legendary Cherokee medicine man Rolling Thunder returned to a public forum in 1987 after some four years of illness. I made plans to listen to his talk at the Celebration of Innovation, a New Age festival held in San Francisco.

Rolling Thunder was no ordinary man. It was said he could cure disease, bring rain, perform exorcisms, communicate telepathically with man and spirit, and even move objects by psychokinesis.

Rolling Thunder once explained how he had received his powers:

> I woke up one morning, and this force was with me for the first time. I'd been doctored—in my sleep—the night before by a sun god and his helpers, and I felt this great power within me! But I had to learn to live with the tremendous force . . . to watch every thought or emotion I had, twenty-four hours a day. . . . It's difficult for a healer to adjust to that newfound power. . . . We all have to learn to guard every thought, every word, and every feeling, since the power could use any such channel to affect someone in one way or another.
>
> I believe the healing force contains the strength of the Creator—or Great Spirit—as well as the energy of the thunder and the lightning and that of all living beings.[1]

Rolling Thunder, known for his cantankerous public speaking manner, didn't disappoint the crowd at his sold-out Celebration of Innovation presentation. The medicine man approached the stage followed by a sizable entourage. Rolling Thunder was lean and tall, wearing a rainbow-colored shirt and a traditional headdress of his tribe. His face had a slightly wan look, but he appeared fit and feisty considering his seventy-plus years and his long illness.

Two women and a man sat on chairs on the stage behind Rolling Thunder. Four men sat in a circle of chairs around a great drum adjacent to the stage. Around the stage and at the corners were his T-shirted body guards, their arms folded and their eyes hidden behind dark glasses.

Rolling Thunder's talk rambled across a range of subjects, from the good taste of a buffalo stew prepared at an area restaurant to the lack of respect some visitors to his camp in the high plains of Nevada displayed by showing up without an offering of tobacco, food to share, or even their own bedroll. It wasn't a lack of respect for him, but of the Great Spirit that used him, Rolling Thunder lamented.

As Rolling Thunder rambled on, my attention turned to the man sitting on the stage behind him. He wore a black hat with a round brim and dark glasses. The glasses and the sweeping brim of his hat gave his visage a mysterious look. His dark skin was offset by the white silken shirt he was wearing. On his thick hands and wrists he wore rings and bracelets inlaid with precious stones. Throughout Rolling Thunder's talk he sat silently, barely moving. Yet a commanding energy seemed to radiate off him.

At one point Rolling Thunder introduced his retinue. He turned first to the mystery man in the wide brimmed hat, introducing him as a great seer, a teller. With the aid of spirits, this man could see into the future as well as explain the meaning of dreams and visions, Rolling Thunder respectfully explained.

After Rolling Thunder finished his talk, I went

backstage to see the teller. I found him in a curtained area crowded with visitors gathered to pay their respects to Rolling Thunder. I asked him if he could spare some time for talk.

"Oh, well, let me first ask Grandfather if it's all right," he said in a soft, lilting accent. He went back into the enclosed area to ask Rolling Thunder's permission to talk with me. When he emerged he nodded that he had some time. We moved outside the circle of people and sat on two folding chairs facing each other.

The teller's name was Ted Silverhand, a Tuscarora Indian from Bertie County, North Carolina. His family lineage was the Sagarrissa family, a line that had produced many gifted seers over the years. Silverhand was so respected that Indian leaders from many different tribes sought his advice.

"What we do is have dreams, or if you decide to come for a reading, I read through the spirits," Silverhand explained. "I have fourteen around me. These are old men. And it didn't start out quite that way. I had to learn a whole lot. And on my twenty-fifth birthday that's when I was taken into a circle. And in my circle were the old ones I used to see in my visions. They were there with my parents and my grandma. She talked to them."

"Did the spirits actually appear during this ceremony?" I asked.

"Yes. And they told me it was my time now to come and do this. You know, we talk in circles, so I have to back up now and say I was reading a little bit at age twelve, but it was not official until I was twenty-five that I was allowed to do this full-time."

"And how did you know you were ready?" I asked.

"Oh, because of the work that I had been doing, and my training. And to where she [his grandmother] said it was the time. You're never really ready because I'm still learning. You don't learn these things overnight like these instant psychics today. It's not that way.

"I use my power stones and my crystal. I'm allowed [by the spirits] to use the tape recorder. I tape everything for people to take with them. That's why so many come back to me, because they see it right on the money. You know, but it all comes through the Creator, Grandfather God. I'm nothing, see. He's everything. And through the use of his people, who are my guides they let me [see]. My guides are the fourteen who have crossed over. Now, it's not that when I sit down all fourteen come into the circle, but there are one or two voices always around at different times."

"Do you go into a trance state when you're reading?" I asked.

"Half and half," Silverhand replied. "Sometimes they speak through me. One time they talked German to a woman. I don't speak German. And you know, I do a lot of work in New York City with the Spanish people. I don't speak Spanish yet—I'm learning, but the thing about it is there are times when the spirit speaks Spanish to these people."

In addition to private readings Silverhand regularly hit the powwow circuit. Before such large gatherings he conducts special ceremonies to empower him to provide accurate individual readings for the large crowds that come to see him.

"When you see the line of people you keep going and going. I don't read their palms, I read their energy. And when it's time for the reading to be over they [the spirits] will pull the plug on me. It has happened at different times. All of a sudden when I start seeing and nothing won't come, that means it's over, it's finished."

To be a successful seer required the ability to tune in and accurately assimilate the information coming in from the spirit guides. "[I have] to understand, because when I get out of here, if I was talking and catching it too fast from them I could catch hell from them when I get back to my room and get by myself. They might say, 'You told that man he's going to be doing something in three weeks and we say three months.' They give me hell, see. Hell, I argue, too, because I try to catch it the best way I can catch it.

"You know, when I get back to a place by myself, they get on me from time to time if I was completely down-the-road wrong. But if I say three weeks and they say three months, that's not much to dicker with. But basically they like to keep me on target, and so far, thanks to my teachers, and of course, Grandfather God, things have been right on target."

Silverhand then asked me to put out both my hands with my palms up. Both his hands made a light pass over my arms and hand. He then asked my birthdate and if I was right- or left-handed.

With his spirit elders whispering in his ear, he then told me past and future things. It seemed nothing was hidden from the spiritual elders who guided Ted Silverhand, the seer. I had to smile. As Silverhand himself might have put it, the reading was "right on target."

It's interesting how much of the New Age is simply a return to the old ways. Traditional tribal cultures and ancient religions seek to access spiritual forces while maintaining a mystic, even loving, union with the natural world. The spiritual traditions of these cultures also manifests in their art, government, mythology—in virtually every area of tribal life. Spiritually starved Americans, whose own culture has separated religion from the other activities of life, are finding that the ancient ways provide the transcendent mystic experiences they are missing. And with the frightening damage being inflicted on the ecology of the planet, it is no wonder the ancient ways, which honor the planet as the Earth Mother, are being practiced once again by modern Americans. Gay Luce, who has studied Eastern traditions and is a consultant to the President's Scientific Advisory Committee, has been conducting workshops in the ancient mystery school traditions of the world since 1982. Luce's program provides initiatory experiences in the ancient and present-day spiritual practices of African shamanism, Native American ceremony, Egyptian rites, and the rituals of Sufism, Christianity, Buddhism, the Kahuna, Celtic druids, and others. Masters of those and other disciplines come to share their knowledge at her workshops.

"[I've seen] a Navajo shaman put live coals in his mouth, and his face change to that of a kachina," Luce says. "Once, in a group, he turned around and became an eagle—everybody saw it. Just amazing. But I don't think the import of all that is 'spiritualism.' I think the import is that we're living in a different universe than we thought, and if we were willing to listen to it, we would be very happy."

The Way of the Essenes is a workshop based on the traditions of the spiritual community that lived in the Middle East over two thousand years ago. The workshop is conducted by Danaan Parry, who left an important position with the Atomic Energy Commission to become a clinical psychologist in 1971. A near-death experience five years later on a desolate stretch of beach on the island of Kauai led him on a spiritual quest during which he discovered the spiritual wisdom teachings of the Essenes.

The Essenes lived in such inner and outer harmony they were able to "absorb and channel the vibrations and healing powers of the plants, the sun, and the four elements of earth, air, fire, and water, for their own nourishment and for the healing of the Earth itself," Parry writes. To renew that ancient way, Parry's workshop participants go on retreats in selected desert locales, following the prayers, diet, and rituals of the Essenes.

The Native American vision quest experience is another ancient tradition favored by many New Age Americans. Vision-quest treks run by non-Indians are often opportunities for urbanites to discover the beauty of wilderness, not to forge a soul-shattering link to the Great Spirit. Such treks often set a timetable of activities and have buddy systems in operation to assure safety.

There are also large gatherings to introduce traditional spiritual ways to non-tribal people. One Native American medicine man specializing in such large gatherings is Sun Bear, sacred teacher and medicine chief of the Bear tribe of Washington state. The Bear tribe was founded in 1970 and is recognized as the first new tribe established in this country. Since 1980 the Bear tribe has been organizing medicine wheel gatherings. Participants not only experience the medicine wheel ceremony, but sweat lodges and other rituals.

Medicine wheels are large circles of stone that symbolize the universe. Tribal peoples have traditionally used the wheels of stone as meeting places for the conduct of sacred ceremonies and the sharing of the spiritual teachings.

Sun Bear claims he was told in a vision to bring back the medicine wheel ceremony. In that vision he saw a circle of rocks at the top of a hill, and what he thought were animals coming to the circle. As he drew closer he realized the figures were human beings, each one singing a song of their path and place in creation. And then a voice in the middle of them said, "Now has come the time for the return of the medicine wheels. Now has come the time for the healing of the Earth Mother."

I interviewed Sun Bear prior to attending the 1987 Medicine Wheel Gathering held in Malibu, California. Sun Bear is a tall, husky man who takes pride in the physical stamina he has developed from years of hard work spent close to the land. With a smile he describes chopping wood for hours, working a plow and butchering his own meat. The natural strength to do that comes from walking the true path of the Great Spirit, he says.

Sun bear credits the Great Spirit for the gift of his medicine powers. He was schooled in the traditional medicine ways by uncles who were tough taskmasters but "much centered into their knowledge." Eventually the Great Spirit gave to Sun Bear the power to use the sacred pipe, the sweat lodge, and other special ceremonies. He says he continues to receive help and guidance from the Great Spirit as well as spirit guides and elemental forces such as the thunder beings, bringers of rain and storm.

"For thousands of years, there's been spirit powers and forces that have worked with humanity," Sun Bear explains. "And these are available to us if we're open, reaching out and communicating with them. What is happening at this time is that some of mankind have forgotten how to communicate with them, or no longer even believe in them. But those of us who continue to work with them, we understand that they're there.

"People have to sincerely seek it and that's how it happens [contact with spiritual powers]. It's where your energies go. If you're putting your energy into building a relationship with these powers and forces, then they will respond to you."

Sun Bear believes that the power of ritual can help in forging direct contact with the higher powers. "Ritual helps you to center your energy and your power. In this society people have lost the ability to center their energy, and their mind is kept so busy spinning in so many different directions they don't have any real ability to communicate or hold their train of thought enough to really get into anything. You have to create a relationship with these powers in order to do anything with them. And you also have to get rid of a lot of your own garbage so you really feel that you're going along a path because you believe in it, and are doing it.

"I pray and the thunder and lightning comes in, and the rain spirits visit me wherever I'm at. Whenever I go someplace, either the rain is coming in or it starts immediately after I leave.

"I pray to the Great Spirit and I ask the spirit helpers who have worked with my people for thousands of years to come and help me. I don't believe in vagaries or canned prayers. I believe in praying for what I need specifically when I need it. And that way you really know if it works.''

I asked him if spiritual forces, such as the Thunder Beings, ever appeared to him in a recognizable form.

''In a form, no,'' he reflects. ''They come as energies and you feel them. You can communicate with them, they're living entities, intelligent beings who can respond and make things happen.

''Once when I was up on our mountain in Spokane [the Bear tribe community], I was standing in front of a big window and there was this big thunder and lightning storm coming alongside the mountain. And I prayed and I said, 'Creator, I'd like to shake hands with my brothers, the thunder beings.' Out there on the side of the mountain there's this big steel bear that had been sculpted as a gift to me—and the next instant the lightning bolt hit the bear. It just whipped back and forth and turned every color of the rainbow. It was the thunder beings saying, 'Hey, we're here!' ''

The thunder beings seemed to follow Sun Bear to the Malibu mountain site of the medicine wheel gathering; hard rains drenched the assembled throughout the weekend.

But Friday was still clear of rain when my sister Katherine drove me to the gathering from her home in nearby Los Angeles. She left me with a special stone of hers to put into the medicine wheel circle. She called it her stigmata stone because two reddish beads on one side reminded her of the ecstatic state manifestations associated with the marks of Christ's crucifixion. I gave her a hug good-bye and promised to see that the stone was thoroughly charged with good vibes.

I had the stigmata stone with me for the night's sweat lodge session. Like many of the over one hundred assembled, it would be my first. Sun Bear had instructed me on the purpose and proper approach for the ceremony during my earlier talk with him.

''When we do the sweat lodge, first we're cleansing ourselves,'' he had told me. ''We're emptying out all our negativity.

"At the same time we're in there praying. Spirits are coming in, and if you're centered and praying in a good way you're going to draw in good energy, good spirits.

"The spirits are there because you're calling them, you're asking them to be there. When you pray for something, and if you're in tune with these powers and forces, then these powers come."

The sweat lodge area was a hike past ranch barns, lodges, and a grassy field where medicine wheel celebrants had pitched their tents, and a few tepees, for the weekend.

Three beehive-shaped lodges had been built on a sandy area marked off for the sweat ceremonies. At the side the sacred fire was heating the sacred stones and sending out waves of illumination through the darkness.

We had signed up for specific lodge groups beforehand. We gathered at the edge of the sweat lodge area at the appointed time, and stripped down to our bathing suits. ("To keep our mind on prayer," it had been advised.)

The sweat lodge leaders were mostly non-Indians trained in the tradition by Sun Bear or other medicine people. We gathered around one of the lodge leaders as he gave us a no-nonsense instruction in the ancient cleansing ritual. The sweat lodge was also known as the Sacred Stone People's Lodge, he explained. The stones being prepared in the fire would represent the Grandfather spirits of the earth and the Great Spirit.

There were a few warnings. Women on their menstrual (or "moon time") period were recognized as already being cleansed and were forbidden from participating by ancient law. Those with high blood pressure, diabetes, or bad heart conditions were advised against participating. That said, we went to our assigned lodges.

To acknowledge our connection with all animal life, we got down on all fours, saying "All my relations" before crawling clockwise through the open flap and into the lodge.

There were thirteen of us sitting in a tight circle. The ceiling was low and it was dark. I had the stigmata stone clutched in my right hand. Two non-Indian lodge leaders were sitting inside on either side of the entrance. They explained they were being trained in the sacred ways. It was an honor for them to supervise the bringing of the Stone People to the lodge's altar pit, to pour the water and sprinkle the sweet sage and herbs over the glowing rocks, to pass the sacred pipe, to beat the drums during the singing, to lead the praying.

When the stones were placed in the pit, the flap would be closed and the water pouring would begin, they said. At the end of a round each person in the circle would take a turn asking permission for the flap to be opened to receive the cooling night air. There would be four such rounds, they explained.

The leader also stressed that the lodge wasn't an iron man activity. They had seen the power of the heat break the spirit of the macho folk who thought they could tough it out. As the leader explained that the lodge might seem claustrophobic to the uninitiated, it suddenly dawned on me—he was right! I felt the warm swelling of panic for a moment.

The leader concluded that the lodge was a place for gentleness, not tension. By focusing into the prayers, the heat would be purifying and not oppressive.

The stones were brought from the fire by shovel; a coleader scooped them up from the shovel with a pair of antlers and placed them in the center pit. I felt beads of sweat already forming and rolling down my skin as the red-hot rocks began to fill the pit. When one of the leaders sprinkled sage over the stones, a sweet pungency filled the lodge. The flap was pulled down. The only light came from a few glowing chips of stone.

When the water was poured over the rocks, a scalding steam went up and the serious sweating began. As the rounds went on I settled into the songs and prayers. I clutched Katherine's stigmata stone in my hand

and silently prayed for her, my family, my friends, the creation, all the world. Sometimes when the heat would press in, prayer seemed to push it away. One woman wept throughout the ritual.

During the final round one of the leaders took his turn making a final prayer. As the man called upon the Great Spirit, the water pourer ladled on a stream of water that sent up a wave of heat that overwhelmed me. I felt dizzy and that panicky feeling came up again. I squeezed the stigmata stone as if holding on for life. The leader was saying his prayers without end. My initial urge was to bolt for the door saying in my pain, "I'm sorry, brother-man but I *have* to get out!" I controlled the urge and saw the ceremony through to its conclusion. It was a powerful lesson. I realized that seeking my own comfort while someone was in a deep prayer to the Great Spirit was very selfish.

As we finished, we all asked permission to open the flap and crawl out. The cool night air provided an exhilarating release. I stood around for a moment, the sweat streaming off me. It had been an interesting inauguration into a new way of praying. Later that night the rain clouds moved in and the storm was on.

The Saturday morning building and consecration of the medicine wheel was held in an open, grassy field under a light rainfall. The ceremony began with the traditional smudging, a "process of cleansing your energy field," according to the Bear tribe press. An attendant held a tray of burning sage and sweet grass; and the participants breathed in and drew the "good energy" of the herbal smoke to them. Thus cleansed, the participants could take their place in the circle.

The boundaries of the circle had already been marked off with a string tied around stakes marking the directional gate to each of the four directions. Small squares of cloth tied with tobacco were hung around the line, the color of the tie cloth corresponding to the specific color and spiritual aspect of each direction.

By the end of the ceremony thirty-six stones representing different powers and aspects of creation had been placed in the wheel. The outside rung of the wheel honored different animal totems. The rocks forming the hub stood for the Earth Mother, Father Sun, Grandmother Moon, the turtle clan (symbolizing Earth), the frog clan (water), the butterfly clan (air), and the thunderbird clan (fire).

In the center Sun Bear placed a buffalo skull representing the Creator.

A huge crystal was placed next to the skull. The participants ringed around the wheel began to visualize power flowing in and out of the crystal, charging it with spiritual energy. Then the participants were invited to leave their personal stones under the tobacco ties. I placed my sister's stone in the side of the circle proclaimed as the spiritual healing side. Then the ceremony was adjourned for the workshop sessions.

The rainfall was relentless. It dampened the body but not the spirit of the gathering. It was cozy and convivial sitting in one of the spacious lounges at the ranch, talking to new friends about the mysteries of the universe while a pouring rain rattled on the roof.

During one such time I met Janet Whitney and her friend Stephanie Dancing Eagle. Janet was another non-Indian who had recently conducted her first sweat lodge after training and participating in Karok, Sioux, and Arapaho sweats. Each experience in the sweat lodge was unique, because each time it was "the raw essence of spirit coming through," Stephanie told me.

Janet Whitney had a few tales to tell about the power of that raw essence: "On one sweat round I became a wolf," she recalled of a 1984 sweat she experienced with Stephanie and another friend in Bluemont, Virginia.

"I didn't think about being a wolf, it just came. I was the eyes of the wolf, I had fur, I had paws, and I was looking out of a cave over a vast desert area. I was experiencing being the wolf. At the end of that round we went out of the lodge and used the water and came back in and closed the flap—and a beautiful silver spirit wolf that was observable to the naked eyes of all three of us sitting in the lodge came in and sat between Stephanie Dancing Eagle and myself! I was in awe and shock.

"Then from outside the door came a howling, and the lodge was lit up inside by the spirit of this wolf. We could only look at each other with awestruck faces at this wolf sitting between us and hearing the sounds of this other wolf howling outside the lodge.

"The energy shifted, and the wolf became this old, old grandmother with silver, flowing hair. An ancient, beautiful grandmother. She was talking through Stephanie Dancing Eagle to me, giving me words of healing that I needed. One of the things she said to all of us in the lodge was 'It's time to get off it and get on with it.' "

Janet laughed. She felt her successful graduation into leading sweat lodge ceremonies was one way she was accomplishing the gentle admonition of her spectral grandmother.

Janet experienced another powerful sweat lodge vision later that same year in a suburb of Baltimore. Over twenty people were huddled inside the lodge, saying their prayers in the darkness, when the spirit broke loose. "All of a sudden the top of the lodge blew open spiritually," Janet recalled, her voice carrying some of the awe she felt that day. "The blankets and tarps were still on, but we could not see them—it was the stars and the cosmos above, and every person in the lodge had the same vision. And then a green beam and a white beam of light came into the center of the lodge from this opening in the ceiling and shone on the rocks. A wave of peace and love flowed through every person in that lodge. And the message that came through was 'This is for your healing. Ask for the healing that you need and receive it now.' People were crying and praying out loud. There was a lot of love and tears and so much beauty."

Saturday afternoon I walked out into a hard rain to the sweat lodge area. The rains were threatening to

cancel the sweat lodge sessions planned for that night.
The tarps and blankets of the lodges had been rolled
up, and the sandy grounds were filling up with water.
A solitary woman in a yellow rain suit was tending the
fire that was still bravely kindling the grandfather
stones.

The fire tender told me she ran her own sweats in
the Los Angeles area. It was difficult for her to talk
about the sweat lodge experience. She smiled, rivulets
of rain streaming down her cap and over her face. She
leaned on the shovel she was using to turn over the
stones in the flames. It was hard to talk about the ceremony because it couldn't be put into words. It had to
be felt from the heart.

She told me that there was a great medicine man at
the gathering who might be able to put the sacred truth
into words better than she. His name was Bear Heart
and the Great Spirit had given him amazing powers.
Bear Heart was speaking at a workshop later that afternoon, and I told her I would listen to his talk. We
said good-bye and I left her in the cold, wind-whipped
rain.

Before going to Bear Hearts' talk I went to the medicine wheel. Only a few people were strolling about
the sacred stone circle. I picked up my sister's stigmata stone and entered into the circle from one of the
directional gates. I walked up to the skull and crystal
rock center, and said some prayers for my sister. Then
I pressed the stone to the surface of the crystal, and a
diffuse glow shone through my hands. I marveled at
that, then returned the stigmata stone to its place in
the circle.

The assembly room was packed when I arrived for
Bear Heart's talk. Bear Heart was sitting in a chair at
the front of the room, the audience sitting on the floor
around him. He was a husky man with an engaging
grin and a robust vitality.

"I'm happy to be here," he told the group. Then he
explained that the literal Indian translation of that
greeting would be the beautiful "My heart was made

glad I come.'' Through such subtle ways he illustrated the richness and diversity of America's tribal heritage.

Bear Heart recalled that the elders before him were at peace with themselves and their environment. They could gaze at the clear blue sky and see the future, listen to the wind and receive news from a faraway place, look at the trees and rocks and read the secrets of the universe.

Bear Heart's knowledge formed a nexus between those ancient Indian ways and twentieth-century knowledge such as linguistics and psychology. He was also learned in spiritual disciplines from Zen meditation to yogic chakra systems.

His medicine training had taken fourteen years. His path of apprenticeship was more than learning how to hold the sacred pipe, or conduct a sweat or vision quest, more than learning the songs and prayers. Like his legendary elders of old, he had to first master himself and become one with his environment before he could channel the infinite power of the Great Spirit.

The training sometimes involved dangerous tests. Once his teacher had told him to remove his shoes and hand them to him. The teacher placed the shoes on the other side of a gully and told Bear Heart to walk through the gorge and retrieve them. When Bear Heart approached the rift in the earth, he saw that it was full of rattlesnakes. As he walked barefoot past the rattlers he kept singing a special song his teacher had given him. It saw him safely through to the other side.

In another test his teacher told him to fling his arms around a tree, and then his legs. The teacher then left him in that odd position. Bear Heart felt puzzled, disgruntled, and ridiculous. What if a friend came by and saw him? After long moments in the position he realized it was a lesson about jumping over the barrier of ego and self-importance. When he realized that, intuitive insights began to flow. He then felt a communion and communication with the tree.

''When I was through training I was told: 'Never call yourself a healer—*He* is the one who heals. You are merely a caretaker of sacred knowledge, dispensing that knowledge to the best of your ability. That's all you are—a channel. So don't go around saying you're a healer or a medicine man. People can call you that if they want to, but you just go around and do the very best that you can.' ''

Bear Heart could perform amazing feats. He could put hot coals in his mouth and blow out healing energy. If he led a vision quest up into the mountains, he knew what songs and drumbeats would help ensure the safety of his people crying for a vision from the Great Spirit. But his greatest medicine was an understanding of how to be at peace in times of joy and adversity. This "inner smile" was all about the unselfish power of love for oneself and others, and the healing strength of forgiveness.

"The way our people look at things—before an arrow can go forward you have to pull it back," he told the group. "Before you yourself can go forward, come back and look within yourself. What is your identity? Who are you? What are you? And then—*why* are you?"

Then he told a beautiful tale, a story that went, as they say, in circles. He began by talking about his youth growing up on a farm in Oklahoma. In that household his mother would rise early to make her prayers to the Great Spirit, thanking the Creator for everything that would come to them that day. From his father he learned how to be a hard worker. At the age of eight Bear Heart could hitch up a team of horses to the plow. When he was ten his dad gave him two acres of his own to use as he wished.

But then his father became sick and bedridden. He asked his son if he would mind staying out of school a year to help his mother run the farm. Bear Heart willingly agreed. He saw to his father's comfort and performed all the dawn-to-dusk duties required of a life on the farm.

Father's Day came around and he didn't have a cent to buy his pa a gift. All during the day Bear Heart worked as hard as he could, hoping that something would happen, that by nighttime a miracle would provide the means for a nice Father's Day present. But nothing happened. And he wept in disappointment when he went to bed.

"In the morning I got up and did my chores, and before I came back with the breakfast tray, I ran into my room and took a piece of paper and I wrote, 'Dearest dad, you're the most wonderful man in the whole world to me, and I love you very much. Happy Father's Day, your son.'

"That's all I could afford! So I took that and put it on the tray and handed it to him and he read it. And then he reached up and embraced me—I can still feel it now! When he embraced me, whatever the glories of the Beyond is, I got a glimpse of some piece of it that stays in my heart. That's the kind of life I had when I grew up."

Some years later, Bear Heart had married and he and his wife eventually brought into the world two children, a son and a daughter. In 1964 his son signed up for a year of isolated duty in the Philippine Islands. But on a flight from Hawaii to Manila the plane crashed. Over eighty young men died, his only son among them.

"Not long afterwards a brother of mine, his name is Raymond Butler, gave a feast and invited me and my family over. And after the feast he said, 'Brother, I call you brother. You helped me put away my mother when she passed away. You shed tears with me at that time. And now I hate to see you shedding tears for your son. I want to share my oldest boy with you so you'll have someone you can call son and he can call dad.'

"He put a blanket on me and put some money in my hands. We made brothers. And that boy became a real son to me, remembered me on Father's Day and a lot of things.

"Then, a year ago last January, Raymond was having a tepee ceremony. His son was fifteen years old and they were having a big, happy meeting for his son. Now, Raymond had the job of being head of the housing program for his tribe, and he had had to evict two families. In retaliation they had been harassing him. So that night they began throwing things at the tepee. Since it was on his property and he was sponsoring the meeting—he was taking care of the kettledrum that we use in that ceremony—he ran out. That was what the young boys wanted. They lured him away, they stabbed him in the back, they stomped his face in, killed him, and ran off.

"He still had that kettledrum stick in his hand because he was offering his prayers to the Great Spirit all night long for his son. He believed in the Great Spirit. So, having that stick in his hand he was loyal, he had faith, he had belief. He died for something.

"So what about forgiveness? We talk about love. Yes, I had love for him. But what about forgiveness for those boys who did it? That was the challenge to me personally. So I had to pray.

" 'Great Spirit, I can't honestly forgive them—I want to because they are your creation also, they have souls like everyone else, but perhaps misguided. I don't condone what they did, but they're still your creatures. So, you keep loving them, but love them through *me* so I might learn how your love really works, that I might learn what love is all about!' "

There were a lot of teary eyes in the audience during Bear Heart's talk. At the end a long line formed with people taking turns to embrace him.

That night, the last night of the gathering, the rain picked up in intensity. The sweat lodge program had been rained out. I visited the site in the darkness. The sandy area was swimming under several inches of rain. But some embers that had settled under one of the stone grandfathers still glowed red in the darkness.

By the concluding ceremonies the following afternoon, the rains had finally stopped. Sun Bear thanked the thunder beings for joining the gathering, and a good laugh went around the stone circle.

When I saw my sister later that evening I gave her the stigmata stone that had been through a sweat lodge and been blessed by the medicine wheel circle and the elements. She took the rock. She suddenly looked up. She transferred the stone to her other hand.

"My goodness, it's throbbing!" She laughed.

And I thought back to the power of that first sweat experience, gripping the stigmata stone and feeling the grandfathers speaking with the hot breath of solar flame.

——————— Part II ———————

Channeling Zones

5

Power Places

During the Harmonic Convergence a number of sacred sites around the world were hailed as propitious points to usher in the New Age. In the U.S. this included Mount Shasta in California, Chaco Canyon, New Mexico, and Serpent Mound in Ohio.

Sacred spots are places of power. The energy at those points can elicit transcendent feelings, visions, even miracles. Many such sites have traditionally been considered gateways to the spirit world. These power places are often located in wilderness areas. Many spiritual seekers throughout time have journeyed to the desert or climbed a mighty mountain in hopes of experiencing the divine.

Power places are not always famous sites enshrined in public knowledge. There are many secret power spots across the land. I had a personal experience with one of them.

I was caretaking a friend's ranch in the High Sierras one winter while he brought his cattle down to the warmer foothill climes. Before he left me in charge, he showed me a spring on his property that had been sacred to the Washo Indians who formerly abided in the area. The medicine people of the tribe once used the spring to access the spirit world.

My friend had known the last of the Washo medicine people. He always let the medicine man come onto his property to visit the spring and make his sacred prayers. Although that last medicine man died from complications due to alcoholism, my friend said the man's spirits were always lifted after a visit to the sacred spring.

One morning I pulled on my jacket, put on my Stetson, and stepped out into a light snowfall for a hike to the spring across the snow-covered land. After crossing a creek that was starting to ice over and walking through a thick forest, I came to a slight rise in the land. A valley of primordial snow and ice spread out to mountains obscured by the silent movement of Sierra snow clouds. A few yards out from the cloistered forest was the spring.

The spring was banked with snow and fringed with icicles. I took off my hat, sat down, and felt the soft snowfall. There was a great, primal stillness in the land.

I got to my feet and looked up into the snowfall. Suddenly the snowfall began speeding up. I felt as if I was being catapulted into the heavens at super speed. I laughed and stretched into it, wondering if I was really flying.

Then the energy shifted, the snowflakes resuming a soft, slow free-fall. I felt the ground once again underneath my feet. I put my hat back on and had an exhilarating hike back to the cabin.

The purity of many power places in the country is threatened in many ways. Whether it is the industrial concerns seeking to mine the sacred Four Corners area or recreation corporations planning massive ski lodge developments on the slopes of Shasta, such interests are drawn to exploit, not experience, power places. The preservation of the sacred purpose of such areas is an issue increasingly on the agendas of legislatures and the courts.

The American Indian Religious Freedom Act was passed by the Congress in 1978, promising protection for Native American religions and access to sacred sites.[1] In 1983 an historic court decision permanently barred the U.S. government from logging or road building in a crest of Northern California's Siskiyou Mountains known as the sacred High Country.

U.S. District Judge Stanley Weigel of San Francisco, who made the decision, observed that the area was regarded by the native Karok, Yurok, and Tolowa peoples as the center of their spiritual world. The ruling pointed out that the twenty-seven-mile area affected was used for important ceremonies, as a spiritual training area for young tribal members, and as a place valued by Indians for communicating with the Creator.

"It was the first time, according to legal experts, that a court has protected an Indian religious site on national public lands under the religious freedom guarantees of the First Amendment," a news report concluded.[2] (Years of appeals led to the case coming before a hearing of the Supreme Court in November of 1987.)

Thankfully, the energy of power places has not been chased away by all the real or imagined threats to their sanctity. Many places held as sacred for centuries still retain their spiritual vitality.

Mount Shasta is a legendary spot that still facilitates visionary experiences. The giant volcano rises 14,162 feet into the clouds. A climb up Shasta is an awsome experience. Once above the clouds, in the rarefied air of the summit, the view stretches for hundreds of miles.

But the mountain can be a foreboding place as well. With its incredible scale Shasta can create its own weather, sometimes with terrible swiftness. A friend once told me a friend of his had died of exposure on the mountain when his hastily erected tent was torn out of its pegs and blown away by a sudden storm.

Such a place also engenders its own modern legends. Some Shasta tales claim the mountain serves as a base for flying saucers and that an entire secret civilization lives deep in the mountain's interior.

Mount Shasta was the site for meetings with the Ascended Masters, spiritual beings who "protect and assist in expanding the Light within mankind upon this earth," according to Guy and Edna Ballard.

In the 1930s, a book entitled *Unveiled Mysteries* was published by the Ballards claiming contact with the Ascended Master Germain. Mr. Ballard, reportedly a former paper hanger, stock salesman, and mine promoter, had come to the little town of Shasta "on government business." Ballard also decided to investigate rumors that a brotherhood of divine men abided in the mountain peaks above the town.

On a hike up the mountain Ballard met a young hiker who, after a closer look, "was no ordinary person." It was Saint Germain, who took Ballard on an astral-body journey into the sky, where he viewed visions of his own past life experiences recorded in the Etheric Records of the atmosphere.

"St. Germain attuned their brain structure so he could project a tube of light to them that they would read in the atmosphere," claims Dr. Jay Scherer, a renowned healer and massage therapist in Santa Fe who knew the late Ballards and calls them "the greatest channels in the world."

A power spot many spiritual seekers feel will be the Shambala West of the Aquarian Age is Sedona, Arizona. *(Outside* magazine in its October 1987 issue mused that the place would be one of the hippest zip codes in the next ten years, particularly for the "spiritual real estate moguls, crystal power, the astrological Heights condo complex" set.) In Sedona, strange, twisted formations and canyons of bright red rock, sandstone and basalt rise up over the high desert country. Ten major areas, with such names as Bell Rock, Coffee Pot Rock, and Boynton Canyon are said to contain power vortexes of incredible spiritual energy.

"Planet Earth is a living, changing, evolving being, that has places of power on it, much like we have acupressure points on our bodies," writes Sedona resident Gayle Johansen in her booklet, *The Sedona Vortex Experience.* "The power points or vortexes on the planet are places where energy can be seen, felt, and experienced. Unusual phenomena often occur at these places."[3]

Visitors to the vortex areas have reported feeling energy surges, seeing visions, and experiencing bursts of intuitive awareness and detailed remembrances of past life experiences. Some visitors, for no apparent reason, are moved to tears when they arrive, as if they've finally come home.

Gayle Johansen felt a trip to a vortex spot was a sacred event. When hiking to a vortex it was important to "find a spot that you resonate with or are called to," her booklet states. It is important to be aware of the spirit world and to ask permission of the guardian spirits before entering an area.

During a trip to Sedona Gayle took me to Bell Rock for a taste of vortex. The "masculine energy vortex" was located in a hilly, red-rock valley off a two-lane stretch of highway.

As we stood on the dirt trail that led over rock and brush to the open rocky rise of Bell Rock, Gayle invoked the spiritual protectors of the area: "Spirits of Bell Rock, we ask your permission to be here. We ask the assistance of the four directions, the east, the west, the north, and the south, to guide us in this journey as we come to experience your energies and to channel these energies today."

We stood there for a moment, marveling at the grandeur of the bell-shaped rock and the red-rock hills that ringed the stony valley. As we stood there I felt a humming rhythm coming up from somewhere deep in the earth. It was a strange sensation.

"It feels good to me," Gayle said, looking over at me. "Let's go for it."

As we walked to where the dusty trail ended and the rise of the boulders began, Gayle mentioned the importance of being centered at a power spot. "You get centered by feeling the energies in your aura and sending roots deep down into the earth, becoming like one of these ancient trees that's here to guard this energy," explained the vortex veteran.

We each began hiking our separate ways. I noticed stone medicine wheels scattered throughout the area.

In one spot someone had used dozens of stones to spell out the phrase: ALL IS LOVE AND PEACE YOU ARE.

I didn't feel the kind of extraordinary hum of energy on the rest of the hike that I had felt through my boots at the entrance to the trail. Perhaps I was distracted by the sounds of automobile traffic below.

As we left, Gayle lamented that she had forgotten to bring the corn meal she usually sifted onto the rocks. It was her way of offering thanks to the Earth Mother after a vortex visit. Before exiting, Gayle did offer thanks to all the spirits and guardians.

While in Sedona I met up with psychics Patricia and Jon Diegel. They had moved to Sedona to continue their psychic studies. One of their undertakings they dubbed "Trinity Power," a tri-level program for personal psychic growth developed through their own extensive channeling.

At the first level one worked with developing latent psychic abilities. At level two the clearing of present-life blocks would move the students to a state of aliveness. At the final stage the practitioner could move ahead into the future to tap into the talents and knowledge of their tomorrow lives.

One night I attended a Trinity Power training session held in the unlikely New Age venue of the Sedona Elk's Club Lodge. The mounted heads of elk and deer looked down on us from the walls as we put our folding chairs into a circle.

In another meeting room of the lodge Jon Diegel was being inducted into the ranks of the Elks, much to the amusement of some of the nearly two dozen Trinity students gathered for the class on The Blueprint for Immortality. Jon did return from his initiation in time to join us in the circle as we joined hands and mentally channeled light energy to cover the lodge with a "golden dome of protection." According to Patricia this kind of "group synergy" would bring a good, healing energy to the lodge and the people and activities held in it.

For a final meditation Patricia said we would perform a past-life regression. As she drifted into a trance state she asked us to close our eyes and return to the lifetime she said we all had known in Atlantis. She asked us to see an Atlantean healing center. She described healing units suspended from the ceiling. There were patients in the units and doctors on the floor who were working devices that directed healing energies into the units. She asked us to visualize whether we were the patients or the doctors.

During the group sharing afterwards everyone revealed strong impressions. Some described in detail the working of the healing units while others had remembrances of ancient healing. I had walked through the healing center and out into the fresh, warm air to stroll through a beautiful garden that surrounded the center. On my way out I had seen a pool of dark water receiving a constant liquid precipitation from the ceiling. Patricia told me later that was the healing pool. She knew her way around Atlantis.

After the evening program I walked out into the chilly night air with Jon to get a ride back to the Diegel household. Standing by the car in the dark for a few moments while Jon fumbled with his key ring I glanced up at the Elk's Lodge roof. I wondered if the golden dome was really up there.

"So, Jon, can you really see the golden dome over the lodge?" I asked.

"I can't even see my car keys right now!" He laughed, finally locating the key.

A spot does not have to have a reputation for miraculous supernatural happenings to be sacred ground. There is a subtle, contemplative force at work in personal power places. Although such a special place may indeed have mystical attributes, the attraction is often an intuitive or emotional connection made by an individual.

There is such a personal power spot that I favor for ritualistic retreats in which the spirit in the land comes through in all its power. I'll call the place Chrysalis Canyon. It is located in a mountain area in Northern California that was once sacred to the Indians. I've been going on retreats there for ten years now. My friends Mike Doran and Brian Connolly are my usual partners in these Chrysalis Canyon adventures. I think of them as my Chrysalis Canyon brothers.

Mike grew up near the canyon and had been trekking to the place years before he even met Brian and me. Jim Taylor, an old buddy of Mike's, had introduced him to the place after discovering the canyon's existence while poring over topographical maps of the region. Thereafter, when springtime rolled around and the tall grasses of the open fields became lush with purple and yellow flowers, Mike and Jim would backpack into the canyon for a weekend retreat.

Several years later I met Mike at college in San Francisco and we became friends. When Mike brought up Chrysalis Canyon in conversation I was intrigued. We broached the idea of a Chrysalis Canyon trip with our mutual friend, Brian, and he was enthusiastic. Being primal, kindred spirits, the three of us had always needed the magical infusions of hope and glory that only nature can provide.

Chrysalis was a balm for Mike, a self-admittedly high-speed character who by day wore a corporate suit and sold computers. By night he wore torn T-shirts, black vests, and drummed his bass guitar licks with punk rock bands in hard-core San Francisco rock clubs. Mike would bring a boundless energy to the canyon that was contagious and the perfect inspiration for exploring the canyon's hidden places.

For Brian, a burly Irishman who sang in clubs, taught music, and was a maestro of the sound technician's art, the canyon spoke to the romantic in him. I had once seen a picture depicting the Hindu god Shiva in a muscular pose, stripped to the waist and sitting yoga style on a tiger skin while meditating on a lonely mountain peak, a union of strength, gentleness, and control that reminded me of Brian. He'd bring that

Shivaistic energy to Chrysalis, as well as the ability to read the canyon's geological formations the way some people read the words in a history book.

And so, every year come springtime, when the first flowers began to open with their sweet perfume, a kind of inner signal would get one or all of us to dreaming about the special Chrysalis experience of the year before. And then the call would go around, we would set the date, and go.

The hike to the canyon begins by climbing over a cattle guard at the edge of a rural road, climbing over a hill thick with gnarled oaks, and then walking a few miles across the expansive tableland (climbing over a few barbed-wire fences along the way). On the horizon is a lone tree stretching heavenward that we aim for. We call it the guide tree. From that point we follow a flowing creek that makes its meandering way to the canyon, hits the rocky edge of the sheer cliff, and becomes a waterfall into the tree-shaded pool below.

On the edge of the canyon is a twisted old manzanita. The branches twist and curl in a horizontal way, forming a natural seat. Half of it is dead, the other half a healthy reddish hue. I call it the meditation tree.

I sit on the meditation tree and gaze into the canyon to the valley of rocks created by centuries of hardened volcanic lava that dried and splintered off from the lip of the great chasm. Past the rocky floor is the thick canyon forest, and beyond that is the edge of the top of a table mountain. It rises above the valley beyond that Mike once dubbed "the bliss layer."

Sitting on the meditation tree I think about life and death, good and evil. It makes me wonder what will win out in the end. I think of the primordial ocean waves and volcanic eruptions that carved out this place of power.

During our canyon haunts we've discussed life and death . . . seen the bare bones of cattle scattered and bleaching in openings in the forest of trees on the top of the canyon . . . debated history and the future while warming ourselves by a fire on the ridge in preparation for a star-filled night and a chance to greet the moon . . . watched electrical storms from inside the open cave on the canyon floor . . . felt rainfall so soft the moisture seemed to evaporate at the touch. We've felt like Stone Age men engaged in the ancient evocations of elemental forces . . . baked like lizards in the rock valley when the sun was high . . . watched hawks fly above the rim and felt ourselves flying with them. . . .

Those are a few of the little wonders that intrigue a trio of Space Age Huck Finns when they visit their place of power.

We all need power places. There we renew that ancient part of ourselves that communicated with the natural world. Power places hold all the makings for the forming of a pure heart. From there flows a path to walk the walk and the hope that only good will follow us all the days of our lives.

The Underground Streams

Two men and a woman were seated on the floor making an occult game out of the *I Ching*, China's ancient *Book of Changes*. One of the men, American journalist and occult researcher William Seabrook, had wondered what would happen if a player took one of the sixty-four hexagrams, visualized an imaginary door, and then mentally pressed the symbol on the door. Could that mental portal then open onto the psychic landscape represented by the hexagram?

Both men had played the game with no results. When the woman's turn came, she selected the hexagram Ko, the symbol for change and the renewing aspect of the celestial and terrestrial forces.

She closed her eyes and visualized the hexagram-marked door. Suddenly the door swung open in her mind. Excitedly she described what she was seeing as her mind crossed the threshold.

She was entering a land of snow. She felt herself walking into it, moving faster, and then realized she was galloping into a sudden snow squall.

Her partners watched in horror as her face underwent a fearful change. Foam licked at her lips and her voice choked off. Then she emitted a wolfish howl.

"What had begun innocently, almost as a game, turned into a dangerous attempt to rescue," a later account of the incident reports. "In trying to recall the woman's spirit her friends shook her, called her name, and slapped her face. She snarled and would have ravaged them if the cramped posture she had maintained for so long had not paralyzed her limbs. It was with great effort that her resistance was overcome. As she calmed down, her face lost its wolfish expression and assumed once more its usual appearance."[1]

The woman had tapped into an atavistic manifestation of prehuman ancestry—just one of the pitfalls that can be waiting in the darkness for the unwary pilgrim strolling along a spiritual path.

"There are a lot of things in the spirit world I don't want in me," a medicine man in Santa Fe told me. "Some of the channeling that is coming through is not real healthy."

There is another viewpoint that considers evil as in the mind of the beholder. "On one level, yes, there are evil forces," opines the Light Institute's Chris Griscom. "But they are only evil in so far as we interact with them. If we don't interact with them, they're not evil. They are simply energetics. The divine force creates nothing that is outside of cosmic law. We, in our manipulation, produce evil."

"You can have evil forces work through you or you can have good forces work through you; that's what we call channeling," therapist Jay Scherer notes. "Evil forces will work through people that allow them. Or good forces can work through. We have free will to choose who will work through us."

But as Ralph Waldo Emerson once wrote, "Things are in the saddle, and ride mankind." And so it can be for those who feel they are being stalked and cursed by black magic forces.

One strange tale of possession by evil forces involves Jelly Roll Morton, the legendary jazz band leader from New Orleans whose star reached its ascendancy in the 1920s. Thereafter the great Jelly Roll mysteriously hit the skids and suffered through rough times until his death in 1941. The jazz man told his story to folk song collector Alan Lomax in 1938, claiming that he had been shadowed by a voodoo curse.

"When I was a young man, these hoodoo people

with their underground stuff help me along,'' Jelly Roll told Lomax. ''I did not feel grateful and I did not reward them for the help they gave. Now, when everything began to go against me, those underground streams were running against me too.''

He sought the help of a medium named Madame Elise. He attended her seances and followed faithfully her prescriptions for curing the evil he felt was ailing him. But all that happened was he found himself thousands of dollars poorer and his luck ''just got blacker and blacker.''

After Morton's death Lomax interviewed Anita Gonzalez, the jazz man's first wife and the woman who nursed him during his final days. Jelly Roll, sick with a bad heart, had driven his Lincoln from New York to Los Angeles in the dead of winter to be with her.

Gonzales said Morton's illness had coincided with the death that year of Laura Hunter, the godmother who had raised Jelly Roll—and who was a voodoo witch.

''Well, everybody knows that before you can become a witch you have to sell the person you love the best to Satan as a sacrifice,'' Gonzalez told Lomax. ''Laura loved Jelly best. Jelly always knew she'd sold him to Satan and that when she died, he'd die too— she would take him down with her. . . .

''Laura died. And then Jelly . . . he taken sick too. A couple months later he died in my arms, begging me to keep anointing his lips with oil that had been blessed by a bishop in New York. He had oil running all over him when he gave up the ghost.''[2]

The fear of black magic has sometimes erupted in hysteria, notably the Salem witch-hunt of 1692. That infamous episode culminated in thirty-four alleged witches being hung by the neck until dead. Witches have been trying to clear their names ever since. (Senator Jesse Helms of North Carolina made a short-lived attempt in 1986 to eliminate the tax-exempt religious standing of witchcraft groups.)

''People who should know better confuse witchcraft

with Satanists, who worship Lucifer and exalt Christian sin. The notion will not die," J. Gordon Melton, director of the Institute for Study of American Religion told the *Los Angeles Times*. "Witches don't devour babies, sacrifice animals, perform black masses, abuse young female victims, or pray to the devil. In fact, witches do not believe the devil exists."

In fact, any of the estimated fifty thousand witches in the U.S. are likely to be students, teachers, attorneys, computer programmers, psychologists, or housewives—a far cry from the legendary caldron stirrers of old. Witchcraft is actually rooted in the Goddess image that exalts fertility and such archetypes as the Earth Mother.[3]

The Satanists, however, indulge themselves in a more sinister form of worship. The satanic black mass seeks to defame the Christ aspect. A good deal of satanic activity ends up recorded on police blotters around the country.

There was the case of four mutilated calves found on the Hayward, California, shoreline. Police investigators assumed that the animals had been wasted by devil cultists during a grisly moonlit rite. Although none of the meat had been cut away, some of the calves had eyeballs, ears, and intestines removed. Another calf had been drained of blood. The hideous corpses had been discovered after a full moon—optimum time for ceremonies in which celebrants are said to bathe with and drink the freshly spilled blood.[4]

The Satanists allegedly target infants or young children for even more ghastly rites. Stories of satanic abuse cases have been turning up around the country. Interviews of allegedly abused school children, conducted by the Los Angeles district attorney's office and L.A. area psychologists in 1987, revealed stories of satanic worship, sexual abuse, the drinking of blood, and even the sacrifice of infants. "The reason kids talk about torture, abuse, and child homicide is because it occurs," psychiatrist Michael Durfee told *Omni* magazine in 1986. "The stories are too patterned not to be true."[5]

Dr. Bill Baldwin, a Carmel, California, psychologist, maintains there exists an underground "international satanic cult" that threatens with death anyone who attempts to expose them. Dr. Baldwin believes that many of the children reported missing each year become the victims of ritual killings and cannibalism by this group. Such cults, he asserts, sometimes use "hypnosis and brainwashing techniques" to add to their ranks. Once ensnared, the person becomes "a slave to the cult." Dr. Baldwin says some "very upstanding" people in society are secret cultists.

"They [the cults] come from fear, not from love," Dr. Baldwin says. "Satan offers power. It's all ego."

Is he afraid of speaking out against such cults?

"I'm not afraid of it," he says. "It makes me very angry that this happens."

The world of ghosts can also be a frightening experience for those on the spiritual path. Ghosts can be defined as the spirits of departed mortals that have not yet passed off the Earth plane. The wraiths of those who have suffered a sudden or traumatic death often wander the Earth, sometimes abiding in the environs of their death experience, or in a place that was a favored haunt during life. Some spirits, seeking the solidity of the mortal shell they inhabited in life, will take possession of another's body.

There are large numbers of ghost hunters and exorcists who have seen and felt what California psychologist Edith Fiore calls the "unquiet dead."

"In my dehaunting of houses I've encountered every type of materialization and manifestation," observes Brad Steiger, a writer and investigator of spiritual and paranormal matters. "I've been with police officers who've had their minds blown away when a ghost materialized in front of them. And I've stopped them from shooting it because it wouldn't make any difference. I've put my hands through ghosts!"

Hereward Carrington, a pioneer of psychical research in the U.S., had numerous jolting encounters with haunting manifestations. One of the most terrifying occurred the night of August 13, 1937, when Carrington, his wife, and five other people spent a night investigating the cause of strange disturbances reported in a multistory house outside of New York City.

The group noticed nothing strange in the cellar or on the ground floor. But they all sensed something unusual on the second floor. Walking along a hall, they found a door that opened up onto a flight of stairs leading to the third story. Carrington decided to take the lead and investigate what might be beyond.

"Glancing up, I could see that the top floor was brilliantly lighted, and that a steep flight of stairs led just ahead of me," Carrington later wrote. "Leading the way, with the others close behind me, I ascended the stairs, and made a sharp turn to the right, finding myself confronted by a series of small rooms.

"The instant I did so, I felt as though a vital blow had been delivered to my solar plexus. My forehead broke out into profuse perspiration, my head swam, and I had difficulty in swallowing. It was a most extraordinary sensation, definitely physiological, and unlike anything I had ever experienced before. A feeling of terror and panic seized me, and for the moment I had the utmost difficulty in preventing myself from turning around and fleeing down the stairs! Vaguely I remember saying aloud:

" 'Very powerful! Very powerful!'

"My wife, who was just behind me, had taken a step or two forward. She was just exclaiming, 'Oh, what cute little rooms!' when the next moment she was crying 'No! No!' and raced down the steep flight of stairs like a scared rabbit."

When they regrouped and climbed back up the stairs they discovered that the eerie force had disappeared and that the powerful room "seemed absolutely clear of all influences, clean, pure and normal."

Later Carrington discovered that a former tenant had committed suicide in that part of the house.[6]

Patricia and Jon Diegel have experienced many hauntings. One strange story involved a haunting that plagued a hilly area adjacent to a broad plateau in Sedona. The solid walls of houses were inexplicably collapsing, and one night a resident sighted two spectral Indian armies warring on the plateau.

"Finally someone got smart and got a Hopi Indian medicine man to come to bless that land and drive off [the ghostly warriors] who were still fighting their war," Patricia Diegel recounts. "The warriors were knocking down the walls of houses from the astral plane! So the medicine man blessed them and sent them away."

Psychics Ted and Jan Robles feel it is important for the exorcist to be centered in a holy light to avoid being overwhelmed by the evil forces. "All you have to do to get [under the control of the dark forces] is to be afraid of them, all you have to do is shine a light on things—and it's no longer dark! Dark forces cannot stand the light. If you get to be afraid of them, that opens you up to the entrance of the dark forces.

"But the dark is going to attack the light at every opportunity. Strange things are going to happen even to the light workers. But it doesn't get to the point of being difficult or dangerous because the guardians [of the exorcists] are there to see that it doesn't."

One dehaunting performed by the Robles was a house in a wealthy suburb of Sacramento, California. A strange chill and an unusual darkness was plaguing the house. The family suffered from constant flus, colds, and other illnesses. The family was finally referred to the Robles, who agreed to see if any evil forces were at work.

During their investigation of the house the Robles discovered that a beautiful, hand-carved antique dresser from Germany contained three little entities that were causing all the trouble. With their psychic eyesight the Robles saw the entities as "little black hairy things."

"We ran a sheet of [spiritual] light through the room and the dresser, and the little entities hung on for dear life as the sheet of light spun around them," Jan Robles remembers. "So we talked with them at some length. They were from a huge oak tree in the Black Forest in Germany, and that cabinet had been made from that big oak tree.

"So we described the Black Forest to them, asking them to remember how beautiful it was. I finally got them so homesick they went back to the Black Forest."

The possession of a human by a ghost or demonic entity poses even more complex challenges to the exorcist than a dehaunting. The intensity of many depossessions (the term in vogue for exorcism) is illustrated in the following account of Rolling Thunder's struggle with a spirit that had taken possession of a doctor.

"The spirit was a very strong spirit with a powerful and dominating will. The doctor's own spirit was there all the time, but the other one completely dominated. I could see both these things—they were both there. . . . Well, this other spirit didn't want to give up; it had to be forced hard, and when it left the man, you could almost hear it. He let out a scream and fell over and then he went into a state of shock. After that the doctor was his old self."[7]

Dr. Bill Baldwin is one of the pioneers in the use of depossession as a tool in professional psychiatric diagnosis and treatment. He travels around the country teaching other colleagues how to use depossession techniques in their work.

Baldwin has assembled a body of case studies that seem to indicate that such psychosomatic problems as multiple personality disorders may often be the result of spirit or demonic possession. Some personality disorders may even be caused when the past lives of a person, usually "folded down into the soul consciousness,'' somehow ''pops out,'' and that past-life personality becomes expressed in the individual's present life, Dr. Baldwin says. In that case, the trick for the psychologist is getting that part of the soul bundle, so integral to the whole of the soul consciousness, pushed back into place.

Baldwin does not offer his current research as the absolute proof of spirit possession, but allows that his work indicates the possibility of such a conclusion. He and some of his colleagues claim the tools of past life and depossession therapy results in complete cures or dramatic improvements in the health of their clients.

Although his clients come from every field and level of society, the most high-risk occupations for spirit possession are those involving work with the dead or dying, such as nurses, ambulance drivers, and morticians, he notes. Drug or alcohol addicts are also felt to be in this high-risk group, although it's not clear to many therapists whether substance abuse is a cause, or effect, of depossession.

A significant area of exploration has been with Vietnam veterans. Dr. Baldwin attributes many of the adjustment problems some vets have faced years after their return from the battles of Southeast Asia to spirit possession. During such depossession sessions the spirits of friends killed in combat, even the ghosts of ancient warriors, have revealed themselves and been exorcised, he reports.

Dr. Baldwin is tall and handsome, with the classic square-jawed features that film director Alfred Hitchcock prized in the leading men of his psychological thrillers. He has a gentle touch with his clients as he puts them into a deeply relaxed state. If the client begins to describe presences, and the client's voice changes in tone or perspective to that of another personality, he is uncompromising in sending what he assumes to be an intruding spirit to ''the Light,'' the heavenly place where all spirits can go for rest or refuge.

Baldwin calls his work ''spiritual psychotherapy.''

He also echoes the viewpoint that his work is not with-out risk to the therapist. Although he has not yet ex-perienced some of the most dangerous manifestations of possession—there are reported cases of possessed children that can lift and throw heavy furniture, and exorcists being hurled against walls by the spirits—Dr. Baldwin recognizes that such physical danger is a con-stant possibility in his work.

"There is a danger to the therapist," he says. "I have to keep my health and energy up. Spirits could attack me. Spirits somehow seem to be able to manip-ulate the physical universe. I'll be doing a session and suddenly I'll start to sway, my knees buckle. I'll call on the God source when in danger."

Possession cases across the country provide detailed descriptions as to the appearance of demonic entities. Hundreds and hundreds of patients have described the demonic forces within them as growling, black crea-tures with sharp teeth. These demons hate humans and God, Baldwin says.

In some depossession sessions, demonic entities dramatically surface from the patient's personality. Pa-tients have described their own fingernails becoming like claws, their voice changing to a threatening growl. Some of these demons give their names. Dr. Baldwin has even found that some of the spirits that possess his patients themselves reveal other spirits and demonic entities within themselves.

Dr. Baldwin claims that the ultimate commander of the demon entities he calls "the little ones" has come through during a few depossession sessions—Lucifer himself. "Lucifer is very sophisticated, precise almost to the point of being haughty," he says. "It knows about the Light, it knows it's deceiving the little ones. But it's got a job to do. When I hear Lucifer's voice, I get a chill that goes right up my spine."

Despite their evil intent, Dr. Baldwin still considers the demonic beings "creatures of God. They have the light within them, too," he says. "Part of the therapy I do is to get the demons to see the light inside. I have them keep looking at it. 'Oh, I'm light—it feels so warm,' they say. So the demons turn to the Light and are taken home.''

The following episodes are select transcriptions of actual clinical depossession sessions conducted by Dr. Baldwin. As in any channeling of entities through a human host, the outside beings can use the person's vocal cords to talk and be communicated with.

In February 1987 David came to Dr. Baldwin with a problem. He had sensed evil entities within him and even claimed to hear maniacal laughter resonating in his being. He was frightened and felt he was losing control.

After Dr. Baldwin put David into a relaxed state he uncovered two spirits of departed mortals who had been clinging to the host body. But the spirits revealed that there was a third presence within the chambers of David's being. It was a thing of the dark, something they feared.

Dr. Baldwin knew time was of the essence. He told the spirits to hold each other's hands and reach out to the lifeline of the Light. Once they were safely gone he began to call upon the protective spiritual entities and forces necessary for dealing with demons.

Doctor: I call now on the whales and dolphins as brothers in light, the demon fighting teams, I call on the presence of the Christ consciousness to be here with us now. I call on the presence of Saint Michael and the forces of Saint Michael gather around us.

Demon: No!

Doctor: And shield each of us humans here in this place, with the shield of Saint Michael, each of us shielded totally and completely by that shield of Saint Michael.

Demon: It will not help you.

Doctor: I'm asking for the spirits of the whales and dolphins, who are our brothers in light, and I ask for the forces of Saint Michael to surround completely so you cannot escape from this place, from this man—how old was he when you joined him in this lifetime?

Demon: Many times ago.

Doctor: Many lifetimes you've been with him. And what is your duty, what is your mission with him, what is your job, little one? What were you assigned to do with this spirit of God now known as David? What is your assignment, because you will surely fail this time as you have failed before. And what happens to you when you fail, little one?

Demon: We cannot fail.

Doctor: You have failed before and you have been punished, is that not true? What has happened in the past when you've failed to capture the ones you've been sent for? You were planted in this one for what purpose?

Demon: To destroy.

Doctor: You have not destroyed! As I say, you have failed.

Demon: I *will* destroy.

Doctor: You shall not destroy. You shall surely fail.

Demon: I shall destroy all things—because I'm the destroyer.

Doctor: You are a tiny destroyer, you are ineffective.

Demon: I'm the king of fear!

Doctor: You have not stopped him. He is a child of light and love. He extends love to others and they can feel it. You have failed, little destroyer, and you shall continue to fail. Who is your master, who's sent you? Who is your commander?

Demon: I cannot say his name.

Doctor: What happens if you say his name?

Demon: We will not allow it.

Doctor: Is he ashamed of it, are you ashamed of it? Do you quake in fear before his name?

Demon: Yes.

Doctor: Remember what it was like when you

were punished. Where were you put? Because you have surely failed before. Remember back—what was it like?

Demon: Pain.

Doctor: What else do you recall?

Demon: Fire.

Doctor: But you didn't die.

Demon: I succumb.

Doctor: You succumb to what?

Demon: I succumb to you—him. No more pain.

Doctor: Look inside little one, look inside. Look inside your own being, for this may yet be a triumph for you in a way you could not know. Look inside yourself, little one. Seek beneath the layers of blackness. Deep inside. For your master has deceived you into thinking that you would die. As you are in this man, what do you see deep within you?

Demon: I see eyes.

Doctor: And whose eyes are these?

Demon: They are his eyes.

Doctor: The one who commands you? Look even beyond that. Deep inside you into your very center. . . .

Demon: I don't understand this. I see—light.

Doctor: Yes. Light. Is it a surprise to you that there is light within your inner being?

Demon: Yes.

Doctor: What did he tell you about light?

Demon: Death.

Doctor: He lied. There is no death. In the light itself is your life. You would not exist if not for that light within you.

As Dr. Baldwin continued to talk to the demon, the light consumed the blackness. The demon's commander, who identified itself as a being of darkness, was also directed to see the light within. During the rest of the session Dr. Baldwin succeeded in convincing not only the little destroyer and its commander to see the light within, but to call forth their legions and

have them look within as well. The session concluded
with an army of demons going into the Light.

There was a final voice that came through, utilizing
David's vocal cords. The entity identified itself as an
angel from the Light and assured Dr. Baldwin that all
spirits and demons had been removed. The angel added
that it would watch over David to make sure he suffered no more possessions.

Immediately after coming out of the trance, David
talked with Dr. Baldwin and a fellow colleague about
the experience they called "psychic surgery." David
remembered the feeling of the legions of evil demons
leaving his body.

"I saw not faces, necessarily, that I could recognize
but I saw many . . . awarenesses," David said. "A
lot of darkness at first. Now that this is over I can
recall several instances of being awakened at home
and I could see his [the commander's] eyes. Animal
eyes. Black as coal.

"Maybe now I can be the right person, I can be me
for a change."

The mother of Jim (not his real name) had died from
cancer in her hospital bed. Years later he suspected
that her spirit was still with him. Troubled by the notion, he visited Dr. Baldwin to find out. Under a trance
he did indeed describe the presence of his mother.

    Jim: I see my mother's face.
    Doctor: All right. Is there any expression on her
face.
    Jim: More like a pain.
    Doctor: Her expression suggests pain?
    Jim: When she was dying she suffered pain.
    Doctor: What's her name?
    Jim: Katherine.
    Doctor: Katherine, are you here now with your
son? Are you here at this moment in time?
    Jim: She says, "Yes."
    Doctor: Katherine, your son felt your presence for

some time after your death, after your passing. You were with him then, you stayed with him—is that true?

Jim: She says, "Yes."

Doctor: Katherine, what is your purpose for continuing to be with your son?

Katherine: Lonely.

At this point the tone of the patient's answers shifted, reflecting the perspective and personality of another entity, identified as Jim's dead mother Katherine. The voice of Katherine revealed that in her last moments in the hospital she was thirsty and the attendants wouldn't give her water because they had removed her cancerous intestines.

Doctor: Katherine, how was it that last day when you were thirsty and they wouldn't give [water] to you?

Katherine: Afraid to die.

Doctor: You knew it was coming, didn't you?

Katherine: (Softly) Yeah. Afraid to die.

Doctor: I think we all are to some extent. Did you have any idea what was on the other side, Katherine? You're a religious person?

Katherine: Didn't know . . . didn't know if I was saved.

The Katherine voice then described floating above her hospital deathbed. The pain was gone for a while and she felt at peace.

Doctor: What did you do after that? Where did you go?

Katherine: Just darkness.

Doctor: There was darkness. . . .

Katherine: (Softly) Yeah. Darkness.

Doctor: How soon after that did you find your son?

Katherine: He was at home and he was crying. I just wanted to comfort him.

Doctor: As any mother naturally would.

Katherine: Yes.

Doctor: Somehow he sensed you around. But perhaps he couldn't hear. You're a strong woman, Katherine, and he sensed your presence somehow. Did you follow him for a long time?

Katherine: Yes.

Doctor: When exactly did you attach to him? Were you outside of his body or inside? Can you tell?

Katherine: Sometimes inside, sometimes outside. It was both.

Doctor: Where are you right now, Katherine—can you tell?

Katherine: I'm inside.

Doctor: Katherine, this is the time when you can speak directly to your son. You're using his voice. He can hear the words that you say. Would you like to tell him anything right now? Would you like to say something to your son?

Katherine: I love you. And . . . life just wasn't fulfilled. It just wasn't fulfilled.

Doctor: Jim, would you like to say something to your mother at this time?

Jim: I don't know what to say.

Doctor: There is a place, Katherine, called the Light. It is the place you deserve to go after you leave the body in the transition we call death. As you've seen so clearly, only the physical body falls away and who you are continues to live, continues to be conscious. The Light, Katherine, is a place where you will learn and grow and become more than you ever imagined here on Earth. When you get there you will rest if you like. You will be taken care of. You will be healed. If you choose once again to have a body in an Earth life you might be able to do that. But at this time you're living in someone else's body, and that is your son—do you understand what I'm saying?

Katherine: Yes.

Doctor: You've heard what we've talked about earlier, the idea that spirit beings like yourself with no bodies can stay around, when you actually deserve to go home to the Light. And beings like yourself stay around because of love, compassion, caring. Others sometimes stay around because of anger or fear. But the result is the same—you are locked in, locked in the Earth plane. Katherine, I want you to raise your eyes, raise your spirit eyes, look up, look around you, look upward and tell me what you see.

Katherine: I see a light.

Doctor: You do see the Light!

Katherine: (In awe) Yes.

Doctor: The guides always come for one who leaves the body in death, Katherine. They were there at the hospital, you simply did not look up because of the caring and concern for your son. What do you see in the Light—is it coming closer?

Katherine: (Softly) Yeah.

Doctor: Do you see anyone there? Are there any beings? Any people?

Katherine: My mother.

Doctor: Your mother's there! Katherine, your mother's there?

Katherine: (Wistfully) Yeah.

Doctor: What does her expression say to you, the expression on her face?

Katherine: She's crying. She's happy to see me.

Doctor: Yes. And are you happy to see her, Katherine?

Katherine: Oh, yeah.

Doctor: It's been a long time.

Katherine: Yeah.

Doctor: Reach out to her, Katherine, reach your hand out to her. Tell me when she's taken your hand.

Katherine: We're hugging each other.

Doctor: All right!

There is the sound of soft tears and sniffles from the patient.

Doctor: Katherine, that is love. Your mother has come for you, to help guide you across. Katherine, are you ready to go with her into the Light?

Katherine: Yes.

Doctor: Jim, is there anything you'd like to say to your mother and grandmother before they go?

Jim: (His voice starts to break with emotion) I love them both.

Doctor: Tell them directly.

Jim: I love you.

Doctor: Do they hear you?

Jim: Yes, they do. They knew anyway.

Doctor: Yes. But it feels good to say it right out loud.

Jim: Yeah.

Doctor: Katherine, are you ready to go now?

Katherine: (With transcendent awe) Yes.

Doctor: We send you to the Light, with love. And thank your mother for coming. Good-bye.

(There is a pause).

Doctor: Jim, describe what you see.

Jim: (Answers, his voice talking fast and excitedly, with a sense of wonder) I see my grandmother and mother, they—they've got their arms around each other, just walking, and there's a lightness. The Light is not what I thought it'd look like. It's bright, but it's got sort of a gold look to it and they just started going up, almost like they're walking up stairs, but it's not—it's hard to describe it. They just went away. It looked sort of beautiful.''[8]

7

The Manifold Path

When the ship *The City of Sparta* departed India for Boston in August 1920, one of the passengers was yoga master Paramahansa Yogananda, who had been invited to speak to the International Congress of Religious Liberals. It was his maiden voyage to the New World—and it filled him with anxiety.

Yogananda was concerned that contact with Western materialism would irreparably contaminate him. It would be safer to brave the freezing cold of a Himalayan storm than to confront a culture that worshipped the illusion of materialism, Yogananda had decided.

So one morning before his trip, he began to pray to God for guidance. He resolved to pray unto death until he received the divine assurance that he would not lose himself in "the fogs of modern utilitarianism" during his visit.

For hours his passionate prayers mixed with inconsolable tears. At noon he heard a knock. He opened the door and gave entrance to a young man clothed in the meager garb of a renunciant. The young man spoke to Yogananda in a lyrical Hindi tongue.

"Our heavenly Father has heard your prayer," the young man said. "He commands me to tell you: Follow the behests of your guru and go to America. Fear not, you shall be protected."

Yogananda was in awe. The humble young man standing before him was the legendary Babaji, an avatar who was said to have retained his physical form for hundreds of years and was working to help humanity from a secret dwelling in the northern Himalayan peaks.

"You are the one I have chosen to spread the message of kriya yoga in the West," Babaji told him. "Kriya yoga, the scientific technique of God-realization, will ultimately spread in all lands, and aid in harmonizing the nations through man's personal, transcendental perception of the Infinite Father."

After Babaji gave Yogananda "a glimpse of his cosmic consciousness" the avatar left. Yogananda went into deep meditation, thanking God for not only answering his prayer, but sending as great a messenger as Babaji.[1]

Yogananda's initial experience in the U.S. proved his fears unfounded. Before his death in 1952 he had many gratifying, fulfilling visits teaching both the raja yoga discipline of body/spiritual meditation, and kriya yoga, which helped the mind attain "an awareness of inner spiritual forces." Yogananda's work in the U.S. carries on to this day through the efforts of the Self-Realization Fellowship.

Yogananda's story is part of a long tradition of non-Western adepts and spiritual teachers who have left their countries to come share their spiritual traditions with America.

The late Jiddu Krishnamurti was another famous Indian mystic who traveled and lectured widely in the U.S. Krishnamurti first came to the America under the tutelage of the Theosophical Society. The organization was founded in New York City in 1875 by Madame Helena Blavatsky, a controversial Russian mystic whose allegedly psychic powers is a point of controversy in occult circles to this day, and an American, Colonel Henry Steel Olcott.

Among the aims of the Theosophists was the study and development of the divine powers latent in people and a synthesizing of world philosophic and religious concepts. (The Theosophical Society would attract such thinkers as Sir William Crookes, Thomas Alva Edison, William Butler Yeats, and Mahatma Gandhi.)

The Theosophists also believed that the coming of a world messiah was imminent, and they were to prepare a path for the illumined being. When the society moved its main headquarters to India in 1882 and discovered the young Krishnamurti, they felt they had discovered their world teacher.

It was during a stay in Ojai, California, in 1922 that Krishnamurti began the yogic initiation of the kundalini energy principle that was to change his life. "In the Indian tradition, the yogi who delves into the labyrinth of consciousness awakens exploding kundalini energies and entirely new fields of psychic phenomenon, journeying into unknown areas of the mind," writes Pupul Jayakar in her biography of Krisnamurti. "A yogi who touches these primordial energies and undergoes mystic initiation is recognized as being vulnerable to immense dangers; the body and mind faces perils that could lead to insanity or death."[2]

For the next several years Krishnamurti experienced the often painful process of opening his chakras, the six energy centers comprising the kundalini energy principle. His successful passage also included spiritual communications with such higher beings as the Buddha and "the Lord."

By 1929 Krishnamurti had renounced the organization the Theosophists had prepared for him, as well as the role of messiah. But Krishnamurti did not renounce his role as a teacher, and his lectures on the attainment of spiritual truths were well received in the United States until his death in 1986. He left behind Krishnamurti foundations to expound his teachings of inner liberation in the U.S., England, and India.

The infusion into America of the Eastern traditions of Yogananda, Krishnamurti, and others planted the seeds of the current New Age movement. These spiritual influences bloomed in the 1960s and 1970s with the widespread application in the U.S. of Zen Buddhism, yogic practice, Sufism, Transcendental Meditation, and other practices.

Writer Jacob Needleman observed in 1970 that

Americans felt a great disillusionment with the traditional forms and trappings of Western religion. Much of the spiritual vitality had been lost in the transplantation of religion from Europe to the U.S., traditions that had already been affected by a scientific revolution that provided a new window on the cosmos. Religious practice had been regulated to "a matter of belief or performance."[3]

"In the East, mind is a cosmic factor, the very essence of existence; while in the West we have just begun to understand that it is the essential condition of cognition, and hence of the cognitive existence of the world," Carl Jung wrote. "With us, man is incommensurably small and the grace of God is everything; but in the East, man is God and he redeems himself."[4]

This Eastern spiritual influence is also reflected in the Asian martial artists that have migrated to America. The Japanese art of aikido provides one example of the transcendent aspect of many Eastern martial arts. Aikido was founded in 1925 during a visionary experience that occurred to martial arts master Morihei Uyeshiba during a solitary walk in his garden: "I felt that a golden spirit sprang up from the ground, veiled my body and changed my body into a golden one," Uyeshiba later recalled.

> At the same time my mind and body turned into light. I was able to understand the whispering of the birds, and was clearly aware of the mind of God, the Creator of this universe.
> At that moment I was enlightened: the source of *budo* [the martial path of spiritual development] is God's love—the spirit of loving protection for all beings. Endless tears of joy started down my cheeks. Since that time I have grown to feel that the whole earth is my house, and the sun, the moon and the stars are all my own things.[5]

Buddhism has been particularly well received in the West. The history, traditions, and cultural aspects of

Buddhism are very complex, but there are two main schools of thought: Hinayana (also known as Theraveda), and Mahayana Buddhism.

Hinayana, also known as the "lesser" or "smaller vehicle," emphasizes the individual's escape to enlightenment from the endless wheel of karmically generated birth, death, and rebirth.

Mahayana, the "greater vehicle," believes that an altruistic love by one for all sentient beings is the greatest path to enlightenment.

The Buddha noted that the world was on fire with desires and attachments that could never be satisfied because of their inherent illusory nature. That attachment creates unhappiness and generates the causative power of karma, which can only be resolved through endless rounds of incarnations.

Buddhism provides a spiritual path to help people see their true immutable and enlightened nature that is beyond all conditioned states. This true nature is infinitely vaster than the transitory, ego-centered delusion of self we inhabit in each incarnation.

Helping to inspire and guide sentient beings on their path from illusion to enlightenment is the Buddha himself and a whole range of spiritual entities and beings. Buddhism holds that beings known as bodhisattvas have progressed to enlightenment and need not become incarnated, but because of their infinite love and compassion choose to return to Earth to help other sentient beings reach enlightenment. These beings manifest the highest ideals of the Mahayana teachings.

Each Dalai Lama, for example, is believed by Tibetans to be a manifestation of the great bodhisattva Chenrezi (also known in Sanskrit as Arya Avalokitesvara). But just as the moon's image can be reflected many times in the rivers, lakes, and oceans of the planet, so can a bodhisattva such as Chenrezi manifest many times on Earth simultaneously.

There are also demons and fields of spiritual illusion that can add to the delusion of those on a spiritual quest. Buddhism takes those spiritual dangers into account in its complex training and techniques. "Buddhism is very strong on that, that we create our own reality, that we perceive our reality by our sense data," observes Doug Powers, a student of Buddhism at the Gold Mountain Monastery, a branch of the Sino-American Buddhist Association. "Spirits have their own reality, but they're as illusory as the world."

Heng Shun, the abbot of that Gold Mountain branch in San Francisco and a *bhikshu* (a traditional Buddhist monk), is concerned that channeling and other extraordinary experiences can create dangerous problems for the spiritual seeker. (Many practicing Buddhists are very reluctant to talk about the supernatural experiences they sometimes encounter in their meditative practices, believing that exalting such incidents is another form of attachment and a deterrent to liberation from the wheel of karma.)

Bhikshu Shun introduced me to the *Shurangama Sutra,* a discourse of the Buddha which details many examples of paranormal states that can delude the spiritual seeker. In the commentary written by the Venerable Master Hsuan Hua, the main abbot of the Sino-American Buddhist Association, Hua provides an example from his experience of the spiritual dangers that can entrap even the most highly spiritual person.

When I was in Manchuria I had a young disciple who had quite a lot of spiritual penetrations although he was only fourteen. He could go up to the heavens and enter the earth. . . .

One day he went up to the heavens to enjoy himself. When he got there, however, a demon king took a liking to him and trapped him in his palace. His palace was totally transparent, as if made of crystal. It was an exquisite place, but he was trapped in it . . . he could see his dharma body being held captive there by that demon king. So he came and told me, "Teacher, I went to the heavens and now I can't get back."

"So you're stuck in the heavens, huh?" I said, "Well, who told you to go there in the first place?"

"I thought it was a delightful place," he said. "I intended just to go there and take a look, but now that god won't let me come back."

"If you want to look for pleasure, don't go there for it," I admonished him. "The heavenly demons in the sixth desire heaven are always intent upon destroying the samadhi power [high meditative concentration] of cultivators. But don't be scared, I'll get you back."

I told him to come back, but the demon king refused to let him go. At that point he got really upset; he was terrified. "What are we going to do? He won't let me come back!"

"Don't be afraid," I said. "I'll get you back." Then I used the section of the Shurangama Mantra called the Five Great Mantra Hearts, which destroys demons. Immediately the demon's palace disintegrated, and my disciple came back. This is something that really happened.[6]

Bhiksu Shun points out that legions of ghosts, spirits, and heavenly demons sought to distract the Buddha during his final stage to complete enlightenment. Such forces also seek to distract others from their efforts at realization. Spirits such as Mara, a demon king who rules a heaven called the Transformation of Other's Pleasure Heaven, can tap into the worldly happiness of mortals and make it their own. Such spirits are said to hate those who seek to transcend the illusions of the world—it deprives them of the opportunity to milk the essence of worldly rapture. Shun notes:

Thus, certain beings throughout the various realms of existence come to disturb the person who has attained a little clarity on the path to Enlightenment. The *Shurangama Sutra* offers important instruction concerning this situation. The only way these unwholesome forces can affect one is if one leaves the door of the mind ajar. . . . If you remain clear, you will not be deluded. Then these demon's devices will have no way to reach you. . . .

It is clear, therefore, that opening oneself up to spiritual forces, as is done in channeling, can be a very dangerous undertaking. . . . For example, in such practices as channeling, people can be possessed by forces beyond their understanding, and in ways not even recognized by those possessed. . . . At first this might seem like a high spiritual state, but after a time, when the possessing spirit loses interest and moves on, the delusional energy sustaining the person to this point scatters and they fall into confusion, depression, despair and undergo great anguish. . . .

Any practice such as channeling that purposely opens us up to being controlled by external forces is to be avoided. Enlightenment is inherent in our true mind, it is not something that we obtain by seeking outside.

Therefore, in the *Shurangama Sutra,* the Buddha said, "The supreme, pure understanding mind originally pervades reality. It is not something obtained from anyone else. . . . It is like a person who has a wish-fulfilling pearl sewn in his clothing without realizing it. Thus he roams about in a state of poverty, begging for food and always on the move. Although he is indeed destitute, the pearl is never lost. Suddenly, a wise person shows him the pearl: all his wishes are fulfilled, he obtains great wealth, and he realizes that the pearl did not come from somewhere outside."[7]

Some of the amazing states the adept can experience include the ability to travel in spirit around the world, to appear and disappear at will, to walk through solid objects, and to be able to see visions of fantastic spiritual realms. Rather than viewing such experiences as transitory states, the practitioner can become deluded into believing enlightenment has been attained and nirvana achieved.

This practitioner can even perform miracles and provide revelations for others—and thus will often attract followings. The *Sutra* observes:

> Demons can also make one believe they are a bodhissatva. He himself believes in what the demon is teaching. His mind becomes swayed and dissipated. . . . He is fond of foretelling calamities, auspicious events, and unusual changes, or of saying that such and such a thus come one has now come into the world. . . .
>
> He and those he is teaching are beguiled and fooled into considering him to be a bodhisattva. . . .
>
> He may enable people to see Buddhalands, but it is a case of people being deceived by the power of the ghost; it is not a true and actual vision.

Master Hua explains that attachment to spiritual states, which themselves are not necessarily bad, can lead to delusion, demonic influence, and powerfully bad karma.

"In general, in cultivation you shouldn't be too greedy for anything," Hua writes in his *Sutra* commentary. "Don't be greedy for the good, and don't be greedy for the bad. The ordinary mind is the Way. You have to keep things on an even keel. Don't give rise to greed."[8]

To be able to avoid such delusions it is considered advisable to have a teacher. Such masters must be motivated by selfless love and compassion to help the seeker. At the same time the student of spiritual knowledge must also develop an inner way of seeing, a wise discernment independent of any attachment to the teacher.

The Buddha talked of the Four Reliances:

1. Don't rely on the person, but the doctrine.
2. Don't rely on the words, but the meaning, of the doctrine.

3. Don't rely on the interpretative meaning but the definitive meaning.
4. Don't rely on the ordinary conscious understanding of the definitive meaning, but an understanding using "an exalted wisdom consciousness."

"The reliability of teachings cannot be determined by considering the person who taught them, but by investigating the teachings themselves," Tenzin Gyatso, the current and fourteenth Dalai Lama told writer John F. Avedon. "In Sutra, Buddha said, 'Monks and scholars should accept my word not out of respect, but upon analyzing it as a goldsmith analyzes gold, through cutting, melting, scraping and rubbing it.' "[9]

A body of powerful Buddhist teachings that have only recently begun to be shared on U.S. soil is the Tibetan tantric tradition. (It is stressed in Tibetan Buddhism that tantric practice should be undertaken only after a grounding in the Mahayana perspective of the bodhisattva path, and an understanding of the concept of Voidness.) Also known as the Vajrayana, or Diamond Way, Tibetans place this body of Buddhist thought at the apex of the Buddha's teachings.

As it originally developed in Hinduism, and later in Buddhism, the tantric practitioners indulged a surfeit of passion to overcome worldly passion. This understandably generated its own problems. Gradually the Tibetans replaced tantra's erotic quality with a more symbolic cast, such as the visualization of male and female deities locked in passionate coupling.[10]

Many tantric teachers have come to the U.S. in recent years to not only discuss the rare teachings, but lead groups in the actual tantric-empowerment rituals themselves.

A ceremony known as the Vajrapani initiation was conducted by His Holiness Ganden Tri Rinpoche, head of the Gelugpa School of Tibetan Buddhism in Santa

Fe, New Mexico, on October 11, 1987. The ceremony, performed only on auspicious occasions, invoked the deities Vajrapani (embodying supreme power), Hayagriva (the wrathful aspect of the bodhisattva Chenrizi), and Garuda (the wrathful aspect of Manjusri, the bodhisattva of wisdom). The deities are believed to provide an initiate with the empowering strength and energy necessary to subdue the egocentric mind.

I attended the Santa Fe initiation, held at the office of Project Tibet, a nonprofit organization that aids Tibetan refugees in the U.S. Some two dozen people assembled in a spacious hall that had been prepared beforehand by prayer and decorated with paintings depicting aspects of the Buddhist pantheon.

Seated on mats and cushions, initiates listened to the Rinpoche ("Precious One") and his words were translated into English by a Tibetan monk. The Rinpoche described the ritual's value in not only subduing the ego, but in curing diseases and dispelling demonic forces. He revealed that as a young man he had suffered a demonic possession—reciting the Vajrapani mantra over 100,000 times dispelled the entity.

He likened the development and storing of the Vajrapani's powers to electric power stations that collect, store, and then distribute power.

"To help other sentient beings we have to store mental energies in our mental continuum," Rinpoche told the initiates. "To become powerful [for the purpose of helping others] we need inspiration from spiritual deities who have already accumulated power in helping other sentient beings. . . . In this initiation we make contact with these spiritual deities."

After the initiates recited bodhisattva vows to guarantee an altruistic intent, the Rinpoche directed that the assembly visualize him as the Vajrapani deity itself, and the gathering place as the very mandala palace of the entity. The Buddha and the highest entities of the spiritual realms were then visualized as being present at the gathering.

Each different layer of visualization demanded different colors, mantras, the evoking of deities, and the constant, altruistic wish that all sentient beings receive the purifying benefits of the proceedings.

At the end of the ceremony was the final, "stabilizing" stage in which initiates were touched at the forehead by the guru with a representation of the Vajrapani symbol.

This ceremony is but one of the four levels of Tibetan tantric practice. The fourth, and highest, level is known as the Anuttara, or Highest Yoga Tantra.

At the pinnacle of this tradition is the Kalachakra initiation, which was performed for the first time in the U.S. by the Dalai Lama in Madison, Wisconsin, in 1981. I had the good fortune to be in attendance at that ceremony.

The Kalachakra (Wheel of Time) is a science involving karmic and yogic principles, visualizations and tantric practice, geography and human physiology, activism of internal energy systems, astronomy, astrology, and mathematics—it seeks to "embrace all phenomenon," notes Edwin Bernbaum, "from the workings of the mind to the layout of the universe, in one all-inclusive system of knowledge and practice."[11]

The Kalachakra initiation was first performed by the Buddha at the request of King Chandrabhadra, ruler of the ninety-six kingdoms of the legendary land of Shambhala. (Tibetans believe Shambhala to be the most highly developed spiritual civilization on the planet. It is believed Shambhala is hidden in the Himalayas and is invisible to all but those with the highest mental and karmic propensities.)

At the Wisconsin ceremony, an open tent was erected for the initiates on a specially consecrated field in the countryside. A covered stage had been prepared for the Dalai Lama and various attendants. On the stage protected by a glass case was a depiction of the multicolored Kalachakra mandala. Tibetan monks had spent hours creating the intricate display by hand out of powdered sand. The sand mandala represented the palace of the Kalachakra deity: a masterpiece of symbolism depicting three squares enclosed within each other, four entrance gates, and some 156 deities.

During the ritual the Dalai Lama was visualized as the Kalachakra deity, a being with four colored faces, twenty-four arms, and two legs, embracing a yellow consort with four faces and eight arms. The deity wears a wrathful expression, fangs bared. In the intertwining of arms they both hold various symbols.

It is said that in the future the "Twenty-five Propagators" who rule the universe will once again spread the Kalachakra initiation. Present-day Kalachakra initiates will be reborn, able to use the Wheel of Time meditation to attain enlightenment. "The higher meditations of the Kalachakra tantra can be practiced only by a select few; but because of past and future events, and in order to establish a strong karmic relationship with Kalachakra on the minds of the people, there is now a tradition of giving the initiation to large public gatherings," the Dalai Lama has written.[12]

At one point in the ceremony a mysterious wind came up out of the stillness, shaking the stage and threatening to lift the tent from its mooring. The Dalai Lama appeared startled for a moment, but then he became still, staring into the gale until it subsided. It was a very propitious omen, I was later told.

At the end of the initiation, everyone filed past the stage for one last look at the colored-sand mandala of the Highest Yoga Tantra. At some point, long after everyone had left, the monks would see to the dissolution of their painstaking work of art by smearing the colored sand together, putting it in a special container, and then pouring the rainbow mixture into a flowing stream, returning the power of it to the universe.

The Dreamer

"This dreaming is a pattern that's much larger than my own life. It's a meshing of many consciousnesses, of life patterns, humans, plants, and things not even connected to the earth."
—Marcia Lauck

Given the fact that we spend a significant portion of our lives in that strange state of consciousness we call dreaming, it's amazing how little import Americans attach to it. We awake and instantly the dream memories begin to evaporate. Perhaps a few nagging recollections will stay with us, and we may shrug during breakfast or office conversation that "I dreamed the strangest dream last night. . . ."

Marcia Lauck, a San Jose housewife in her late thirties, with a husband and two young daughters, does more than shrug off her sleep state each morning: Her dreams take her beyond time and space, and upon awakening she incorporates those visions into her waking life.

I had been introduced to her by people who said Lauck had even been channeling messages from the spiritual caretakers of the planet in her dreams. I met her at the home she and her husband had been living in for twelve years. It was in the matrix of that house that her serious dreaming had begun. As the dreams began to flow, so did the work on the life of her family, on the house, and the garden.

Her neighborhood is in a quiet, tree-lined family area that doesn't see many moving vans. Her house is a California bungalow built in 1906. A white picket fence surrounds the grounds, and the gate opens onto a short walk to the two-story home with its bay windows and gingerbread fringe. Marcia's dream house.

Inside the house the feel of the early part of the century is preserved, but without the dust and mausoleum somberness of a museum. The past and present history of the house seem to exist in vital union. Each room has its own colors and functions, wallpaper and decorations. Some of the trappings of the house were created directly from her dreaming, such as an Indian prayer shield hanging in her study.

The dwelling is as perfect as a miniature dollhouse crafted by a genius toy maker. The internal ordering of her dreams helped build the house, and led to an evolving understanding of a sacred and ceremonial approach to life, Marcia said. "For me it was knowing that everything in our house was alive and that to really be a steward of the things that had been given, or had come to share their life in a very different form of consciousness with us, I had to honor all of that and learn to care for it in ways that were very intentional."

The things she was caring for, which she had been steward of these past few years, was the information contained in her dreams.

We sat down at her kitchen table, next to a sliding glass door that afforded a cheery view of her back porch and garden, and Marcia described the path of her dream life.

She had been feeling deep spiritual rumblings ever since her childhood in a small town outside of Pittsburgh. As a girl she loved to climb a special backyard tree that was as tall as their three-story house. Up there in a majestic fork of branches was a special energy she could tap into. For her it was "like being inside a church sanctuary when no one else was there."

The intangible spirit that shadowed her throughout the early part of her life took many forms. In high school the spirit found its expression in the dreamlike ballets she would experience doing jumps on the trampoline. In college at Penn State's speech communications department it manifested as a sense of purposeful activity resulting from the civil rights and antiwar movements. While at Penn State she became fascinated with the dynamics and collective consciousness of small groups and what allowed them "to be empowered." Years later she would be apply this early interest while coordinating her own dream circle groups.

But that wouldn't come until after some disappointments. During a graduate school stint at the University of Colorado "the resonant field fell *flat*. There just wasn't anything." It was a feeling of isolation, of doors closing. Other than her husband, Tom, whom she had married while at Penn State, it was all a "black hole" time of being in Colorado, twenty-five hundred miles away from the friends and experiences that had always inspired and defined her. They moved to the West Coast when Tom was hired to do some technical writing for an industrial firm near San Jose.

All through this period the nameless kept following her. She felt as if she was constantly "pushing the boundaries of what is normal, what is sanity." But then she met a woman she felt comfortable telling her troubled thoughts to. Marcia paid her new friend a visit and during a marathon four hours of talk, tears, and tea she finally unburdened herself of the feelings she had always dwelled on deep inside. Her friend assured her she wasn't crazy. She asked Marcia if she had ever looked into her dreams.

"I knew I had been waiting all my life for someone to ask me that question, and it was like all the sound came back—my body was just singing!" Marcia recollected. "And I said, 'That's it. That's my path.' "

Suddenly the underlying patterns that had whispered to her in the childhood tree sanctuary, that had exhilarated her on the trampoline, and had challenged her in her college life became apparent. She was, and had

always been, a dreamer. In dreaming she would experience the unfolding spiritual dimension she had always been seeking.

She began to prepare for her dream work like an
explorer readying to trek through unknown territory.
She apprenticed with a Jungian dream scholar to understand how to move through the dream zone. After
a year she took a twelve-week dream workshop, where
she learned how to keep a dream journal, how to meditate, and other techniques of consciousness travel.
Marcia even did advanced work with a white woman
who had studied with an Indian medicine woman from
one of the Plains tribes.

In 1975 the extraordinary dreaming began, dreaming in which she felt herself outside of time and space.
"My dreams began to emerge from a central core of
indescribably brilliant light whose very essence was a
deep and abiding love," she later wrote in a journal
of her dreams. "Gradually, this light clothed itself in
images, in vision, and in story, and splashed out into
the events of my life and the lives of others. Far from
being personal, subconscious dramas, these dreams
had become a rich commentary on the evolution of
consciousness."

The breakthrough dream, which in 1975 set her on
the dream work path, was titled "The Rabbit, the
Rainbow, and Me." She described the dream to me.
The setting for the dream was her own house, the
dream house where we were talking. She encountered
a grandmotherly sorceress who asked Marcia if she
was Houdini. When Marcia replied, "Illusion is not
what I'm about," the grandmother vanished in a puff
of smoke.

In the next sequence Marcia found herself in the
bathroom of her new house. Her four real-life brothers
appeared and began moving the bathtub into its proper
position. Before leaving, one of the brothers told her
there was a seal that only she could put into place.
Marcia understood it was a seal to her own inner
workings. "I just very matter-of-factly put the seal in

place and the minute that happened, I'm just thrust into this dimension of living color,'' she remembered.

She found herself landing in the foyer of her house. Lounging contentedly in her living room was a nine-foot-wide, six-foot-high rabbit. The rabbit, who called himself Charlie, communicated not through words but with a telepathy that filled her with the essence of the strange being. Charlie revealed that a rabbit was not its usual appearance. The entity felt that Marcia, who loved animals, would be less threatened by a rabbit, albeit one as big as a room. And then the giant rabbit began speaking out loud, but in a beautiful alien language that sounded ''like the finest symphony orchestra taken out into light-years.'' She translated the communication as ''It is within you, little one.''

Marcia reached into her heart and pulled out a rainbow-colored butterfly. A flash of light exploded, and she felt all the rainbow's colors radiating from within and without her. She knew she was ready. Then the dream ended and she awoke.

The next day she received three different phone calls from friends asking her to conduct a dream workshop. From those early days evolved the process of forming a union of inner knowing and outer works, of applying care and sensitivity to every activity.

The physical building of the dream began then, too. Marcia, her husband and friends replaced walls, repaired cracks, sanded floors, painted rooms, and added a second story. They rebuilt the collapsing back porch and then set to the asphalt-paved back yard. They jack-hammered the asphalt, revealing earth that hadn't breathed in forty years. They marked out a garden plot and sifted by hand the fresh soil. In Marcia's dreams the seedlings she was planting came one by one to tell her they appreciated the sacred intent of the garden work.

''I started to dream things and it was just a case of watching them happen out here [in waking reality], and then moving into my life,'' Marcia remembered.

"It was a way of real training, of seeing that all aspects of life are sacred."

During the creation of the garden Marcia impressed upon all the helping hands the importance of not doing harm to any of the other plants, particularly the ivy that hung down from their backyard fence onto the outer areas of the asphalt rubble being cleared away. But one day a friend accidentally hacked some of the ivy while turning over the soil. That night the deva (in Hindu myth, a good spirit) of the ivy appeared to Marcia in a dream.

"In the dream I'm aware of this being that's very wild-looking with leaves and brown, shaggy skin standing there at the fence," she recalls. "I said, 'Oh! You're the deva of the ivy! Please forgive us for what happened. We weren't intending to hurt the plant in a conscious way.' And he said, 'That's okay. We meet this kind of reaching out on the part of human beings with such excitement! And we are glad as the ivy to be part of the experiment. We will watch from the fence. We will add our support, but we will keep it to the fence.'

"And all the time we had the garden the ivy only grew on the fence. It never came down into the garden space. It just observed and added its special support."

The dream circles also began around this time. In the dream circles small, intimate bands of friends learned how to conduct their dream voyages. Marcia initially charged for her services in coordinating the group dream work, but then she realized the group experience was too powerful and pure to be bought and sold. The money exchanges ended, and the dream circles prospered.

In 1978 she was approached in a dream by what she knew to be a manifestation of the planet's racial consciousness. Unlike the brightly lit and colored texture of her regular dreams, this dream was a summons to a shadowy meeting place. Marcia found herself in a cave surrounded by a circle of beings she recognized as Indians. Their faces were lit up as if by campfire light, the rest of their forms obscured by darkness. She knew they were spiritual elders and that the great circle was an important gathering.

The meeting was brief. They all talked to her, yet she perceived the message as one thought: "We're watching you, we're watching your work. We'll be in contact."

The next morning, while reflecting on the strange meeting, Marcia thought it curious that a gathering of spiritual elders would be contacting her, an Anglo-Saxon Protestant woman. Other than a friend who had apprenticed with an Indian medicine woman she had never had any contact with Native American people or their culture.

Nine months later, the elders again met Marcia in her dreams. "They said to me, 'We want to build a bridge.' " Marcia recalls. "The bridge I understood to be a two-way bridge (between Anglo and Indian cultures). Because I was . . . an Anglo-Saxon Protestant woman—somehow that was an important element. Something in the merging of these two cultures was really central to this bridge building. Also, the range of my own awareness, of what I had been working with and dreaming was important.

"That night in the dream I crossed over the bridge. I heard, I knew all their tongues, I could speak to all of them in one language. That was the beginning of the travel across the bridge that has continued now for nine years."

She was starting to dream of ancient tribal traditions. Marcia described a meeting with Twylah Nitsch, a Seneca medicine woman who told her she was "dreaming the universal dream" as well as experiencing the sometimes secret ceremonies of different tribes.

Her traditional notions of time and space were beginning to break apart. She began dreaming planetary events before they occurred. Her dream work involved meeting people and visiting different parts of the Earth and other dimensions. At times she moved through different dream layers simultaneously. Sometimes guides would accompany her on the dream journey, notably an Indian shaman. But she never forced a dream subject to come up. The elders might come to her, but she never sought them out. She felt her job in dreamland was to go in and wait for the experience to unfold.

"I get called places. I always wait until the call comes. It's almost like a magnetic radar, like things are lining up and pulling and I just follow that thread and it takes me wherever the dream work is supposed to be.

"But it's a process that is so organic and natural, the dreaming unfolds into the waking and the waking unfolds into the dreaming. That has been the really special thing about exploring this territory over the years. The more I move into myself and my work, the more the correlations are there in the seasonal rhythms of the planet, the tides, and lunar cycles—all of that is so interwoven. I allow myself to surrender to a wisdom that is greater than my own that is unfolding this pattern. And I trust it."

She has journals full of the detailed accounts of her dream adventures. One collection, ''At the Pool of Wonder,'' reads like a captain's log from a great journey. The journal covers some of the nine years of dream channeling she's experienced since she crossed the bridge presented to her by the ancient elders.

May 23, 1980

I am in a remote primeval rain forest. Moonlight filters softly down through the dense vegetation, and the night air feels cool and moist against my skin. I am sitting in the driver's seat of a car. . . . I sense it is important to the context of the overall night's work that these two levels merge within me—a synthesis of primal earth power and modern technology. . . .

Suddenly my flesh rises up with pinpricks of alarm. . . . I watch as the air behind me parts. Stepping through the crack between realities, into the seeming solidity of the backseat, is a wild and powerful jungle cat—a jaguar. . . . Her low growl tells me that I must not turn to approach her. There is a test here: I understand that I am to sit quietly, opening as I can into the deeply underlying entities of creation. In unshakable calm I am to radiate my bond with and love for the earth, for the earth's creatures, and for this jaguar in particular. I am to do so, in the imminent threat of her untamed wildness. . . .

After what seems like hours of reaching and sustaining this deep communion, I feel the brush of whiskers against the nape of my neck—a soft, gentle caress. Slowly she steps over the seat that separates us and sits beside me . . . she lifts one of her paws into my field of vision and firmly places it in my lap. . . . As I watch, the paw touching me shimmers and transforms into a woman's hand. In an instant the transformation is complete. She is no longer a jaguar, but a woman of great power, a shape changer dressed in jaguar skins. . . . We talk mind to mind, no words exchanged in the usual sense, and I bring none of our communication back for now other than the agreement of our meeting. I wake with the skin of the dream wrapped around me, and continue to be stirred deeply by it all day.

July 3, 1983

I am in a grassy, unpopulated plains area, scene of many meetings with Native Americans. . . . I become immersed in and part of the land's living awareness. It feels like I/we are reaching back into distant, shadowed memories . . . but as my awareness is more wholly merged with the land, the shadowiness lifts, and the story becomes clear.

The birthing ground was established when humanity was young. It has been the fertile womb where the new seeds and innovations of each stage in the evolution of human consciousness have been cared for. All possible expressions have been nourished here; all conceivable courses of development assessed for their potential to bear the fruit of a species awake to the richness of its divine heritage. . . .

I see that I have been working with a man my own age, making sure that all that is presently newborn and potential in this time is properly nurtured. Before long, we walk to an area where I see various eggs and embryos of a great bird—all of which have died or aborted due to improper genetic or environmental conditions. . . .

I feel the fluid acceleration of my consciousness, and this portion of the dream becomes a springboard for another, more expanded one. In rapid flashes of vision I plunge into the history of the Plains tribes. But as my inner velocity increases, the images blur and then open out, thrusting me into the rich bed of generativity for all the Indian cultures and the ancient wisdoms by which the societies were shaped. It is then that a voice begins to speak through me, overlaying all levels of the dream:

"This bird is an entry point to great power and generativity for the planet. . . . It is known as the firebird. . . .

"At each new stage of cultural development—as far back as your human story line reaches—you have sought to bring forth the firebird. What you see here are the attempts, each of which seemingly failed. Yet in truth there was no failure, for with each new attempt you gained new knowledge that allowed the building to proceed through the following stages of your culture's development.

"You who seek to embody the sacredness of God's creation in everyday life are, collectively, a womb in which the embryo of a new civilization has taken root. . . . Through this communion which you and others of similar purpose sustain, the firebird of a new world will rise on wings of pure light. All the conditions have been met once again, and as you

near the full equinox, *listen,* for the melodic essence
of the firebird's return is being sounded once again.''

April 24, 1984

I am standing on what appears to be an enormous
natural bridge. My eye scans the sweeping arch,
noting that rather than spanning oceans or bodies
of water, this bridge soars upward, vaulting into
seemingly endless dimension, fording layers of increasingly expanding consciousness. One end is
earth—anchored, the other stretches into unknown
realities. . . .

I suddenly become aware that another presence
has joined me. . . . I turn to see an ancient totem
moving toward me. Its power is stunning. I can't
remember ever seeing anything like this. Not only
is it painted in what I intuitively know is a Native
American design, it is also *alive!* In the exact instant
that I understand this aboriginal deity is a lion, it
springs toward me with a deafening roar. An inex-
orable force compels me to meet it. I, too, leap,
opening myself to its power. As we collide midair,
I hear an explosion of sound and we are spun diz-
zyingly into some faraway vastness.

When my feet meet solid ground, I find myself
standing next to the medicine man so much a part
of my dreaming these past years. I understand he
has brought the totem to life, and that through the
lion's power we have leaped through the worlds into
an ancient, lightless cave. I send out feelers, tendrils
of awareness, sensing into every nuance, every vibration which emanates within this underground
lodge. Gradually my vision clears and the cave becomes filled with light. Some sort of cryptic message is chiseled into and covers the smooth, rock
walls, like the hieroglyphs found in Egyptian tombs.
Impulse tells me that we are to place our hands on
these precisely tooled symbols. Together we approach the walls, astonished to discover that these
stone symbols are alive. They begin to press them-

selves into our awareness, transmitting their information through patterns of vibration which are directly assimilated into our genetic coding. . . .

When our bodies have fully absorbed the cave's teaching, the medicine man and I find ourselves once again on the bridge. We are deep in conversation, walking back toward the earth-end where my husband waits in our car for me.

"I can't even say I'm frustrated or impatient for the next sign," I say, "Because I know everything unfolds in only the most perfect of times. All I know to do is wait until the sign comes."

"That is what I'm here to tell you," the medicine man says earnestly. *"This* is the time—the sign has come through the totem. I *know* it. I dreamed it, I dreamed *you* this night!"

With these words, we reach the end of the bridge. He takes my shoulders in his hands, our eyes meet, and I awaken.

October 28, 1985

. . . I find myself over the ocean, being drawn toward an island. . . .

In a flash of insight everything clicks into place: This is the island of Iona off the coast of Great Britain. With this information the time frame of the dream settles, and the night's work becomes clear.

There is a thin, gleaming, crescent moon overhead, and the air is scented with the sea. I am with a small body of robed people. There are several men holding up flickering, smoking torches, and I observe with some curiosity that I am the only woman present. I peer through the haze and the leaping shadows, noting that we are in a courtyard surrounded by a stone abbey or monastery. There is power here. I feel it pressing against my skin, letting me know by its touch that this is the heart of an ancient power point.

The historical period places us in the Dark Ages. . . .

I listen to the intent of our meeting, and again the times get blurry. I am not certain whether we are interring something of great potency in the earth or exhuming it. . . . In the rapid flashbacks I see that both have occurred in other times, depending on the need of the planet. When time's spinning stops, it is clear that tonight we are to bring concentrated power out from within the earth. . . .

At the moment when the exhumation begins, I am propelled into another time connected to my present life. As this happens, I am aware that only one portion of my consciousness comes back . . . another is still on the island involved in the work. As I am lifted out of the torchlight, a voice is ringing in my ears:

"This place is hallowed ground. Since the earth's beginnings it has been wholly devoted to worship as a place where the developing consciousness of mankind could have a direct connection to the divine vision for itself and the earth. Much power has been stored here, and for many years it has been unactivated. Because these energies were to remain untapped until a certain stage of planetary readiness was reached, no one with inner knowledge was called to waken them. The need is present now in your time. . . . That is why you have been called here."

December 5, 1985

. . . I waken into the unfolding of a vast story. At times a voice is speaking; at other times I am given a gestalt of images and sounds. Everything in me stretches to bring this story home:

There were beings of unimaginable breadth of consciousness and creativity, propelled from the heart and mind of God, who came to the newly forming earth to assist the divine impulse creating the human race.

Certain aspects of divine awareness which emanated from these beings were to be imprinted in the new race and within the physical body of the earth. These awarenesses would then be triggered and released at specific, synaptic firing times, when a new evolutionary pattern in human consciousness was to emerge. It was understood that in our present time, when the greatest of these expansions in consciousness would be undertaken, humanity would experience crises potent enough to destroy itself and life on the earth. In the most intense and critical periods . . . these imprints would leap the cellular gap, striking home like lightning, firing their way into human awareness. In this great synthesis of consciousness and racial memory, these imprints would assist humanity to waken to the divine dream within itself, within the earth, within the universe.

These vast beings knew that knowledge of the sacred dimension—of all life's inherent divinity—would need to be rooted in the very soil and marrow of the earth itself. . . .

So they seeded the forming earth's elements, encoding portions of themselves within matter—spirits of mountains . . . of wind . . . of trees . . . of creatures. They implanted essences which, when met with and penetrated by human love and consciousness, would reawaken humanity to our common origins and divine purpose. . . .

To ensure that the fundamental links with the sacred in nature were never lost, direct bonds containing this knowledge were established within the root peoples, the native, indigenous tribes of each continent. . . . On our continent, the Native Americans have been the bearers of that wisdom. . . .

I waken, feeling immersed in the power of the natural world and the medicines that the Indians have observed and worked with for many generations. . . . They are the teachings given to us through the agency of our Creator and the divinely inspired, fully aware being which we call the Earth.''

September 18, 1986

As I prepare for sleep, the white orb of a full moon casts a soft radiance through our bedroom windows, creating a silver patch at the foot of the bed. I settle underneath the covers, wondering what the night's dreaming will bring. . . . There is the now familiar sense of rapid passage away from my known surroundings, and I feel my dreaming self launch into the unknown, drawn to an appointed destination.

I surface after an unknown period of time, sensing into the nature of the space . . . underneath and overlaying everything is a brilliant light. . . . I am without body or form, a spark of pure knowing swimming in a vast, omniscient sea. . . .

Out of the formless radiance, wavelike bodies of awareness assemble and express themselves in ways that enable me to identify them. This is a great gathering of many expansive, yet familiar, collective consciousnesses—the human race, the nature kingdoms, the animal kingdoms, the living earth, the full moon, the fiery sun. Then, as if blown by a solar wind or some unknown breath of the spirit, these consciousnesses converge, rising into a towering wave. They crest and break, washing over and through me, infusing my awareness with their very essences. Luminous, multicolored transparencies and images emerge into my awareness. . . .

I watch, spellbound, as the earth's story—all possible patterns and combinations of planetary evolution, past, present, and future—unfolds in images unbound from the linear constraints of time. In a majestic, surging dance they interweave, each of us, and all of us combined—man, woman, animal, plant, moon, sun—as part of a great cooperative endeavor forming the earth we know. We are coded within each other's genetic material in ways that make for unceasing communication between us all, if we but learn how to listen to it.

I gasp as the powerful figure of a shaman suddenly emerges out of the center of the spiral. His eyes catch and hold mine, commanding my attention as the ribbons of light change into the curling smoke of a medicine pipe. Without warning he transforms into a massive stag, though his eyes remain the same. . . .

And under the deer man's penetrating gaze, I am opened to a great flow of information:

Shamans from all times are directing the movement of these spiraling, luminescent images, bringing them forward in response to the great challenges we presently face. These travelers of the inner dimensions are focusing their wisdom, their knowledge of the imperishable truths of existence, and all their skill toward the earth, in creating a constant stream of energy, power, and information to assist us in this time.

As part of their message, I am given insights concerning my relationship to them and the wisdom they bear. . . . These concern my work as a type of receiver/transmitter that allows this knowledge to be communicated, that translates cosmic sound into images and information coherent to the people of the earth. The knowledge communicated through these beings is to assist us in penetrating through the camouflage of the outer universe into the central mysteries at the heart of creation. . . .

I waken, feeling stretched across the multidimensional images of the dreaming, trying to orient myself to my body and to the coming day. The energies which opened me to the shamanic stream had their greatest impact in my chest, and as I come to record this three days later, I am still working to balance my body. Each night now, following the dream, I have continued to work with and further expand what was opened, clearing pathways for the wisdom which is seeking entrance.

We interrupt our dream talk to walk around the corner to meet one of Marcia's daughters at the school bus stop. It feels good to step outside into the warm day and look up at the blue sky.

The bus arrived just as we turned the corner. Marcia's daughter bounced off the bus and skipped over to her mother. She excitedly talked about the events of the day. As we walked back to the house she skipped ahead, stopping to stroke the soft fur of a favorite neighborhood cat. As we waited, I asked her if she was a dreamer, too. She giggled and nodded, telling me about the pink squirrels she had played with in dreamland the night before.

Back at the house Marcia had a special dream to share with me. The dream had come on February 13, 1987, her thirty-seventh birthday. The date was not only a Friday the 13th, but a full moon, total lunar eclipse—auspicious signs for a night of good dreaming.

She picked up her dream journal and read me a dream.

February 13, 1987
I am without form . . . immersed in what I can only sense are vast fields of cosmic energy, energies that are profound, highly evolved orders of consciousness. I am somehow a midwife or mediator of these energies. . . . I travel through many successive realms, gradually bringing these energies . . . into dimensions progressively closer to the earth. At each level I work to stabilize and anchor these energies as they approach the earth, creating as I do so a stable structure and an open channel so that these orders of consciousness can be absorbed into the planet's life without cataclysm. When I am at last within earth's dimension I become aware of a small group of others who, like myself, are engaged in this same task. We've just completed the grounding within human racial consciousness, and now I am heading into the next location of the night's work. . . .

As the mists clear what I notice first is this layer is stewarded by those who are guardians of the sacred

earth. . . . Gradually form and substance gather. . . .
This particular intersection of consciousness is the
training ground for the initiates into the sacred earth
lineage, which the indigenous people of each continent steward. The elders and medicine people I am
shown here are American Indians. . . . They have
called in the next generation of people who will be
called to assume the responsibility for the unbroken
connections between God, earth, and humanity. . . .

I'm given to understand that there are three major
areas of instruction. . . . The first concerns dreaming.
I see that this is the largest entry-level group. The
second group is somewhat smaller and is taught the
art of shield making. And finally, the most advanced
of the groups is involved in boat making. The making
of the boats is hard to describe, for it's a calling of
these vehicles out of the formless realms. They're carriers of the deep truth of existence in and among all
cultures of the earth. Only two people are currently
able to sustain this level of complexity and mas-
tery. . . .

The outward signs . . . can hardly convey the power
and knowledge that must be mastered at each step,
whether to bring a dream to feed the people, or to heal
through the power of the shield, or to transmit knowledge over oceans of consciousness so that the teachings by which the world is continuously renewed may
continue to be planted in each new generation. . . .

There are clear, insistent, inner instructions I am to
become visible here, to assume some sort of bodily
form. . . .

I am aware that I'm still blurred around the edges,
though now I am in the midst of the action. Everyone
is deeply immersed in the trainings. I wander around,
trying to see why it is I have been brought here. I stop
near the two who are beginning boat makers. They are
exploring the underlying consciousness necessary to
allow a boat to emerge.

I feel a tug inside and sense that I am to sit here. A
sheet of paper materializes. I hold my hand over its

blank surface. With a sweep of my palm a sea-blue ark appears. A second motion calls up a series of shimmering, golden waves. . . .

The dream crashes open and I am plunged down, inward, hands stretching deep into unnameable creativity, calling up the boat—my boat. Every cell is charged with fire, calling the formless into form. Flesh begins to shape itself around me, and suddenly the dream explodes into a baptism of water and fire. A powerful wind is blowing, shaping my body once more.

"My whole body is singing, for I have united with my boat. I am standing on the back of a great blue whale, and we are speeding across the ocean, heading for land. I look down at my feet, and the joy is nearly unbearable. Blazing on the whale's back is my shield, a sun seal of my work. In my hand is a tall shepherd's staff. The wind curls my flowing robe around my legs. The whale, the sun-drenched sea, and I fuse into an exquisite song: "We come, we come."

And then abruptly I am back staring incomprehensibly at the symbols on the paper, struggling to orient myself here again. In my hand now is a small brooch, a version of the sun seal. It slips off my hand onto the paper. I am still half in, half out of the dream of the whale when I feel hands placed on my shoulders. All of me arrives back. I rise and turn to find I'm ringed by the elders of this dimension. They're all looking at me and at the sun seal.

The one who has touched me speaks for them all: "We have been waiting for you. You need to make yourself visible."

I waken, coming back slowly with their words echoing in my head. I do not yet know how or why this is to happen but I trust I will be shown the way.[1]

—————— Part III ——————

Down to Earth

The Cynics, the Seance, and the Seeker

Changing television channels one night, I happened upon the departed ventriloquist Edgar Bergen (alive again!) and his wooden pal, Charlie McCarthy. They were both gazing into a crystal ball. Edgar was outfitted with a swami's turban. Irascible Charlie was demanding of mystic Edgar whether he could really foresee the future.

"I don't think—I know," replied the confident Bergen.

"I don't think you know, either," one-upped Charlie.

Like Charlie and that famous man from Missouri, many Americans have a show-me attitude when it comes to the claims of psychics and channels. And then there are other folks who'll believe without question anything that has a little star dust sprinkled on it.

A national survey of two thousand adults by the Public Opinion Laboratory at Northern Illinois University concluded that horoscopes and numerology found more favor with a large number of Americans than the hard sciences.

"If a newspaper runs a story about how a newly discovered chemical changes the molecular structure of a compound, at least two-thirds of the readers will not understand it," Jon D. Miller, director of the Public Opinion Laboratory, wrote concerning his organization's 1985 poll. Miller concluded that for twenty-five million Americans without high school diplomas the world was a strange, hostile place. This group was most likely to believe in signs and luck, astrology, and omens. Overall, two-thirds of American adults followed astrological reports at least periodically.[1]

Many mystic merchants, cognizant that there's a big market in fortune-telling, promise not spiritual truth but worldly riches for their clients. Consider this pitch from a French seer that took up a full page in the New York *Daily News* in 1987:

SHE'S HELPED FRENCHMEN WIN MILLIONS. NOW SHE WANTS TO HELP YOU!
My revelations are reserved exclusively for those who wish to win a major lottery prize ($1,000.00 or more) . . . a Bingo jackpot . . . big money at the track or in a casino . . . or any game of chance based on winning numbers. If you are one of these people, and if you mistakenly believe you have little chance of ever winning thousands—even millions— of dollars, this message is for you.

One assumes that this woman would have long ago followed her own lead and now be soaking up sun on the Riviera instead of buying ads in the *Daily News*.

Those looking for a quick cure, or revelations from psychics to make a complex world simpler, are often prone to a good fleecing from spiritual shysters, critics contend.

A good example is the self-styled New Age Zen master who in the 1980s has been filling auditoriums from Los Angeles to New York with the philosophy of Zen for the competitive edge. His Zen sell tactics have included national magazine ads decorated with a beautiful blonde meditating atop a Porsche. His resume is a generous listing of his spiritual accomplishments in past lives.

Parody to some, a prophet to others, the story of this Zen master took a darker turn when a November 1987 report in the *San Francisco Chronicle* alleged he had pressured female disciples into sex with him against their will, bilked followers out of thousands of dollars each, and manipulated one female disciple/ companion with LSD and assertions that she was possessed by demons.[2]

Unfortunately, the stakes, and the damages, inflicted by sham shamans only gets higher. Take, for example, this 1987 clipping from the Philadelphia *Inquirer* titled: "Men Die Obeying Priestess: Africans Go to War with 'Bulletproof' Oil." The report concerned a young Ugandan woman named Alice Lakwena who "is able to cast spells. It is said, too, that she is instructed by spirits. And it is said that those who disobey her are driven to madness by her curses."

Formerly known as Alice Auma, she was said to have disappeared after attending a teacher's college, reappearing forty days later with the name Lakwena (holy spirit). She also claimed to have undergone a spiritual rebirth that imbued her with occult powers. Reportedly, she convinced the men of the Acholi tribe that by smearing their bodies with a magic oil they would be impervious to the bullets of government troops.

"According to the government . . . well over a thousand Acholi, loyal to Lakwena's Holy Spirit Movement have died in battles in the past year," the news item said. "Most of them have been mowed down while bare-chested, smeared with oil and swinging clubs."

Closer to home there are faith healers who purport to be channels for healing energy. At faith healing gatherings the auditorium floors are often littered with the vials of medication that sick people have thrown on stage, believing a divine force has, or will, cure them.

Debunker James Randi in 1986 exposed as a fraud TV faith healer Peter Popoff. In Popoff's TV healings the minister was said to be able to correctly identify strangers in the audience, diagnose their diseases, and cure them. His followers proclaimed that his gifts were the result of prayer and fasting so that the spirit of God could work through him.

The Randi investigation discovered that before a Popoff miracle show, his wife and lieutenants would work the crowd, getting exact names, addresses, and medical diagnostic information. At the start of the revival Mrs. Popoff would be sequestered in a trailer outside the auditorium, watching the proceedings from closed-circuit monitors and feeding Popoff all the information he needed through a transmission hookup to a hearing aid receiver in Popoff's ear.

As for the "healings" many were short-term, a temporary release during a remission time period, or the more complex placebo effect.[3]

Psychic debunkers maintain that mediums are channeling their own subconscious or are complete frauds who liberally borrow the tricks of the magician's trade. The so-called "cold reading," where a psychic reveals a client's secrets, is an example of what investigator Ronald Schwartz calls "the skilled use of ambiguity" by the psychic fraud. The skilled wording of questions and comments by the fraud can often elicit valuable information from the subject himself. This unknowing complicity on the part of the subject provides all the information the fraud needs to fashion the seemingly psychic revelations.

"A number of psychological principles are operating which contribute to the ESP effect," Schwartz writes. "Specifically, investigation into the artifacts in behavioral research has shown that more dominant experimenters effect greater inducement of their expectation on their subjects than less dominant experimenters. Also, it had been demonstrated that experimental subjects generally try to comply with the demand characteristics of the situation, that is, try to be good subjects."[4]

One famous fake medium would give amazingly accurate readings by simply targeting his clients and thoroughly investigating their backgrounds beforehand. The fraud was young Harry Houdini, who in the late 1890s posed as a medium. Houdini's regret for that period of psychic subterfuge was undoubtedly an impetus to the medium busting he would perform later in life.

Houdini always had an interest in the supernatural. He cultivated the mysterious in his act, his books, and his films. In *The Man from Beyond,* a film in which he was writer, producer, and star, the hero is released from a bloc of Arctic ice that has held him in suspended animation for two hundred years—just in time to be reunited with the reincarnated love of his first century.

In a feat his program handbills proclaimed "A Feat Which Borders on the Supernatural," Houdini would escape from a tank of water in which he had been submerged upside down with his ankles clamped.

One of Houdini's most mystifying feats was causing a ten-thousand-pound elephant to completely vanish from the stage of New York's Hippodrome Theatre.

J. Hewat McKenzie, president of the British College of Psychic Science, wrote in 1916 that the American magician was a true psychic who "for years demonstrated dematerialization, and the passage of matter through matter upon the public stage." If so, that was news to Houdini. Although he certainly encouraged the occult air around him, he was a showman, not a shaman.

Houdini even used his shows as forums to expose mediumistic fraud. At the New York Hippodrome, the same stage where he made elephants seemingly disappear, he exposed the mediumistic effects of the time by duplicating them. While tied to a chair inside a curtained cabinet, he still caused tambourines to jangle, hand bells to ring, as well as make megaphones rise and float while his hands and feet were controlled by associates.

The magician's crusade even took him to Washington, D.C., to endorse anti-fortune-telling legislation in 1924. (None of the bills passed out of their legislative committees.)

The magician believed that spiritualism was not just a benign superstition, but that vulnerable family and friends of the recently departed were being bilked for millions by despicable frauds claiming contact with the departed. In his book, *A Magician Among the Spirits,* Houdini angrily called mediumistic frauds "moral perverts" and "human vultures."

But Houdini always proclaimed the desire to believe in spiritualism. Harry Houdini even made arrangements for receiving spectral contact. "I have made compacts with fourteen different persons that whichever of us died first would communicate with the other if it were possible, but I have never received a word," he wrote. "The first of these compacts was made more than twenty-five years ago and I am certain that if any one of the persons could have reached me he would have done so."[5]

A national television audience got the chance to see if Houdini himself could make it back from the grave during a live seance broadcast on October 31, 1987, the sixty-first Halloween since the magician had died. From the stage of the Orpheum Theater in Los Angeles, host William Shatner promised that the "trance contact" seance would reach from "across the sands of time and space" to contact the famed illusionist.

The seance group sat on one side of a table. The table's circumference was illuminated, and a darkly lit backstage provided contrast. Bill Steiner, president-elect of the Society of American Magicians and head of the group's occult investigation committee, served in the role of medium. Those seated included a *Los Angeles Herald* reporter. The seance was also joined by James Randi on a stretcher. Randi had suffered a compound fracture of the vertebra while rehearsing Houdini's famed water-filled milk can escape. To add to the anticipation, background music played haunting, eerie tones. Then came the moment for the live seance broadcast to begin.

"Oh, spirits from the world beyond the grave, we're trying to communicate with Harry Houdini," Steiner began. "Please, we earnestly request—let this message get through. . . .

"Oh, Harry Houdini, can you hear us from this side of the grave? We have gathered here in an attempt to communicate with you . . . if you could just send us a sign, a word, a message. . . . Anything, Harry Houdini. Just to let us know there is a link between the living and those who may be living beyond the grave. . . .

"Are you there, Harry Houdini, can you hear us? If we hear not from you we must of necessity conclude that the claimed communications do not exist."

At that point, with the eerie music providing the background, the cameras went back to William Shatner, who announced a commercial break.

Upon the return, Shatner was at the table with the rest, all concluding that old Harry apparently wasn't going to show up for the party. "You waste your life and you give up your self-esteem if you follow the mystics," Steiner concluded. "Do not follow it! You're hurting yourself if you do."

James Randi was bemused that people had been writing in all week, convinced the seance would bring in demonic forces. The reporter hoped that the following year the group could give Elvis a call. Shatner concluded that perhaps somewhere the master magician was looking down and smiling.

However, there are other approaches to the conduct of a seance. A proper seance usually opens with a few moments of silent meditation. A minimum of an hour is needed to open to, and receive, supernatural forces. As the book *Genuine Mediumship of the Invisible Powers* observes: "One of the most common faults of the sitters at a circle is to become unduly impatient, and to try to force matters to a clear manifestation of phenomena almost from the moment of the start. This is all wrong, and is frequently the cause of many failures to obtain the higher phases of mediumistic phenomena."[6]

But beyond the cynics and the superstitious are those

spiritual explorers who burn with the need to experience the spirit in the land. They thirst for spiritual transcendence, for union with the divine. Their spiritual quest can be a disastrous one. I knew such a seeker:

I'll call him Jonathan. (His name and those of others mentioned herein are fictitious, exempting references to myself.) He was in his early forties, working at a small California college in the Sierra foothills when I met him in the mid 1970s. He had come to California from the East Coast. As a twenty-year-old artist in New York City, he had been hailed by *The New York Times* as the next Picasso. By the following year he had attempted suicide. The fast track of the high-profile art scene was not for him.

His move to California actually accelerated his artistic output. He worked in many media, from pen and ink to bead work, sculpture, and dyes. But his great love was painting, especially watercolor.

He enjoyed celebrating nature, particularly the strength and beauty of trees. He painted at his house, which was perched on a hill above a wild river near an old, but still bustling, gold-mining town. He would take his easel or sketchbook, find a place in the sun or a fine tree to sit under, and paint or sketch the day away.

The house itself was a triangular-shaped wooden marvel with a centerpiece chimney that ran straight up from the lower level to the second level and through the roof. On either side of the upper-level part of the brick fireplace, staircases gracefully curved to the lower level. Picture windows liked out on a wooden deck and a view of the forests, the snaking river, and the mountains beyond.

On the deck Jonathan displayed his wood carvings or pieces of wood and rocks he had found on hikes around his land. Chinese wind chimes suspended from the branches overhanging the deck echoed the movement of the wind and prisms caught and danced with the rainbow sparks of the sunlight.

It was Jonathan's own little world.

He used the power of the house, the surrounding forests of oak and pine, and the wild river for more than inspiration for his art: The place became his personal laboratory for contacting spirits, practicing magic rituals and ceremonies, and attempting to unlock the secrets of life and death.

Jonathan also had a manic-depressive personality that wasn't helped by the alcohol and marijuana binges that often accompanied his escape into ritual. His disdain for the medicine prescribed for him (he believed his mind could control his matter) didn't help his mood swings, either.

But the real mental deterioration would not come until later. On most days he was charming and delightful. He loved to play with the small circle of friends he would invite over.

His best friend (they were really like brother and sister) was Elizabeth, the mother of my best friend Sean. Elizabeth's husband, Frank, would often join them on weekend romps by the riverbank for magical evocations of childhood.

They would spend the day with paints and charcoal, marking the rocks with African tribal designs. In the house, with a nice fire in the fireplace, Jonathan sometimes brought out his treasure chest of costumes to lead his party in a masquerade ritual, or bring out his old set of Tarot cards and see what fate would say about their fortunes.

But around 1979 his mood swings became more erratic. One terrible day he even broke into Elizabeth and Frank's home and broke up some of their furniture in an inexplicable fit. Afterward he was chastened and contrite. Elizabeth and Frank repaired the damage, and would stand by their friend, but they were concerned. They knew Jonathan would bear watching.

One night Frank, Elizabeth, and Sean were driving near Jonathan's house and decided to check in on him. They drove down his winding dirt driveway and saw the house lights were on. They parked by the garage.

They all got out of the car and knocked at the door. There was no answer. They tried the doorknob, found it open, and walked in.

In the lower floor they found Jonathan prancing around, painted up and dressed in woman's clothes. He was drugged out, disconnected, but still lucid enough to be startled that other people, even though his dearest friends, had intruded into his private world.

They got Jonathan to relax into conversation. But Elizabeth and Frank decided Jonathan shouldn't be left alone that night, so they asked Sean to stay over to watch him. They said good-bye and drove away, planning to return in the morning.

Their departure suddenly ignited another burst of madness in Jonathan. He ripped the telephone out of the wall, determined that Sean would be a captive witness to his battles with demons. Raging and out of control, at one point Jonathan picked up a carving knife and threatened Sean, who ran out to the garage and locked himself in. As Jonathan stood outside, pounding on the door, trying to get in, Sean grabbed a handy piece of firewood and in fear and exasperation shouted that if Jonathan tried to break in, he'd bash his head.

After long moments of silence Sean heard Jonathan walk away. Sean cautiously unlocked and opened the door. There was a stillness in the chill night air. Sean saw that the front door of the house was open and he walked back in.

He found Jonathan crying in front of the fireplace. The knife had been cast aside, and a fire was glowing and smoking in the hearth. Jonathan had taken a manuscript detailing his spiritual quest he had spent years writing and consigned it to the flames. Sean stood by his weeping friend and watched the pages being eaten alive.

There were other incidents, but they were anticlimactic after that frenzied night. From then on, Jonathan was subdued and regretful. He drank more than ever, usually at the saloons in town. Even his dear friend Elizabeth was having trouble communicating with him. Perhaps Jonathan felt God had deserted him.

It didn't surprise me when Sean called a few days after New Year's Day, 1980, to tell me that Jonathan was dead. His car had hit a tree on the side of the country road leading from town to his place.

Elizabeth was crushed at having lost her best friend, but she bravely took on the task of executing Jonathan's estate and arranging a sale of his personal art. Among the furniture, books, and art were notebooks Jonathan had been filling in an attempt to get the record of his spiritual voyages back on paper. Elizabeth asked me if I would go through the material and edit it into a coherent whole. I told her I would be happy to look through the material.

It was an eerie thing being left alone with the most secret thoughts of one newly departed. In his journals Jonathan described the rigors of his search for salvation. "The body is dismayed at the voyage," he wrote. "It is at this point afraid for its mortal life. It is here that the nerves are torn and one's personal concepts are destroyed. It takes a long time for one to build and rebuild as a bridge to cross this level. One cannot escape this level—one must always go through it."

Jonathan was cremated, according to his wish. A small band of friends met at his house for a short ceremony. They were each given some of his ashes to sprinkle in a special spot of his beloved land.

I was living some distance away at that time and wasn't able to attend the ceremony. Sean called and asked me to make a special trip the following weekend. The two of us would then go out to Jonathan's land and give him our own special good-bye.

Although the National Weather Service predicted a thunderous storm was moving in, we weren't about to change our private vigil plans. I arrived by bus under cloudy, but still dry, clouds. Sean picked me up at the station and we set out on the one hour drive to Jonathan's land.

Sean made one stop by his parents' house to pick

up the keys to Jonathan's house. His parents weren't in, so he left a note saying we had borrowed the keys and were gone to the place for the afternoon. Before leaving, Sean picked up a pair of Tibetan cymbals and an afghan. They seemed important talismans, since they had belonged to Jonathan.

As we drove up to the foothills, serious storm clouds were coasting in on a fast, chilling wind. As we exited the freeway and got on the lonely rural road that led to Jonathan's home, I asked Sean to stop at the spot of the fatal accident. Sean slowed down as we came to a bend in the road. We drove around the curve and then the road straightened out. Halfway up, on the opposite side of the road, Sean pointed out the spot. He pulled the car to the side of the road and parked.

We walked over to the spot that had been the body of a graceful old tree until Jonathan's car had slammed into it. We walked around the grassy field, circling the blasted stump and figuring out how it might have happened.

It didn't seem possible that he could have lost control coming around the curve, we reasoned. The point of impact was too far up the straightaway. There were no skid marks, either. Since Jonathan had been driving back from the town, we considered his late penchant for motoring into town and drinking in the saloons was the probable cause for the accident. It was just another statistic for the "senseless tragedy" files.

We arrived at the house, and Sean unlocked the front door. It was strange to walk into the once magical house stripped of the art, the books, the furniture. Sean walked out on the deck and gazed down at the river.

I sat by the fireplace of the hollow house wearing Jonathan's afghan and holding his Tibetan cymbals. I remembered the good times there. Looking out the picture windows, I could see the storm already falling in the surrounding hills.

Suddenly I had a strange feeling about being alone in the house. I rushed out to the deck, down the steps to the soft earth and jogged out, catching up with Sean, who was meandering toward the river.

''He's in there!'' I exclaimed.

Sean grinned. Little drops of rain were beginning to fall as we began our hike down to the river. Then Sean turned and gave me a compacted, crystalline substance, a little chip off Jonathan's mortal coil.

We meant no disrespect, but for some reason Sean and I started laughing in the rain. I pocketed my little piece of Jonathan, and we continued down to the river. Along the way I clanged the cymbals together, listening to the vibrations echo out and disappear into the rain.

From the trail we could see that the season's storms had already swelled the river. Then the clouds above us burst and the rain increased to that of a thundering tempest. We were both drenched by the time we completed our descent to the riverbank. But we paid the storm no mind. We were thinking of Jonathan, feeling the cold wind, the soft grass, and muddy earth, smelling the sweet scent of the trees, daring the rainstorm to break us.

Stepping from the riverbank across a path of half-submerged stones, we made our way to the boulders that rose out of the middle of the river. Finding some flat surfaces, we sat down only a few feet above the maelstrom around us.

I then stood up, took the ash of Jonathan out of my pocket, and tossed the speck into the rushing waters. I sat down again as Sean climbed onto another rock.

Sitting there, I tried to meditate on the form and spirit of the river. I imagined a picture of the Buddha serenely floating through the power of river and rain. After a few minutes of staring into the depths of the river, I turned to talk to Sean.

He was gone.

I stood up and looked downriver, expecting to see him seated on some other rock. He wasn't in sight. I called his name. Only the storm and river sounded a reply. I called again, louder, but still there was no answer.

I scrambled off the boulders, crossed the stone path across the river, and began scrambling up the muddy bank. My calls of "Sean!" seemed to echo off into infinity. I suddenly realized—he'd fallen into the river!

I looked up the hill to Jonathan's house impassively staring down. I knew the phone in the house still wasn't disconnected. I would head to the house, call his parents, tell them there had been an accident. . . .

And then I saw him, walking back to my direction along a tree-covered trail. With an expletive I threw up my hands and fell to my knees. Sean rushed over to me. He had a big grin on his face when I looked up. He saw me weeping. His smile disappeared and he gripped my shoulders.

"I thought you had fallen in," I muttered as we embraced.

We stood up and felt not the roar, but the silence of the storm.

"Let's leave this apocalypse," I said. We looked up at the house looking down at us and started hiking back up to it.

On the muddy trail back up, Sean asked if I had the Tibetan cymbals with me. I waved them at him and he mentioned the belief that the sound of clanging cymbals can call the dead. I nodded. I had been ringing them all afternoon.

As we got up to the house we saw headlights bouncing up the driveway. A car had pulled up.

"My God, Sean—it's your parents," I exclaimed.

I rushed up ahead of him. I could see Frank at the wheel. Then the door on the passenger side facing us opened, and Elizabeth started to get out. The first thing she did was point to the sopping afghan around my shoulders. Her mouth was just starting to open with an exclamation when I reached her and took hold of her hands.

"We're all right," I said.

"Hold me," she whispered as we embraced.

In the house Sean and I warmed up by the fireplace. After the battering by the elements it was wonderful to appreciate the storm through rain-drizzled windows with friends and a warm fire. There was some tea in the cupboard and Elizabeth brewed up a pot.

As Sean and I sipped our tea, she explained how she had arrived home and saw the note that we were off the Jonathan's house. She knew Sean and I were too fearless and foolhardy to postpone a hike in a storm that turned out to be one of the worst in memory. Fearing the worst, she and Frank had come up looking for us.

The good feeling of family gave me the urge to make a long-distance phone call. I asked permission to use the phone and then excused myself to call my parents. My mother answered my call. I didn't give her the details, but said vaguely that I was with Sean and his folks, and I just wanted to call to tell them I was doing all right and that I wanted to give them my love. It felt good.

Once back home I plunged back into Jonathan's strange journals. "Here's a stone that's the heart of a deer," he wrote in a sequence describing the little treasures crowding his deck. "I used that stone to show a young man his ancestry. He picked up an imaginary sword from the Arabian carpet on which the bloody heart fell and remembered a whole past.

"By the stone are two pieces of wood. When my spirit severed into a million parts, those two pieces of man-shaped wood helped me gain back my form."

Further on he wrote about the Tree of Life, of rain giving the look of emerald velvet to wet moss, of hallucinatory colors vibrating out of stones, the grass, the California oaks.

"Recently I find myself being drawn to trees. I'm learning from trees. They are my teachers, just as my mother and father were. When I'm good and clear I know they're here with me. These teachers are teaching me about 'It.' 'It' is asking an amazing question.

"We get shown our teachers finally, and at death we

no longer insist on such singular forms for who they are—at that point I'll see more of my teachers.

"I'm working on a painting now. It is of a tree that becomes a total spirit. It comforts me. It is a true way of sleeping with trees."

He wrote of the soul-body-spirit, of the search for God, of reaching out to the spirit world.

"There was a night three years ago where I had come home and I was really aware of presences all around me. It was really strong. I really sensed something. There was a voice in me that said, 'Solomon's Seal is upon this' and it was an effort to understand. But I sensed that I had support from many, many people. I sensed it. I sensed that my eyes could even put a seal down onto paper . . . a curious moment of just sensing presence and power and wonder."

From the writings I discovered that Jonathan had begun experimenting with calling forth spirit beings and entities. He seemed to make no distinction between outside sentient beings or atavistic creatures from his subconscious.

He helped the cast of characters "emerge" with silk scarves and masks. To banish the energy he had only to doff the scarf or remove the mask. "The devil mask was always a test. It was a mask I had bought in an old costume shop. I was drawn to it, drawn to a strange aspect of it. I gazed at it for so long the shop owner became strangely hesitant to sell it to me.

"The devil mask. When you put it on and take it off, what was the face underneath? Would you succumb to that ironclad form of face. Could it—would it—destroy you?

"Monks and magicians in the countryside are told to journey to high mountain cliffs and find the truth of their selves over waterfalls, to discover the mysteries in an isolated place. Of course, I was isolated too. But I had all these things to do in this world, and a profession to maintain."

I spent hours poring over the material. It was just

short of an obsession. It was as if Jon were in my head, expounding on the points as I read them.

He wrote of how he once "blew up on the rocks of too much ritual."

"I sometimes feel a need to scatter myself totally out into the world as if I were ashes. . . .

"I paint trees. An old forest surrounds my house and there are many dead trees that have died and opened themselves up layer by layer. Seeing into those trees, that though dead still live, I have been given an incredible vision. They are not dead. I think of them as the Tree of Life.

"We call trees 'trees,' we don't call them spirits. We don't have the experience of them as spirits. And when we do have the experience of trees as spirits we don't know how to name them. . . .

"I think my paintings are a mark, my way of marking my space as I move through time. I think the trees show me a space that is beyond death. For me it's fascinating."

And then like a lightning flash going off, it hit me. I read the line again:

" . . . I think the trees show me a space that is beyond death. For me it's fascinating."

The picture rolled off like a film in my head. Jonathan driving in the dark night on a road driven so often, anticipating the tree just down the road, approaching the curve and coming onto the straightaway, then aiming for the tree and gently pressing down the accelerator. . . .

I wondered—had he had enough? Did he finally decide to prove his theories and take that fatal step into the bridge world and had his beloved trees shown him the way?

I made one halfhearted effort to discover if Jonathan had made it to the Other Side during a 1987 reading at a spiritualist church in San Francisco.

It was a plush brick building with Doric columns on the exterior and a carpeted interior with polished wood pews and fine antiques. It felt like a museum piece to old-time spiritualism.

That night was the night for the billets, where questions concerning the departed would be answered by one of the mediums. I wrote my question, asking if Jonathan was doing fine on the Other Side, sealed it, wrote my initials on the envelope, and dropped it into the billet basket.

During the billet reading the church medium picked my envelope out of the basket and announced my initials. I raised my hand. The medium made eye contact, smiled, and touched the sealed billet to his forehead. In a stentorian voice he described some strange vision of an old man and a young kid riding a bicycle. But no word, no response, to my query about Jonathan. The medium was so far off the mark it was almost funny.

But a billet bulletin from Beyond would not prove or disprove anything, anyway. The path and progress of the ultimate journey into mystery that begins at the grave is not yet ours to follow. From there the tracks of those that go before us become lost and we can only hope—and wonder.

"After the fire consumes, when this great body-form goes into the soil, the seed will grow again," Jon wrote. "For it's not that we're dust in the wind—we are dust that *is* wind."

10

The Neon Palm

One day, during a conversation with Florida mediums Fred and June Bowermaster, the subject came around to the big-money New Age channeling. They decided it was permissible for mediums to make a living giving psychic readings, but June drew the line at the "neon palm" people.

It's hard to miss those neon signs of displayed palms that advertise the business addresses of psychics across the country. Many were reputable, but June had heard a few horror stories about some of the psychic shysters in operation.

She recalled a story about a troubled welfare mother in Atlanta who had gone to "one of those neon palms" for spiritual solace. The psychic told the woman a plague of evil spirits had taken possession of her, and it would only cost her $1,000 for an exorcism. The psychic explained she wouldn't make any money out of it because the ceremony involved the lighting of one thousand candles at a cool dollar apiece. When the welfare mother broke down and wept bitterly that she couldn't afford it, the neon palmster told the woman to cheer up, she had a sister down the road who could perform the same ritual for only $750!

"That makes me mad!" June frowned. "Now the skeptics equate those people with us."

That incident is an extreme example, but there is no doubt that a lot of New Age spiritualism comes with a price tag attached. Virtually overnight, channeling has become a big business. Although it is probably impossible to come up with an exact figure, estimates of gross revenues from seminars, tapes, and books on channeled material run from $100 million to $400 million a year.[1]

Personal appointments with a prominent channel can range from $450 to hundreds of dollars for a one-to-two hour session. A weekend "intensive," where the channel works with a small group, is usually a minimum of $300–$500 per person, much more if the program is held in a wilderness or vacation spot.

When the total product line of the New Age is considered, the gross numbers become truly astounding. The numbers for total consumer dollars spent on crystals alone totaled an estimated $100 million in 1987, with millions more spent on crystal books, videos, and seminars, according to *Forbes* magazine.

With that kind of money involved, the New Age business atmosphere can often be charged with something more than good vibes. A California dealer of New Age products provided an uncomfortable look at the competitive side of the business in a personal column of his forty-eight-page product catalogue/magazine: "For over twenty years, my work has constantly been copied and criticized," he complained in a 1987 column. "In 1976, I launched the first hypnosis tape catalogue, and now hundreds of companies have copied our lead . . . and most of our titles. If we come out with a catalogue with Sedona on the cover, three months later, two or three other companies follow suit—from seminar formats to little things like adding the 'send a friend' space to the order form. If we do it, so do our competitors.

"I wouldn't change this if I could. We never get upset about it—we laugh and accept what is."

Competition isn't unknown in channeling, either. A spokesman for one major channel once told me that a famous movie star, popularly identified with another channel, had recently come over to their camp. "Everyone moves on," was the spokeman's satisfied evaluation of their celebrity coup. When I told my sister

Katherine of the conversation she reacted askance, "Back stabbing in the channeling business!?"

Major channels have even been known to hire lawyers to advise them on interview requests, book projects, and product ventures.

Many New Age products and channeling consultations are offered through free catalogues sent through the mail or given away in stores. Perusing the catalogue of the California company mentioned earlier, there are listings for a wide variety of New Age books, tapes, products, and services.

Some of the metaphysical tapes include the "Trance Prophet Hypnosis" album "to assist you in channeling otherwise unavailable information"; taped seminars such as the "Battle for Your Mind" (exposing brainwashing techniques); the "No Effort Weight Loss Subliminal Video" (lose weight while watching TV); "Aerobic Exercise Music—With Subliminal Suggestions;" and, of course, "Erasing Someone from Your Mind Programming" album: "If you want to eliminate the pain usually associated with the ending of a relationship, this album . . . uses the three most powerful techniques available to assist you to successfully *mentally detach from anyone.*" [Emphasis added.]

There are books for exploring past lives and the "higher self." Seminars are also listed, including "Transcendence Training," in which the seeker can change his life or rid herself of "self-defeating masks and hang-ups"—for $295 per.

For those wanting access to a channel, there are many options and styles to choose from. In Sacramento you can "Dial a Channel" for a personal telephone consultation. If you're in Los Angeles, you can "channel yourself through art" at a "transformational art" class designed to reveal the meaning of past-life memories and dreams. Also listed in the Los Angeles psychic want ads is a mystic Akashic Records reader who describes herself as a "psychic to the rescue." Then there's the "metaphysical teacher and practitioner" with the ultimate reference line: "If you want to know what my credentials are, ask your guides to ask their guides about me."

Maybe you want to learn how to do some of this mystic stuff. If so, there are opportunities such as the apprentice program in the shamanistic practice of Hawaiian Huna. In that program the spiritual novice can learn how to "use shamanic healing methods . . . avert or diminish natural disasters" and use "power animals and inner worlds"—in a two-day workshop. (Those who successfully complete the entire two-day program receive a certificate recognizing them as an Apprentice Shaman.)

There are tours to psychic power places around the world. You can fly from New York to visit the sacred spots of Egypt, including the temples of Luxor and the Great Pyramids, for $2,195 complete. If you're on a budget, a mere $525 is all one needs to spend a week with the Huichol Indian shamans of Mexico.

A whole line of products is available to help provide an instant altered state. A device known as the Synchro-Energizer, marketed by the Institute for DeHypnotherapy in California, is one of a number of devices that promise to build consciousness the way Charles Atlas once promised to build biceps. Special Synchro-Energizer goggles provide the strong visuals that can take one into a higher meditative state. In that stimulated state, intuitive visions or past-life information can flow, they say.

I tried the Synchro-Energizer experience at a 1987 New Age Expo in San Francisco. I lay down on a mat in a room lined with mats for a group experience (only one other voyager was there during my session), fitted the Synchro goggles over my eyes, put the headphones over my ears, and settled in. A woman on a raised stage sat lotus-style and worked the controls that fed meditative music into the earphones and released the all-important high-frequency lights into my goggles.

The flashing lights produced constantly changing kaleidoscopic patterns and colored shapes. There were a few images I noticed, mostly crowds of people that seemed to bubble up dreamlike into the surface of the hallucinatory landscape I was viewing. According to the product's developers no two people interpret this rush of data the same way.

For me it was a fun if not transcendent experience. But developers of the product have high hopes that the device could become one of the indispensable products of the New Age. "There is an incredible market out there," enthused Denis Gorges, exulting over the Synchro-Energizer in a 1987 *California* magazine interview. Gorges, a "self-described biomedical researcher," estimates to have sold more than six thousand of the devices at $6,500 apiece within two years.

The Synchro-Energizer or variations are even being promoted as centerpieces for new consciousness-raising "brain/mind salons." One such institute, which opened in 1984, reportedly grosses over $250,000 a month. "We envision the gray-flannel executive coming in on his lunch hour for a quick brain tune-up," the Institute's director told *California*.[2]

Such metaphysical make-over centers are popular avenues for New Agers seeking spiritual tune-ups. One retreat is the Blue Mountain Center in Colorado, run by the Spiritual Sciences Institute, a private, nonprofit organization based in Santa Barbara. Institute director and trance channel, Verna V. Yater, purchased the forty-four acres of forested Rocky Mountain property in 1978 after she was led there by her spirit guides. She says she later discovered the land was in alignment with global meridian lines that connected with such power spots as Machu Picchu and the Great Pyramids, giving her land "a special vibrational power."

"Join with others to experience the spiritual and physical beauty of Blue Mountain, as participants live in tents on the land, while working with a series of five teachers, channeled spirit guides and seminar leaders" reads the Center's brochure.

Actress and New Age activist Shirley MacLaine is

preparing to open up a retreat of her own on three hundred acres of Colorado property she has dubbed "Uriel Village." (Uriel is one of the archangels noted as "regent of the sun" in Milton's *Paradise Lost.*)

"I want this to be all mine, my energy, my control," MacLaine explained to *Time* magazine in 1987. "I want a big dome-covered meditation center and a series of dome-covered meeting rooms because spiritual energy goes in spirals. We'll grow all our own food and eat under another dome. I want to turn a profit with this so I can build another center and another. I want to prove that spirituality is profitable." (Some might argue that spirituality has always been profitable.)

MacLaine, who has been praised for her role in publicizing the metaphysical, has also been a lightning rod for critics of all New Age money changing. MacLaine's 1987 nationwide "Connecting With The Higher Self" seminars was noted more for the $300 per person ticket price than for the program content. One writer noted that seminar participants had to sign release forms allowing their voices to be used in any possible audio productions. "This has created the suspicion among her listeners that Shirley MacLaine is readying herselves [*sic*] to become to the spirit via audio and videocassette what Jane Fonda is to the body," reports *Money* magazine reporter Marlys Harris.[3]

Regardless of the price tag, the MacLaine seminar was a huge draw across the country. The ballroom of the New York Hilton accommodated 1,200 believers, who spent the weekend meditating on their chakras, visualizing with psychic sight, and accepting the notion that they were, one and all, God.

Of course, not every New Age undertaking is solid gold. In November 1987 the San Francisco ESP World Fair, promoted as the largest psychic fair ever to hit the city, was a financial failure. *San Francisco Chronicle* reporter Mick LaSalle couldn't resist asking in his lead paragraph why, with all the psychics involved, someone couldn't know beforehand that the program would be a flop.

But when all the New Age showmanship and entrepreneurial streaks have been laid end to end unto the astral levels, we should ask if all this spiritual biz is really resulting in happier, more aware people. Or is the underlying message that spirituality can be bought, that truth comes packaged in fad products, that enlightenment is a prospect for only those with the healthiest bank account?

Many channels want to demystify the psychic and bring spirituality down to earth. As such, some channels feel that the services they provide are no different than that provided by a psychologist or personal and career counselors. Increasingly, psychic and spiritual concepts are being applied to fields outside of the traditional function of religion. Those inroads are themselves shaping the evolving face of the New Age.

11

Psychic Sciences

"Noetic quality.—Although so similar to states of feeling, mystical states seem to those who experience them to be also states of knowledge. They are states of insight into depths of truths unplumbed by the discursive intellect. They are illuminations, revelations, full of significance and importance, all inarticulate though they remain; and as a rule they carry with them a curious sense of authority for aftertime."

—William James
The Varieties of Religious Experience

In February 1971 astronaut Edgar Mitchell piloted the Apollo 14 lunar module to a soft landing on the moon, and thrilled to the experience of walking on the surface. But that was to be only the beginning of that mission's outer space adventures.

During the 240,000-mile voyage home Mitchell had a peak experience in which the "presence of divinity became almost palpable and I *knew* that life in the universe was not just an accident based on random processes."

According to Mitchell, this insight came directly, or "noetically," as he would call it. "Clearly, the universe has meaning and direction," he would write. "It was not perceptible by the sensory organs, but it was there nevertheless—an unseen dimension behind the

190

visible creation that gives it an intelligent design and that gives life purpose.''

In that peak experience Mitchell realized that a transformation to a new consciousness was needed if humankind was to survive its proclivity for destructive technologies and war. That metamorphosis would entail a dramatic move from an ego-centered self-image to a truly cosmic consciousness.[1]

Mitchell had also brought on board, without the knowledge of his NASA superiors, a set of cards designed with geometric images. During rest breaks from his return flight duties Mitchell attempted to telepathically communicate the image sequence of the cards to four co-experimenters on Earth.

Mitchell's associates guessed the correct card sequence twenty-five percent of the time—slightly but not dramatically above the twenty percent accuracy rate representing the minimum accounting for pure chance. But Mitchell wasn't discouraged.

''People want and desire an explanation of ESP (extrasensory perception), if one can be provided,'' he said after his return to Earth. ''I think it can.''[2]

Mitchell began the effort to explore the outer limits of consciousness with the formation in 1973 of the Institute of Noetic Science (IONS). The formation of IONS is keeping with the American tradition of parapsychology—the scientific study of phenomena such as ESP, precognition, out-of-the-body experience, telepathy, and other manifestations of the paranormal.

One of the earliest parapsychology organizations in the U.S. was the American Society for Psychical Research (ASPR), established in 1885. (The group was an offshoot of the Society for Psychical Research (SPR), founded in London three years earlier.)

American psychical researcher Dr. Joseph Banks Rhine, who cofounded the Parapsychology Laboratory at Duke University in 1935 and has been called the father of the scientific study of the paranormal, has noted the difficulty in developing a scientific study of the psychic. ''There was a long period of struggle over whether science could extract and liberate these [parapsychological] principles from the institutions to which they had become so essential,'' Rhine once wrote. ''Gradually, however, the parapsychological elements were pulled away from mesmerism and hypnosis, and later psychical research achieved its independence of the spiritualist movement.''[3]

Magic, spiritualism, and the occult formed the original structures for discovering, examining, and even controlling the mysteries of nature. Experimental science would evolve from that background and become the dominating paradigm for studying the mysteries of life in the twentieth century.

There was a scientific method to the occult researches of old. The Key of Solomon, for example, formed a famed medieval collection of spells and ritual incantations. Such ''grimoires,'' as they were called, provided practical instructions and devices, such as astrological pentacles, for summoning spirits.

In the legendary science of alchemy it was believed that base metals could be transmuted into precious gold and silver. As far back as the ancient Egyptians there was a belief that certain alloys were imbued with magical powers.

Astrology existed in India as early as 1500 B.C. The ancient Greeks also cast horoscopes and their philosophy acknowledged, and expounded upon, the theory of transmigration of the soul. Even when Johannes Kepler (1571–1630) established that the Earth was a minor planet and not the center of the universe, astronomy was allied with astrology. Kepler himself drew horoscopes for the aristocracy.

Kepler and other scientists of his and earlier eras had inherited a tradition of science/mysticism. The Pythagorean brotherhood that reflected the views of the Greek philosopher Pythagoras (c.570–c.500 B.C.) ''sought by rites and abstinences to purify the believer's soul and enable it to escape from the 'Wheel of Birth.' '' The universe, in the Pythagorean view, was supreme, divine mathematics.[4]

The current scientific methodology of experimenting and demonstrating evolved out of occultism. Robin E. Rider writes in *The Show of Science:*

> Demonstration experiments evolved against a background of ritual magic. Natural magic, with roots in antiquity, still boasted an enthusiastic corps of advocates and practitioners in the Renaissance. . . . Both [science and magic] invoke the forces of nature and the influences of stars. . . .
>
> In many Renaissance books it is hard to tell where natural magic leaves off and science begins, or vice versa. Magic was often proclaimed the key to nature, and its defenders went so far as to claim that natural magic lay at the heart of the natural sciences.''

Rider observes that by the end of the seventeenth century, institutions such as the royal Society of London were starting to extract, and denounce, the mystical elements that had influenced scientific research. Sir Francis Bacon, in particular, was an ardent denouncer of the occult's influence on experimental science.[5]

But the idea that science could not only unlock the material workings of the universe, but explore the divine mysteries believed to empower those physical workings continued to have its fascination. Many famous works of literature reflect this melding of occult and science. Goethe's *Faust,* written between 1773 and 1831, describes how the brilliant Dr. Faust, a man learned in philosophy, jurisprudence, and medicine, desired to see ''what secret force [hides] in the world and rules its course.'' Locked in his study, Faust poured over ancient occult texts and meditated on the mystic symbology before calling out: ''You float, oh spirits, all around/ Respond to me, if you can hear me.''[6]

Robert Louis Stevenson's *Dr. Jekyll and Mr. Hyde,* published in 1885, immortalized Dr. Jekyll's discovery of a chemical that unlocked the physical and psychological character of Mr. Hyde within him. "And it chanced that the direction of my scientific studies, which led wholly toward the mystic and the transcendental, reacted and shed a strong light on this consciousness of the perennial war among my members," Jekyll explained of his researches into the duality of good and evil in the human race.[7]

Frankenstein, which has thrilled generations since its publication in 1818, presented another learned man who combined science with mysticism. As Dr. Frankenstein mused on his experiments in the creation of life: "It was the secrets of heaven and earth that I desired to learn; and whether it was the outward substance of things or the inner spirit of nature and the mysterious soul of man that occupied me, still my inquiries were directed to the metaphysical, or in its highest sense, the physical secrets of the world."[8]

As the twentieth century approached, mainstream science rapidly moved away from any mingling with mysticism. But parapsychological studies by respected scientists would continue. One such scientist was the famed physicist Sir William Crookes (1832–1915), who discovered thallium and invented the radiometer. Crookes's attention was drawn to the field of spiritualism, which was in its heyday. He decided to investigate mediums "with no preconceived notions whatever as to what can or cannot be . . . believing, as I do, that we have by no means exhausted all human knowledge or fathomed the depths of all physical forces."

But despite acknowledging an open mind to the subject of mediums, Crookes has also written: "The increased employment of scientific methods will produce a race of observers who will drive the worthless residuum of spiritualism hence into the unknown limbo of magic and necromancy."[9]

His fellow scientists and the English press were confident that this learned man, considered one of the greatest physicists of the nineteenth century, would expose spiritualism as a fraud. But the skeptical Sir William became a true believer after investigating the mediumship of one Daniel Douglas Home, considered the greatest physical medium in the history of modern spiritualism.

D. D. Home (1833–1886) was born in Scotland, but went to Connecticut at age nine, where he was reared by an aunt. His early psychic experiences included the ability to have visions of dead spirits, including his mother and a school chum, and to hear spectral rappings.

Home became a celebrated medium. Adding to his renown—that continues to this day—was the fact that not once were his manifestations of spiritual contact proved fraudulent. Going against the mediumistic protocol of the day, he held seances in broad daylight. During those sessions Home caused tables and chairs to move without apparent cause. It was said he could cause spirit hands to materialize and play musical instruments.

In 1868, at the home of Lord Adare in Buckingham Gate, London, Home reportedly performed his greatest feat: a levitation out of a third-story window, reentering through another window, much to the astonishment of Lord Adare and two other witnesses.

In 1871 Crookes's investigation into the psychic claims of D. D. Home resulted in the eminent scientist concluding: ''The phenomenon I am prepared to attest are so extraordinary, and so directly oppose the most firmly rooted articles of scientific belief—amongst others, the ubiquity and invariable action of the force of gravitation—that even now, on recalling the details of what I have witnessed, there is an antagonism in my mind between reason, which pronounces it to be scientifically impossible, and the consciousness that my senses, both of touch and sight—are not lying witnesses when they testify against my preconceptions.''[10]

Sir William's skeptical colleagues were not amused.

Crookes's report to the Royal Society on June 15, 1871, was not accepted since it did not expose spiritualism as a fraud.

The scientific study of mediumship—and the attendant controversy—continues to our day. Psychologist Julian Jaynes, in his 1976 book, *The Origin of Consciousness in the Breakdown of the Bicameral Mind,* ascribes the art of oracles, mediums, and channels to disturbances of the brain's left and right hemispheres, resulting in hallucinations. In ancient times such deliriums were thought to be the voices of the gods, Jaynes believes. Modern-day trance and conscious channel states are simply a vestige of this ancient, hallucinatory inner voice, he concludes.

"Channeling is a difficult area to study," observes Jerry Solfvin, a professor of parapsychology at John F. Kennedy University in Orinda, California. "In 1975 I did some studies with a trance channel in Michigan. While she went into trance and several personalities came through I monitored her brain waves with very sophisticated EEG equipment.

"During the presence of each of several different trance personalities the EEG reading was different for each. But the data doesn't tell a whole lot. Brain waves also change during biofeedback."

Solfvin admits that for someone like himself who specializes in process-oriented research the ultimate question of whether a channel is bringing through another entity may be impossible to prove. The next possible step to validate channeling would be to analyze the channeled information, but that would require months, perhaps years, to corroborate what is often very subjective information.

IONS has recently commissioned psychologist Dr. Authur Hastings to prepare a study of the phenomenon of channeling. Dr. Hastings's initial research has identified various models for approaching the subject. Channeled messages could be coming from disembodied beings, or the channels may be making contact with, and personifying, inner or archetypal forces. Dr.

Hastings also entertains the possibility that channels are simply using telepathy and clairvoyance (if one assumes the validity of those models) to obtain information from a cosmic source such as the Akashic Records. Dr. Hastings writes after some initial observations of the phenomenon:

> If messages do indeed come from non-physical beings, then the implication of the reality of other domains wants to be explored. If the messages, which are often spiritual and inspirational, come from another part of the Self, the implication is that there is a deep part of consciousness that is profoundly concerned with noetic values and attitudes. If this model is held it implies that there are amazing potentials in the unconscious for creativity, insight, and eloquence that are rarely tapped by the conscious self. . . .
>
> Learning more about channeling holds the promise of deeper understanding of human abilities and the realities of consciousness.[11]

One organization seeking to bridge the hard sciences with the information potential of channeling is the Center for Applied Intuition (CAI) in San Francisco. The organization was founded in 1970 by Dr. William Kautz, a Massachusetts Institute of Technology graduate and former staff scientist at Stanford Research Institute, who began his parapsychology work after thirty years in the fields of mathematics, communications, and computer science.

The CAI has been applying its intuitive researches to archaeological researches, investigating infant death syndrome, AIDS, societal transformations, and advising Japanese business interests. But Kautz points out that some of their most popular work has been private channeling counseling and training people how to develop their own intuitive skills.

The CAI has developed a method of inquiry that seeks an ''intuitive consensus'' from channeled sources on subjects ranging from medicine and societal transformation to the study of ancient history. In this methodology a CAI team prepares questions for a particular area of research and presents them to as many as seven channels (CAI calls them "expert intuitives"). The answers are tape-recorded, transcribed, and examined for correlations.

In Kautz's opinion psychic sources are " all telling us the same things. This doesn't prove it's right, but it allows for a high credibility. The goal is to pull together this information, not so much as fact that we can offer the world, but as hypothesis, a new way of looking at subjects."

Kautz, like others, believes access to higher information is a natural human function, albeit repressed in our modern world. "Channeling is a deliberate putting aside of conscious thinking," he explains. "Information then starts to flow out that is clearly not in the conscious mind, and we believe not in the subconscious memories, either, but seems to come from a higher source."

Kautz notes numerous accounts of the revelations that can be produced in intuitive states. Many scientific problems have been solved through the insight of direct knowing.

There was Friedrich August von Kekule, a professor of chemistry in Ghent, Belgium, who in 1865 was working unsuccessfully on solving the problem of how atoms formed themselves into molecules. Dozing in front of the fireplace after another winter day of fruitless work, he dreamed of a snake seizing its own tail. He suddenly awoke, a revolutionary idea coming to him—certain compounds can form closed chains or rings, not the previous model of an open structure. The insight helped pave the way for the development of organic chemistry.

Melvin Clavin, who in 1961 was honored as a Nobel laureate in chemistry for his work in photosynthesis, reported an intuitive insight that came to him while he was waiting in his parked car for his wife to return from a shopping trip. "In a matter of seconds, the cyclic character of the path of carbon became apparent to me . . . the recognition of phosphoglyceric acid . . . all in a matter of thirty seconds."[12]

"We open our eyes, we see what intuition will do—and there it is." Kautz smiles. "We can go in and work with an expert intuitive who has no prior academic or prior conscious memory knowledge of a subject and pull out information that could take scientists years to extract by their methods."

But Kautz, whose professional life has been steeped in the paradigm of modern science, feels that the majority of scientists are not yet prepared to accept intuitive consensus as a research tool. "With the rise of modern civilization, a science was there to conduct us into that, and which we now operate with," says Kautz. "This method of operation says that the way to come to knowledge is through reasoning and linear thought, sense-related activities. If you can't see it, touch it, or hear it, then it isn't valid. Now, most people throughout history haven't operated this way. They put a great deal of emphasis on other ways of knowing.

"We've grown up a model of physical reality which is superb. It's given rise to our technology and all that—it's great. But the thing is, it doesn't deal with the issues that are most central to human beings. You can't run your life this way.

"Science has practically nothing to say about the most important things that ever happened to you. These have to do with your feelings, your subjective impressions of people and the outer world. It has to do with maybe peak, or mystical, experiences which are sporadic throughout your life, with relationships. Science has nothing at all to say about these things even though it's held up as the authority to whom we turn when there's a social issue."

"There's a lot of public misunderstanding about channeling," Kautz says. "I guess in a broad way the image of it coming out is something spectacular, phenomenal—whereas it isn't that at all. It's something very ordinary that everybody does to some small degree, and could do to a larger degree if they wanted to or had the right understanding.''

Lawrence LeShan, a psychologist who wrote *The Medium, the Mystic, and the Physicist,* observes that as long as the paranormal is viewed as unusual or invalid, it cannot be activated, and hence, never proven. ''It is certainly clear to all of us that clairvoyance and precognition are impossible,'' LeShan rhetorically writes. ''They simply cannot exist in the world as we commonly know and respond to it. . . . The problem is that they do occur. The evidence, and it is there—hard, scientific and factual—for anyone who looks at it, is not refutable. We must do something about the paradox.''

LeShan suggests that although one way of looking at reality may be valid, that shouldn't preclude another reality from being equally valid. LeShan describes an integration of ordinary and non-ordinary reality perceptions as ''Clairvoyant Reality.''

''In the Clairvoyant Reality there are no separate entities or events,'' he observes. ''Things 'flow' into each other instead of being separate: they are overlapping subfields of larger entities. Space cannot be a bar, under these conditions, to the flow of being an 'information' between them.''

In that mystic reality time is not chopped up into fine linear bits that have a past, present, and future—there is only ''Now'' and things simply ''Are.''[13]

Roger Sperry, a Nobel laureate neuroscientist, has written that the subjective phenomenon of inner experience ''that had long been banned from scientific explanation'' is now accepted as having a relationship with the conscious experience. Sperry even states that such ''holistic thinking'' has gone from a fringe, eclectic concept to that of ''the majority practicing paradigm of the behavioral sciences.''

This holistic shift in the behavioral sciences has not yet caused a change in the ''more exact sciences such as physics, chemistry and molecular biology,'' where

Sperry believes the exact sciences still largely adhere to a materialist, mechanistic view of reality. The scientific materialist merely views the natural order as being "governed from below upward following the course of evolution" as part of a "strictly physically driven cosmos. . . . By this long dormant physicalist-behaviorist paradigm there is no real freedom, dignity, purpose or intentionality."

Sperry believes a paradigm that allows for freedom and transcendence is not only needed but is currently evolving. "Is the consciousness revolution a revolution for all science? I believe it is and that the behavioral sciences may be leading the way to a more valid paradigm for science in general."[14]

Quantum physics is one of the hard sciences being heralded as helping to lead science to a new and more transcendent prototype. Advances in this area are even being touted as bridging Western science with Eastern mysticism. "In contrast to the mystic, the physicist begins his inquiry into the essential nature of things by studying the material world," Fritjof Capra writes in his classic, *The Tao of Physics*. "Penetrating into ever-deeper realms of matter, he has become aware of the essential unity of all things and events. More than that, he has also learnt that he himself and his consciousness are an integral part of this unity. Thus the mystic and the physicist arrive at the same conclusion: one starting from the inner realm, the other from the outer world. The harmony between their views confirms the ancient Indian wisdom that Brahman, the ultimate reality without, is identical to Atman, the reality within."[15]

Gary Zukav in *The Dancing Wu Li Masters* agrees. In this look at the new physics, scientist Zukav points out that quantum physics itself proves the world is more than the solid, independent force we believe is the only reality. Zukav notes that the scientific worldview is moving away from the traditional, logical symbology toward an open-ended mythos that does not separate observer and observed.

A powerful awareness lies dormant in these discoveries: an awareness of the mind to mold "reality," rather than the other way around. In this sense, the philosophy of physics is becoming indistinguishable from the philosophy of Buddhism, which is the philosophy of enlightenment. . . .

A vital aspect of the enlightened state is the experience of an all-pervading unity. "This" and "that" are no longer separate entities. . . . Everything is a manifestation of that which is.[16]

Dr. Willis Harman, president of IONS, a member of the University of California board of regents, and senior scientist at SRI International, agrees that the accounts of paranormal phenomena throughout history and across cultures require a change in science itself to accommodate those viewpoints.

In a keynote address before a convention of the Association for Past-Life Research and Therapy (APRT), held in Sacramento in 1987, Dr. Harman observed that views that were only recently anathema to the scientific materialist, such as the concept of unconscious mental processes, are becoming more acceptable.

"The idea of objectively looking at things doesn't fit when we get into the mind and spirit," Harman says. "Out in culture a widening group of people are basing their lives on the idea that the processes of mind seems to only be limited by our beliefs. That turns everything around. All experience is feedback. Grasp the implications! It's the most exciting news tip you can possibly have. It means everything is up for grabs!"

As such, we can create our own reality—a major point of New Age channeled information. Under such a view we don't have to accept the logic that an environmental price must be paid for a society to function, or that a war and starvation is an inevitable human condition. This creates an openness to infinite possibilities. The adventure, the exploration, the growth never end.

Another group on the frontier of consciousness research is Findhorn, the experimental community on Scotland's north coast. The community, which has inspired similar experiments in the U.S., believes there are nature spirits and elementals that can be communicated with. Findhorn has collected the communications from these entities and devas. As a "lettuce deva" once explained: "We can control the life force in individual plants, speed it up or slow it down. . . . We have been given certain powers, and within our limits we wield them. In your [Findhorn] experiment let us aid you all we can."[17]

The result of this divine connection between humans and nature includes plants that are "growing out of sand and blossoming in the snow," according to poet William Irwin Thompson.

> Whether we speak of kachinas, devas, djin, angels or spirits, we are invoking a cosmology that is much the same around the world.
>
> Industrialization tried to drive that cosmology out of men's minds. . . . Urbanization and nationalism have reached their limits to growth along with industrialization, so the culture of the presently emerging future is one of decentralization of cities, miniaturization of technology and planetarization of nations. . . . Animism and electronics is the landscape of the New Age, and animism and electronics is already the landscape of Findhorn."[18]

"Reputable scientists not only in physics but in many other fields are convinced that the old mindless, mechanistic picture of the universe is inadequate," writes environmental writer Harold Gilliam. "In the words of Sir James Jeans: 'The universe begins to look more like a great thought than a great machine.'

"How to get in touch with that thought whether by talking to trees [Gilliam earlier notes the Findhorn success] or meditating or exploring the microworld of the quanta—may be the major human project of the coming century,'' Gilliam concludes.[19]

Dr. Harman writes,

The full implications of the ''global mind change'' associated with emergence of a science that adequately treats the human mind and spirit are no more apparent than were the implications of the scientific heresy in the middle of the seventeenth century. We can be sure, however, that they will be no less profound. If indeed the ''new heresy'' involves changes in basic assumptions at the same deep level as the scientific heresy, it means that the world of the twenty-first century will be as different from ours as the modern world is from the Middle Ages. There is no sector of society, and no institution, that will not be affected. We have an interesting time ahead, to put it mildly.[20]

Turning on the Channel

*"They shall train themselves to go in public to
   become orators and oratresses,
Strong and sweet shall their tongues be, poems
   and materials of poems shall come from their
   lives, they shall be makers and finders,
Of them and their works shall emerge divine con-
   veyers, to convey gospels, characters, events,
   retrospections, shall be convey'd in gospels,
   trees, animals, waters, shall be convey'd,
Death, the future, the invisible faith shall all be
   convey'd."*

—"Mediums" *Walt Whitman*

To get to the class it was a short walk along the
Powell Street cable car tracks to the bustling hotel and
shopping environs of San Francisco's Union Square,
into a hotel decorated in Florentine splendor, past a
chic lobby restaurant, and down the carpeted stairs to
a meeting room where several dozen people were already seating themselves in the rows of chairs.

But this was no ordinary class—in this room we were
going to learn how to channel.

The course, An Introduction to Channeling, would
be taught by Loretta Ferrier, Ph.D., a second-gener-
ation channel active in the psychological/metaphysical
field.

"Did you know you have within yourself the ability

to tap into a hidden wellspring that can bring you increased happiness, creativity and well-being?'' her course description read. ''You can find this inner source through the process called channeling. Channeling is an altered state that allows you to tap into a higher consciousness—your own higher consciousness—and to communicate information from that source to others.''

At the appointed time Loretta Ferrier, tall, blonde, and attired in a flowing yellow gown, waltzed into the room, accompanied by two young women assistants. Like many channels she is a large woman, but also like a lot of channels, she moves with an assured grace and energy. She had a smile that was beaming goodwill. I had already known she was upbeat. Days before, when I had talked with her on the phone regarding her class, she had remarked that her mother had ''gone to the Light.'' She said it with such sparkle that I was momentarily puzzling over her meaning. Then I sheepishly offered my condolences. With the same sparkling tone she replied to the effect that Mother, who had been a channel and healer, was still with her, only now working and communicating from the Other Side.

Loretta began the class by asking the assembled to put their chairs in a circle. She explained that the spirit used her as a conscious channel. She would enter into a state similar to deep hypnosis, but her mind would not be detached. She felt this made her more engaged and reactive with her life.

She observed that more and more people would be learning how to channel in response to the coming Earth changes. Channeling was also preparing the way for a ''messiah that will become incarnate.'' The light emanating from this being would be too bright to stand unless people began to open up to their spiritual and psychic dimensions.

''Vibrations moving through the earth now are very heavy and difficult,'' she noted. ''Our technology is now moving against us. The Earth is dying from lack of nutrients and love of the human spirit.'' Only if more and more people opened up the intuitive capacities of the right brain (''our connection to the divine'') would we be able to survive. She asserted that respected people she knew, from Harvard psychologists to Episcopalian church leaders, were now channeling. ''Channeling is a technology. It can be taught.''

She began to channel for us, describing what was happening to her. She closed her eyes, resting her hands on her knees. She described heat moving through her body and up to an ''energy muscle'' at the top of her head that would open. Although some people channeled through their subconscious, spirit channeling would ''come in primarily through the back of the neck. We feel an energy begin to descend into us. A ghostlike part of us reaches up into that energy field.''

She was going deeper still. Finally her voice changed to a distant, impassive tone, and she invited questions from the class. After answering a few tentative questions she opened her eyes.

Now it was time for the class to do it. She broke the group up into partners. One partner was instructed to describe some problem they were facing while the other tried to intuitively arrive at a solution or analysis of the dilemma.

During the activity Loretta mentioned a sudden energy shift. She felt a wave of warmth flow over the room, which meant the spirit energy was there. She said during a channeling program she would sometimes get fire-hot and begin perspiring in a cold room from the spiritual heat. Although I didn't feel any outside energy come into my being, there were a few startled observations among the class that some unusual energy had been felt. Loretta was smiling, nodding and encouraging the assembled to be open and aware to the little breakthroughs.

After the class some of Loretta's friends who had been in attendance went up to greet her. One young couple took me aside to rave about Loretta. They had been at the funeral for Loretta's mother and they described how amazed the mortician was at the demeanor of the crowd—instead of a dirge they were dancing!

Loretta credited her mother with helping make things interesting when she was growing up in Paris, Texas. Their psychic talents made them both standouts in Bible Belt land. "When I was a little girl I had [spiritual] playmates," Loretta told me later. "I knew I wasn't talking to a person, but some energy system that looked like a body. Sure, I touched them. We could feel energy. So, to a child's mind it was as real as what we call reality. That ended when I was about seven.

"I played with my mother and her guides once in a while. My mother was an interesting woman, a lot of fun. She had a guide called Master Lotus, who she said was a small Oriental woman.

"Now, when I channel it's an energy that takes my system over. It's warm and loving and I feel my heart's open, my head feels like it has space. All my cares and concerns disappear. There's a lightness.

"Information comes by light and what happens is, my conscious mind is very much in the background and the channeling state is in the forefront and impulses come very rapidly. I just turn myself over and the guide translates it out so you can hear it.

"We've now moved to an evolutionary place where people can channel. Because of that there's less of a demarcation between our world and the channeled world than there used to be.

"Now, for mankind I feel that more and more people are being guided to this union and that more and more people are reaching out to bring the divine to the earth."

Edgar Cayce (1877–1945) the so-called "Sleeping Prophet" was sometimes asked how an individual could develop psychic ability. Under a trance Cayce noted that psychic meant "the expression to the material world of the latent, or hidden sense of the soul and spirit forces, whether manifested from behind, or in and through the material plane.''

To develop psychic abilities Cayce urged a union, not a separation, of mind, body, and spirit, so that ''self may be a channel through which the Creative Force may run. How is the current of life or of modern science used in the commercial world? By preparing a channel through which same may run into, or through, that necessary for the use of material things. So with the body mentally, physically, spiritually, so make the body, the mind, the spiritual influences, a channel—and the *natural* consequence will be the manifestations.''[1]

The Association for Research and Enlightenment, Inc. (A.R.E.), a branch of the Edgar Cayce Foundation, was formed to collect and study the trance readings Cayce made during his life. Research into the Cayce readings has produced some guidelines for developing channeling and other psychic abilities.

Everyone is connected to the universe, A.R.E. research maintains. We as human beings are multidimensional creatures, with many psychic capacities and potentials. We have a spiritual body that is open to the psychic realms and exists beyond the casual awareness of our five senses. Our thoughts have energy—''mind is the builder and that which we mentally dwell upon has reality.'' A positive attitude toward the existence of this spiritual nature is the first step in the journey toward unlocking their infinite capacities.

The purpose of our natural psychic side is to aid in fulfilling our spiritual growth and karmic purpose on the planet. Since we are all spiritual beings with previous incarnations, we carry talents, including psychic powers, from one lifetime to the next. The most gifted channels, it can be surmised, have simply been acknowledging and developing their psychic side over many lifetimes. But a psychic potential is still the birthright of all.

To be a pure channel requires that the physical and

spiritual forms be pure and healthy. A.R.E. urges that the body be kept in tune through exercise and diet. A diet conducive to channeling avoids high cholesterol, fried and processed foods, and red meat. A diet heavy in fruits and vegetables is recommended.

Spending more time in nature is also helpful in increasing one's attunement to the invisible forces. Regular meditation, the keeping of a dream journal, and involvement with a spiritual growth group are other useful tools.

A.R.E. feels the seeker should develop a clear idea of who they are, noting personal ideals, interests, and aspirations. It's also important to practice discernment when attempting channeling states. A galloping rush of random, disconnected thoughts does not constitute a psychic revelation.

Sedona psychic Patricia Diegel, for example, gets clear, three-dimensional pictures in her head of a client when she does channeling preparatory to a session. If she is working on a client's past lives, she will enter into a conscious, but very deep, trance state. In such an altered state she sees things as vividly as if she were there. If what one deduces to be a psychic insight has a flat, two-dimensional look, like viewing an image on a movie screen, it's likely to be a fantasy, according to Diegel.

The U.S. Yoga Publication Society book, *Genuine Mediumship of the Invisible Powers,* provides guidelines on achieving the channeling state. Author Swami Vishita explains that many people were "naturally sensitive to Spirit influences, and therefore mediumistic." But most people do not utilize this potential because they hadn't received the proper instruction in "psychic law and self-control," developed the proper spiritual qualities, and properly attuned their nervous systems to channel spiritual energy, Vishita writes.

Other than spontaneous mediumship, in which persons not claiming to be channels suddenly access spirit beings, Vishita recommends the spirit circle, or seance, as a useful way for the novice to learn how to open up to the spirit side.

Such a circle is "a company of harmonious, earnest, sympathetic persons joining their psychic powers for the purpose of aiding the medium to establish the lines of psychic communication between the earth plane and the planes of the Spiritual World."

The group will of a seance can also guard against the entrance of undesirable forces into the physical plane.

> When these fraudulent spirits appear, the atmosphere of the circle should be made very sacred and high in character. Evil spirits, and those of low characters, cannot endure the presence of elevated and high thoughts, and by the holding of thoughts of this character the circle can soon rid itself for good of these troublesome entities—and it should do so without fail.[2]

"My God, I've worked with people who took channeling classes and they brought forth earthbound spirits—the instructors have to be very aware of this and often aren't," warns depossession expert Bill Baldwin. "True guides from the Light are infinitely loving and never serve themselves. A guide cannot be exorcised. It's a different energy that's there for a good purpose.

"But the earthbound entity is clumsy, more like a parasite, it drains the host of energy."

Dr. Baldwin describes a channeling class in which the students were asked to open themselves up through meditation, asking for spiritual energy to come through. During the exercise one of the students became possessed by the spirit of a recently deceased woman, and Baldwin had to perform a depossession.

Demons and earthbound entities can be masters of deceit, very seductive, he warns.

Such a demon entered a professional channel he knew who normally channeled only pure, loving entities. When Dr. Baldwin put the channel into a trance state and attempted to exorcise the demon, the entity transformed into the form of an innocent child.

"I will not tolerate deception," Dr. Baldwin admonished the crafty spirit before finally exorcising it and sending it back to the Light.

It is because of the possibility that a channel may be utilized by a manipulative spirit that the A.R.E. recommends a thorough channel check before using the information. "Does the channeled information encourage you toward a balance of attunement and service?" A.R.E. asks. "Is the message helpful and hopeful?

"Does the information point beyond the channel and its source to the Spirit within and to our sense of God? Does it ring true with your own inner voice?"

Therapist and healer Dr. Jay Scherer, who teaches how to channel healing energy, has some guidelines for bringing in good forces and dispelling evil forces. "A general rule is to ask that everything be under divine control. Ask God to take command of the whole situation and see that energy is used in the proper manner, that it is not used to glorify the human personality. Jesus was the greatest example of how to channel energies. He let God work through him. But if you think you're the big shot and the doer, you can get into trouble. Bad energy can come in.

"If [a being] comes to you and says, 'I'm the Archangel Michael,' or 'I'm So-and-so,' and says they want to channel through you, say—'Show me your light!' Now, if they can't show you their light, you say, 'Now, you get the heck out of here!' If they can't prove they're who they profess to be, you dismiss them.

"If they're from the Higher Being, and they teach you about the Light, of love and kindness and perfection, then they're a true being. You have to evaluate it. There's a certain amount of discernment that people have to learn to see what forces are acting, whether they're evil forces or good forces.

"You see, an evil force never uses love. He'll use

wisdom and power. But he can't use love, because then he turns himself into a divine being.''

Lin David Martin, a California trance channel who brings in a spiritual presence (the entity does not give a name, just wanting to be called ''Spirit''), has channeled a body of information on how a person can open up to his intuitive reality. The following are some recommendations from Spirit that were channeled through Martin during a 1986 channeling session:

''Whether it is a spirit in the sense of a teacher or guide, or it is the spirit in the sense of your own inner being that is divine in nature makes no difference. As long as you open to that inner source you are connecting to that common point, that common origin, and the energy flows,'' the entity reveals.

''The outer mind wants to know all the pieces, how does the puzzle fit together? The inner mind is satisfied just to know the desire is there to be a vehicle. That's enough. And outwardly, whatever form appeals to you, and you can relax into, that enhances the inner mind's ability to align itself with the greater universe.

''Now, by such suggestion I don't want you to think that your teachers are not involved—of course they are! But you are not a puppet at the end of a stick. They aren't making you do a dance or something. You are your own vehicle, you are your own consciousness on the very deep level. And it is that alignment with the spirit that they work to achieve with you, whether consciously or unconsciously. If your outer mind can accept that there is the potential for divinity it will be a more conscious work.

''And so the inner knowing begins to surface, begins to be advanced to the point that the outer mind can accept its presence. Your spirituality then becomes conscious. It is born within you and the outer mind accepts it.

''Just allow the presence of the spirit in as many ways as is possible. It calls for balance of your intellect, your wisdom, of your knowingness, of your sense or desire to be at one with the universe. And at the same time acknowledge that you will not always be functioning at that level, that it's okay to function in the normal state as well.

"So, a sense of balance—which brings tremendous joy. The world stops being chopped into so many little pieces. You begin to see that there is a unity of consciousness, that all those who have gone before—that you have termed the saints and sages and masters, avatars, irregardless [sic] of what culture they move through—you begin to see a common thread of truth linking you with them and with everyone else. You begin to sense that yea, even I am a son of God and I too may bring forth that which we have termed miraculous. I too may bring forth a greater power of creativity or love. And that is not for the ego to say 'Aha! I'm helping God to get the work done.' The ego will want to do that.

"But it's enough to enjoy the process. It's enough to know you are linked with the human race. And whatever you can do to advance your consciousness, to come to grips with your fears and doubts, to lay aside the poison of the past if such there be, and let it be healed . . . whatever you can do to alleviate the sorrows, the problems, the sufferings of others, that too will begin to build the totality of human consciousness in such a way that mankind finally, collectively, wakes up.

"[That] is the threshold you now stand on—the awakening of humanity. As Jesus said long ago, 'There will be wars and rumors of wars.' Wherein does the war exist? Is it not within the self first and externally projected?

"When there is integration with self, the true being that you are, you don't see others as separate. You see them as unique individuals moving in the path of their own progression, but still linked to you. And therefore, they cannot be your enemy since they are a part of your being.

"As you awaken, the intuitive mind is well rounded in a balanced state of inquiry into self, and your past, your present, and your future. The balanced inquiry into what's happening to others.

"And perhaps [ask] the Divine, 'What would you have me do? Oh Father, Mother God, what would I do that would be truly of an awakening state?'

"Think on these things in their simplicity. Feel them out with your inner self, with your feeling state, but not so caught in the intellectual analysis of truth that you have to understand how it works. Embrace it, allow it as a lover would show you its own beauty. Joy is there, wisdom—all that you deeply long for is to be found in that state of inward linkage.

"Gently now, woo the lover of life, which is the divinity that you seek, which is yourself on a vaster scale, which is everything, which is the universe."[3]

— Part IV —

Millennium Bound

13

New Age Paradigms

New Age channeling is full of buzz words, catchy phrases, and esoteric concepts. The range of ideas presented can be bewildering to the uninitiated: Reincarnation; the legends of Atlantis; "You are God"; "You create your own reality"; extrasensory perception; You don't need gurus; crystal power; Everyone has a psychic side; All is One; "Expect a miracle"; the Earth changes; the Age of Aquarius. . . .

"You know, our culture has waves of interest which gather and subside," observes San Francisco publisher Hank Hine. "But one thing is assured—when people have forgotten what that word 'channeling' means, when it's all over, there are going to be Native American people looking after things in North America. And they'll continue to do that, that's their function."

Zora Neale Hurston (1901–1960), who chronicled the African cultural experience from its transplantation to the Caribbean and the U.S., has reported on the vision-quest rituals of black Americans. Much like their Native American counterparts, those quests involve seeking visions and signs from the spirit world by going to desolate places to fast and pray.

Calling to the spirits and having them channel through is called "shouting," Hurston writes. Derived from Africa, where the priesthood considered such channeling as a sacred entrance by the gods, the implication in America is still the same. "It is a sign of special favor from the spirit that it chooses to drive out the individual consciousness temporarily and use the body for its expression."[1]

Asian cultures have brought their complex cosmologies of spirit worlds and supernatural forces to this country as well. For example, at any Chinatown across the land one can see public rituals such as the lion dances to drive out evil spirits and bring good luck.

Auntie Lani, a Hawaiian woman who teaches the hula dance in all its sacred tradition, believes that her dances invoke the power of spirit and her ancestor's spirits. "I share in the dance that works, and whatever feelings there are, of that Great Spirit that's come to me," Auntie says. "And my ancestors come and sit with me during that time, and this is where I get my inspiration for the dancing."

Author Brad Steiger sees all interpretations of spiritual essence as interconnected manifestations of the Oneness. Steiger believes the evolution of the New Age will lead to a conscious opening of personal intent and connection with this Oneness. "We're seeing [in the New Age] a rebirth of individual shamanism," Steiger says. "We need magic, we need mystery. But as long as we put it into a practical, pragmatic, and direct application, then this is a facet of creativity, and why don't we use it?

"When people say, 'Oh, that's only a dream' or 'That's only your imagination' to me, that's the greatest capacity we have as human beings. Everything we're doing here right now began with a dream, with imagination. And that's what I'm working about, to encourage people to develop their true selves, their higher selves, and extend that to the greater self. To have people pray, become more complete, become their own healers, become everything.

"But by the same token, not to regress into a non-tech. We live in the Space Age, but there's something within us that is as primeval as it could be, and we need to have peace with both aspects of ourselves. That's the balance. And to me, that's the challenge."

There are many examples of spiritual knowledge and

technique being drawn out of the traditional parameters of religion and applied to many fields of society. Like the samurai of old, who used meditative techniques to sharpen their focus for battle, many business executives are using meditation to prepare for the strategy and conflict of the boardroom. Some executives have adopted as their bible *The Book of Five Rings*, the legendary treatise on spirit, philosophy, and military strategy written by Miyamoto Musashi.

Some business people are trying to use meditative techniques to look at their careers in less combative terms. Relaxation techniques, applied intuition training, Zen, yoga, even channeling are being used as tools by individuals and even corporations. An entire growth industry in firms teach New Age concepts to all corporate levels to make workers more relaxed, focused, and productive on the job.

The Optimal Performance Institute in Oakland, California, is one such firm. As the company notes: "Success begins on the inside." This philosophy has gained positive results for such clients as Holiday Inn, TRW, and Pacific Bell.

The company was founded in 1980 by Dean Anderson, a star athlete at Stanford and seeker of the spiritual. His background in athletics was particularly important in convincing him of the benefits, and positive results, of inner focus. Anderson was the first ten-year-old in the world to swim the hundred-yard freestyle in less than one minute, and the first twelve-year-old to swim the two-hundred-yard freestyle in less than two minutes. At Stanford he was a four-year All-American swimmer. The inner concentration of his athletic pursuits made him naturally open to his own intuitive inner voice.

During trips around the world this natural feeling was broadened by his contact with other spiritual traditions including Zen meditation and Indian yogic practice.

Spiritual texts speak of enlightenment as a state of being one with the moment, where you blend so fully into what is occurring that you become it. You lose all sense of separation from the experience. Such an experience transcends the normal state of consciousness. It's an altered state. . . . Being one with the moment is heightened concentration. That's why "enlightened" people, those who can fully engross themselves in each moment of an activity, are true optimal performers.[2]

Sports is a field that celebrates optimal performance and that produces many events of extraordinary reality. In my own athletic experience, which includes martial arts competition and long-distance bicycle riding, I've experienced that paranormal quality of sport. During a solo four-hundred-mile bicycle ride I made down California Coastal Highway 1 several years ago, I experienced a trance state on my second day of riding. In my travel journal I observed that the experience was "akin to the Indian dances when the celebrants would dance themselves through exhaustion and into the spirit world.

"I had stopped at a place of brush and tall eucalyptus trees on a cliff above the ocean. It was a garden where trees formed shaded tunnels with their branches. I sat down, ready to call it a day even though it was almost four hours to sunset.

"I didn't sleep but I went to a place. . . . my body just shut down for an hour while it went about the work of recharging. In my trance I saw—nothingness. Nothing and everything existed as the hypnotic sounds of the ocean set the chant for my view of the trees and flowers, whose colors held me with a beauty not of this Earth. I shook myself and arose, refreshed and ready to continue."

When I had snapped out of the reverie and glanced at my watch, I was astonished to see that instead of five minutes, over an hour had passed.

The sports page of the daily newspaper regularly

records examples of the paranormal. During the football season, for instance, many post-game, big-play reflections describe virtually telepathic communications between players, amazing feats performed by sheer transcendent will, and even precognitive comments by athletes claiming to have dreamed the game's result the previous night.

A list of sport's mystical side has been collected by Michael Murphy, cofounder of the famed Esalen Institute, as part of an effort he has termed the Transformation Project. The effort is an assemblage of interviews and over eight thousand articles from scientific and popular journals that talk about kinds of bodily transformations mediated by consciousness. Murphy, himself a golfer and long-distance runner, noted in his 1978 book *The Psychic Side of Sports*: "The idea that there is something more profound in us fits many athlete's reports of inward knowing and transcendence—they sense something that secretly supports the superficial being and enables it to persevere through all labors, sufferings and ordeals."[3]

"I think sports, particularly modern athletics, is the greatest laboratory of bodily transformation in the history of mankind," Murphy told me in a 1983 interview. "Never have so many people tried out so many different physical possibilities on so vast a scale as in modern athletics. There's a constant testing of the limits of the body and records are being broken as we go further and further."[4]

Many professional athletes are using visualization, meditation, and other techniques to be able to call up at will the peak performance state. In high-stake game playing there can also be a little psychic hard ball. In the 1987 world chess championship between challenger Anatoly Karpov and defending champ Gary Kasparov, Karpov reportedly complained about the champion's "psychological and psychic disruptions." *Sports Illustrated* reported that Karpov "felt turbulence in his brain . . . which he believes was caused by a parapsychologist on Kasparov's team." Such accusations of psychic foul play are not unheard of in the high-pressure climate of world-class chess.[5]

Russell Schweickert, who served as lunar-module pilot for the Apollo 9 Earth-orbit flight, had a dramatic experience during that mission when he played in space a music tape he had listened to during the long period of his preflight training. "It brought the reality of being up there back to those periods of preparation," Schweickert has said. "[It] integrated the two. . . . It almost jerked me bodily out of that spacecraft."[6]

There is a growing New Age influence in the medical field as well. The use of visualization, mental techniques, and diet have all produced miraculous benefits for patients without resorting to Western drug therapy.

The channeling of divine energy is also being used in the healing process. Native Americans have been using such methods for centuries, and the larger culture is becoming more receptive to that approach. At eighty, Dr. Jay Scherer has been channeling healing energy for the patients at his Academy of Natural Healing in Santa Fe since 1979. During his healings he uses divine energy and receives the assistance of spirit guides.

"I usually invoke a whole group of guides [during a healing session]," Dr. Scherer says. "I invoke Archangel Michael, and legions of angels, and I ask Saint Germaine, the Master Jesus, Quan Yin, and others to stand by, to help. Because on our own we could not generate enough power to [heal]."

Channels and psychics have long been involved in helping to locate things, whether a missing person for a police department or an ancient buried temple for an archaeologist.

Psychologists such as Raymond A. Moody, Jr. and Elisabeth Kubler-Ross have extrapolated their documentation of patients' near-death experiences into complex studies of the possibility of life after life.

The Association for Past Life Research and Therapy, a nonprofit educational foundation, promotes the acceptance of reincarnation and the recognition that some present-life traumas can be due to the lingering effects, or karmic states, from past lives. Acknowledging that, the APRT trains professional psychologists and doctors in the use of past-life therapy for their patients.

Some New Age tools are even being used in the military. The U.S. Army has contracted training programs to provide Green Berets with visualization and meditation techniques.[7] During a 1976 interview with famed psychic Uri Geller, the controversial spoon bender, telepathist, and clairvoyant, provided me with a disturbing look at the possibilities of psychic warfare: "Lately I've been doing government stuff with the United States Naval Surface Weapons Center," Geller said. "I bent a metal alloy they had invented. I changed the molecular structure of the alloy. This metal has memory cells, which means if you bend it with your hands, it springs back to place. After experiments with me it not only didn't spring back to place, but continued to bend farther.

"Every government institute or laboratory, like Lawrence Radiation Laboratory in California, is always interested in such areas [of psychic research], since in the future there will only be psychic warfare.

"America is making a critical mistake in not investing more money in psychic research. I'm afraid the Russians will develop, in a hundred years or so, a man who will block radar or knock weapons out of the sky with brainpower.

"I've also learned Americans are interested in what the mind will do in a protective way, such as protecting a president with psychic powers that could detect an attack seconds before it occurs."

I talked to Dr. Willis Harman, president of the Institute of Noetic Sciences, about the use of psychic powers for warfare. Dr. Harman, who had served as a consultant to the U.S. government, commented that the Pentagon was interested in the possibilities of "remote viewing," in which psychics "see" distant objects. Soviet counterparts were busy exploring the possibility of psychically "scrambling people's minds." But Harman said that neither side was getting the results they wanted. The psychic tests conducted by the Defense Department, for instance, were not coming close to the one hundred percent accuracy desired.

"Something about the [psychic] process is that these things aren't as effective when they're being used to kill other human beings," Harman concluded.

I asked a Florida psychic who claimed he could travel in mind or astral body to distant places if it was conceivable for him to astrally invade the top-secret confines of the Pentagon. He told me he probably could if he needed to, but it didn't interest him. "Believe it or not, the government does have psychic protectors," the psychic explained, crediting other psychic and spirit sources for the information. "Ever since Nixon the psychic protectors have had to protect the president. They have no choice. The Russian psychic investigators got to Nixon, influenced him, and caused him to make mistakes that led to his resignation.

"So there are guardians out to protect. But if there's no harm being done, a person can go around them [on the psychic levels], and the guardians wouldn't even be aware of the person. If the entity has a negative intent, the guardians would probably instantly know and be aware of it, so the person wouldn't get around the block or shield."

As we talked I was reminded of the early Doctor Strange comic books, in which the Master of Black Magic would leave his body behind in his Greenwich Village manse and travel to the astral realms to punch it out with some psychic bad guy. I asked the psychic if this battle of intruders and protectors on the psychic level took that form. He shook his head. Fist fights on the astral plane were low-level. But a conflict did occur during such confrontations, almost like a cosmic chess match.

"On the higher levels you don't have a physical

body, you're just energy, just essence," the psychic said. "You're just gaining knowledge. If you're blocked on that level, you can go around it. You can go up several levels and come back down, or you can go underneath them. If you want, you can ask to be shown the block and it will symbolically manifest. You can then go around it if you choose to. See, anything the mind of man can set up to prevent somebody from doing something, the mind of another man can figure a way around it."

The most obvious flowering of the spirit in the land is at the various New Age retreats and think tanks actively involved in developing and exploring the techniques of psychic and spiritual transformation. The Light Institute, located less than an hour out of Santa Fe in the sleepy little town of Galisteo, was founded in 1985 "for the purpose of assisting the individual in the illumination of their path toward the inner being."

Christine Griscom, founder and guiding light, had "developed highly effective techniques which allow each person to experience their holographic, multidimensional self, thereby gaining access to a reservoir of unlimited potential," according to institute informational material.

The work was considered an evolutionary process since "every person is at a different stage on their spiritual journey." And initial program involved an emotional body-balancing session, a minimum of three, three-hour multidimensional past-life sessions, and other activities designed to accelerate expansion of consciousness. The program required a minimum of four to six days at a cost of $650.

Shirley MacLaine's book *Dancing in the Light* featured an account of her visit to the Light Institute. While there, Chris Griscom conducted MacLaine into the mystery of an esoteric acupuncture treatment that unlocked a patient's past-life experiences. Griscom escorted MacLaine behind a glass-enclosed greenhouse full of fruit trees and herbal plants to the stonework building that housed her clinic. MacLaine lay down and Griscom pulled the sanitized golden acupuncture needles from their containers. She told MacLaine she would be inserting the needles into the proper psychic points with the help of her spirit guides.

"Her [Griscom's] guides were proficient in body meridians and energy points of the body," MacLaine wrote. "The primary guide was an ancient Chinese doctor who was always present when she worked.

"As soon as I relaxed, I could feel the presence of the other entities in the room. . . .

"Chris went into the meditation as she tuned into her guides. I felt a cold air pass over my body, which always accompanies the presence of a spiritual guide into a room."

With the power of the needle points and the help of the guides, MacLaine released some trapped past-life experience memories. The needles even put MacLaine in contact with her higher self; "the unlimited you that guides and teaches you throughout each incarnation."

Intrigued by such reports, I made an appointment to meet Chris Griscom during my stay in the Southwest. I drove out to Galisteo, made a turn at an old church, and went down a dusty road that ended at the few weathered one-story structures comprising the institute's facilities. The rugged, undulating land spread out in all directions under the hot sun and the bright blue sky. I met Griscom and we went out to talk on a rare patch of unshaded green lawn behind the greenhouse and clinic.

Griscom is petite, with flowing blonde hair and the high cheekbone look that could probably light up the cover of a fashion magazine if she was so inclined. But not a dab of makeup masked her features. She wore a simple cloth dress, walked barefoot on the grounds, and was as rugged as the land. When MacLaine met her, she was over eight months pregnant—and had been white-water rafting the week before. Despite the amazing nature of her work she prides herself on being a practical person. As a single mother of six she had to be, she said, smiling.

Workers were busy digging out an area adjacent to the lawn that would accommodate a new building for the expanding institute. Farther on in the distance, across a chaparral that stretched to a hogback would be the site of the Nizhoni (Navajo for "beauty way") School for Global Consciousness. That Light Institute project had been "conceived in a vision" to help young people aged twelve through twenty access and "live the profound wisdom that lives within them through the guidance of their higher selves."

I was surprised to hear Chris tell me she only rarely performed her acclaimed past-life acupuncture work. "Everybody became addicted to the needles." Chris laughed. "When Shirley wrote that book everyone thought, 'Oh! If I could just get the golden needles I'll be enlightened.' So, it forced me to let that go, because it's a level of integrity. I would be cheating you if I said to you, 'It's my golden needles.' It's not. It's inside you. When I stick a needle into you, I'm taking control. You're going to have to give your power away for me to do that. And I'm opposed to that. You must take responsibility, you must participate.

"The needles are specifically wonderful for when you've done a lot of emotional clearing, when you want to holographically access dimensions that are beyond channeling. Needles do act as spin points to trigger the brain to do that. But once I'd done that twenty thousand times, I'd figured out how to do [it without the needles]. I've trained all the people in my institute to do this work without needles. It's within the human nature [to do it]. It's a matter of our focus."

The needle work had first begun when she was on the faculty of a healing school in Santa Fe. During an acupuncture presentation to the assembled faculty, the instructor began discussing a secret acupuncture method that connected the Chinese elite of olden days to the powers of the heavens. The talk of the ancient windows to the sky instantly triggered a past-life recall for Griscom. She remembered that she had been a disembodied entity in those ancient times who had actually channeled the psychic-point information to the Chinese people. She then went into a long remembering pattern of the location and function of all the points. The remembering was an important step on the road leading to the formation of her Light Institute.

The past-life aspect of the work involves bringing back to conscious memory the stories, trials, talents, and terrible deaths of significant past lives. "We're here to find past lives, and we're here to get rid of them so you can become part of the universal *now*," Chris says. "To discover the lessons which are not in your head. The lessons are held within the memory packets of the cells of your body.

"I did a lot of body work first and I discovered that the body does have those past-life memories. It has images and pictures in it."

This clearing process can even change our physical look, she maintains. The bodies we incarnate with often hold the look of a particularly influential past life.

Griscom believes that past-life realizations help the individual realize that each incarnation experience is determined by personal choice. This power of choice includes one's physical body, family, friends, and social structure. The great guardian that facilitates this incredible process is an individual's higher self.

"You can't come into body without the higher self," Chris explains. "The higher self is not like a spirit guide, they're totally different. The higher self is like a megaphone for the soul.

"The soul is part of the universal energy. But as you funnel into body on this planet you bring certain patterns of energetics—that's the soul. The soul comes into this dimension so it can communicate with us here in body. We're only one little speck of the hologram when we're in body.

"The higher self is that channel through which the unlimited can communicate to us and make contact. What is realy exquisite is it not only brings that into us, but allows us to begin to experience our own multidimensionality. Our brains have that capacity! We can trigger the brain to perceive in different ways.''

"How does the higher self manifest itself?" I asked.

"The higher self manifests in terms of its visuals according to what our repertoire is," Chris explained. "If you think a spirit has to be a being with a cloak, then your higher self will be a being with a cloak. If you think the higher self is going to manifest as a bird, then it'll manifest as a bird. Again, it's like the thread of communication around the hologram. So, you get a higher self and by contacting that image of the higher self you begin to dialogue.

"As it makes that communication and goes on, [the higher self] changes form. Suddenly it may come in as a blue triangle. That blue triangle may be the next spot on the hologram of your multidimensional consciousness. So, maybe the blue triangle relates to some cosmic octave of reality, or other planetary or galactic reality, or some other civilization's understanding. By accessing that blue triangle you begin triggering a frame of reference, a memory that comes into the brain. And it is an energy that begins to guide your life, begins to awaken you.

"We have to learn to bring that in so we can use it. That's the same thing with channeling: Bring it into this dimension so we can use it in our daily lives."

This daily application has some profound implications. In 1986 Chris was psychically alerted to a sudden surge of radiation that had occurred on the planet. She had felt the deadly leak from Russia's Chernobyl nuclear power plant disaster. "I got it [the information of the leak] from the birds in Arizona," she says. "They told me. All the animals went, 'What's this?!' This is a part of us, it's within our brains to do this. We're simply so locked into patterns of external behavior that we can't hear the messages that are there around us."

Another example of a real-life application of psychic consciousness involved a mercy mission she took to a drought-stricken area of Africa. She brought to the continent an eighty-two-year-old Hopi woman to perform the rain-making ceremony. The woman had been chosen because her brother, who would normally have performed the ceremony, couldn't leave his land. She wasn't even a medicine woman, but as the last daughter of the sun king, she was part of a tradition that honored the ability of human beings to tap into the spiritual realms.

"You harmonize with the spirits, you ask for the gift, and you're given it. That's a whole different consciousness," Chris observed. "You hold that sacred. You live a life that allows for the gift to be given."

"And did the rains come?" I asked.

"Of course the rains came! It was very simple. You just hold the intention. The intention was to be pure enough to bring the rain."

The woman had brought a blue corn seed with her as a gift from the Hopi people to the African people. She stuck the seed in the ground at a special place. She and Chris went a distance away to fast and pray. Then the Hopi woman was ready. She began to wave a feather to the sky—and the heavens opened up. "It was raining so hard we were all holed up in that place," Chris recalled.

Since the ceremony involved getting back to honor the spot of the newly planted blue corn seed, they made an effort to travel through the deluge. After three days they managed to get to the plot where they had performed the sacred planting of the seed. "I thought it would take three weeks for that seedling to come to the top if it even came to the surface at all. But that little corn seed that had been stuck two feet down"—Chris held her hand several feet above the ground to indicate its height.

"It's called a miracle. And that Hopi woman is nobody special. She's an eighty-two-year-old woman who trusted that she could be a vehicle. That's a powerful message to the world.

"We separated out from the great divine arm of the divine force, so that we ourselves could create a flower or bring the rain or stop an earthquake. That's what time is on Earth. We've pushed ourselves to the brink.''

As we talked a roaring tractor began digging up the earth for the foundation of the new building. We made knowing glances at each other, smiled, and decided to move.

We headed across an open field to the ruin of an old stone building in the distance. As we walked, the tractor noise receded. Chris explained that the energetics and the auric field were incredibly expansive in Arizona and New Mexico: Galisteo was an epicenter of that great regional energy. The Galisteo basin held the ancient ruins of some six pueblo communities. Their petroglyphs celebrated images of sky, spacemen, mystical snakes, and strange animals. The pueblo people had settled there because of the multidimensional nature of the place. ''The spirits of the old ones are still here,'' Chris said as we walked.

She pointed out an area where the institute had attempted to dig and plant a marriage tree to honor a wedding celebration. A foot into the earth the shovel started hitting charcoal. Farther down they discovered the bones and corn of a prehistoric burial site. They covered up the hole and left the burial area wild and free. In another part of the field they had discovered the buried ruins of an ancient kiva.

We arrived at the stone ruin. Three sides of the roofless, square structure were standing. The large, perfectly shaped stones that formed the walls had been put in place by the Spaniards during their occupation of New Mexico. The perfect shape of a doorway still framed one wall. The doorway looked out on a gentle desert savannah that rambled out to the horizon's blue sky edge.

I thought of the Spanish people who had once stood at that spot and looked on the same pastoral scene. What were the dreams of those Spaniards and the Indians before them, and where were those dreams now?

''The expediency of each culture is to use the energy of the one that was there before—you know what I mean?'' Chris commented. Standing there in the Spanish ruins, under a strong sun and embraced in the soft silence of the rugged landscape, Chris Griscom echoed the talk of a new era coming.

''We are on the brink of a tremendous expansion of reality. What was impossible yesterday is possible today. We're in a place on the evolutionary ladder where we can access more of our brain's capacity.

''When I was a little girl of five, and people would ask me, 'What are you going to be?' I would say, 'I'm going to be an explorer of the mind.' There's a great adventure going on and it's not out there—it's inside.''

14

The Spirit in the Land

When my old friends Ted and Jan Robles invited me to join them in Florida so they could show me the psychic sights, I jumped at the chance. They were both learned in mystic matters and Ted was a card-carrying pastor for the Tampa area Universal Life Church, Inc., a "Metaphysical Learning Center."

Ted is a physical scientist who had served a notable stint during the 1950s as chief chemist and chief physical scientist of Nouasseur Air Depot in Europe. He's a tall, husky man with a quick wit and an self-admitted gift for gab.

Jan is short and sweet and given to long, reflective silences. She seems happiest when she can sit down and work for hours on the necklaces and charms she fashions from the fruit of her rock and gem hunts.

They had also been channeling spirit beings since the 1950s.

When I arrived at the Tampa airport, Ted and Jan were there to meet me, along with Dennis Dort, a tall man in his early forties with a light beard and moustache. He was a co-pastor with Ted in their Universal Life Church ministry, a high school physics teacher, and, I would soon discover, an expert channel.

The Robles lived in California a few months of the year, and then would pack up their mobile home and drive it cross-country for their Florida stays. They lived in a cozy corner of a Largo trailer park. For the first few days of my visit, the trailer was command central for our planned foray into Florida's psychic territory.

One of our destinations was Cassadaga, a small town in central Florida. Cassadaga was one of the few towns in the country founded upon and devoted to the tenets of spiritualism. The town founder, George R. Colby, was reportedly led to the spot in 1894 by his spirit guides, Seneca, the Philosopher, and the Unknown. The town became the location of the Southern Cassadaga Spiritualist Camp Meeting Association, a psychic village of one hundred mediums who live in their own homes.

The Cassadaga definition of spiritualism, adopted in 1920, recognizes it as ''the science, philosophy and religion of continuous life, based upon the demonstrated fact of communication, by means of mediumship with those who live in the Spirit World.''

According to local mediums, a protective psychic net had long ago been placed over the town so that the community could peacefully go about its spiritualist business.

Cassadaga's supernatural reputation has attracted sincere seekers of spiritualist truth as well as the merely curious. There is also the fear, mostly among religious fundamentalists, that the town is engaged in the devil's work. Some of the area legends hold that Cassadaga's psychics can fly through the air, storms never pass over the town, dogs can't bark there, and a car parked on a hill will roll upward. The town has been besieged in recent years by ghost-hunting tourists, urged on by seasonal Halloween stories in the media. The good-natured mediums have responded to the Halloween automobile traffic jams and hay rides by opening their town hall and serving up refreshments instead of ghosts and goblins.

Ted, Dennis, and I made the trip to Cassadaga. Jan elected to stay home and work with her gem collection. We arrived by evening and checked into a hotel outside of town. I spread my sleeping bag on the floor while Ted and Dennis each took one of the two double beds. As Ted proceeded to drift off to sleep, I talked with Dennis about his psychic side. He was wide awake and wired on what he called "universal energy."

I asked him about a remote healing I had seen him perform with Ted and Jan a few days before. During the session Ted and Jan described to Dennis a sick friend on the other side of the country who needed treatment. Dennis had closed his eyes and instantly began supplying a detailed diagnosis and recommendations for treatment.

He explained that during a remote healing he had a feeling of being in a place and seeing the person he'd been asked to contact. The process involved an energy link between himself, the person present making the request, and the individual he was diagnosing at a distance.

After years of developing his natural psychic abilities he found this process would occur automatically when he requested the help of the "higher positive universal forces" or "God energy." His band of spirit guides helped him connect with those cosmic powers. He described contact with his entities as usually a transparent picture in his mind. Sometimes the spirits would manifest "like high-fidelity movie-screen stuff" with such power that for a few moments his awareness would totally merge with his mental pictures.

I was curious what made a physics teacher commune with spiritual entities. Dennis said his metaphysical interests were no secret around his school. He was personally careful never to promote his interests as a religion, but he often had students, and sometimes a parent or two, drop by his office to ask about the spiritual realms.

He described his entities as performers of assigned tasks. He had a gatekeeper he called Prairie Flower, who helped facilitate loving, joyful energy. The gatekeeper also initiated "contact between the conscious mind with the etheric realms, the spiritual world." Prairie Flower could manifest in different appearances, but usually appeared as a woman pioneer from the days of America's overland expansion.

In addition, Whitefeather was an American Indian entity whose job was to lead Dennis physically through life, to watch, protect, and guide him. There was the Bronze Man, an ancient bronze-skinned Egyptian who served as an alchemist, transmuting Dennis's spiritual essences to access "higher realms far away from the Earth plane." He also counted as a spirit advisor Aaron, first high priest of Israel during biblical times. There was Jester, who took the appearance of a medieval court jester and often greeted Dennis with a funny face whenever he appeared in his mind.

"Sometimes I think Jester gets lost when I get too serious," Dennis said, lying on the bed in his pajamas, leaning on his right elbow, his chin buried in his right palm. "I'll say, 'Jester, where are you?' Other times I'll be thinking of nothing in particular and I'll suddenly get a grin on my face and get silly and it'll lift my spirits and I'll say, 'Okay, Jester, what are you doing?' And he'll show himself to me in my mind in some odd position or making some obscene gesture that is really ridiculous.

"The main personage that I deal with is a doctor/teacher. These beings are coordinators and intellectual mediators of all your guardian angels and spirits. My doctor/teacher's name is Dr. Randolph Holbrook, a very proper British physician who often appears dressed close to the conservative British attire of the World War II era. Dr. Holbrook at one time was literally an English physician and gentleman. He had incarnations on the Earth plane just recent enough so I could recognize them.

"When he first checked into the scene he often sat at a bench with test tubes and chemical vials. I'll recognize him as if I'm stepping into his laboratory. Other times I see him on the bank of a river in sunshine contemplating why people are so cruel to other people."

There was also a divine personage he tapped into, a powerful spirit that resided at a level above even his guides. "This being is a representative of the positive deity energy for the universe," Dennis said. "He appears as a very gentle, positive person who floats in the air or rests lightly on a fluffy cushion in a cross-legged position. Energy and light and absolute love streams out of him. My guides and I touch in with him. We experience him or give him greetings and acknowledgment for being what he is.

"Also, through your guides and helpers you can become aware of the Christ consciousness people like Jesus, the prophets and teachers of the other realms and religions, and get a feedback of their essence and their loftiness and continuing help toward fellow entities on and near the Earth plane."

Dennis had had powerful psychic experiences as a normal part of his growing up in the Largo area. The environs were all farms and wilderness then. (The farmhouse he grew up in is now a concrete ditch along a highway.) Growing up on the land, with the nearest neighbor almost a mile away, he could sense when someone had entered the property. But such experiences were considered the normal sixth sense developed by people living in the country.

But at an early age he also began having psychic experiences that were extraordinary by any definition. "I was in the third grade and daydreaming in the classroom when I looked out through the dimensions of the ethers toward our farm three or four miles away," Dennis recalled. "I saw that the house had caught fire and was burning. Instantly, in psychic body, I went there.

"I tried to pick up and save things from being burned, but I couldn't grab hold of them because I reached right through.

"I then became aware of my mother, who was trying to put out the fire and was straying too close to the flames. So I started pulling on her, trying to pull her physically out of harm and danger. I didn't have much success, but I noticed that on the spiritual levels there were all kinds of little imps and thought forms, personifications of little demons and things that were trying to pull her toward the fire to die! So I pulled them off, and threw them and chased them away. My mother then got herself out. The house burned to the ground.''

He often used his psychic abilities to observe the physical universe. ''I remember in junior high school sitting on top of the roof of a flat porch where the sun shone, and watching drops of dew on leaves fall on the porch and seeing the prismatic colors in them. I studied and stared at them intently. As I watched, they seemed to get much bigger and I could see the details of the minute droplets. I realize now I was psychically tying into the structure of the water molecules and the light energy going through them.''

Dennis acknowledged that guides could be manifestations of the subconscious, or real entities, but they could also be nonlinear vibrational emanations across time and space. He felt that was the case with Aaron, his spirit guide from biblical times. ''Aaron was the last guide to come to my conscious mind awareness. It seems I wasn't ready to perceive him until very recently.

''I was at a formal anointing to bless a plot of land according to Hebrew tradition. The rabbi had his staff of Aaron that he had carved himself by inspiration. He had ram oil, a combination of animal, plant, and exotic spices made in the Near East. The rabbi applied it to the forehead of each participant.

''When my forehead was anointed I had spontaneous feelings and recalls as if I was a young man, Aaron of simple origins who had been sought out by the prophets and anointed for God's holy purpose. I felt very troubled by this perception. Each person who ties into Aaron experiences these turmoils and helps Aaron in that time of history to handle them.

''There's this idea that time from ancient history to present to the future is all happening at the same time. Away from the Earth plane time doesn't flow, doesn't pass, it just is. All is happening at the same time. So as people recall or experience these things of antiquity, it's very likely they're helping those people from ancient times handle the trauma of the situation as well. And as a result the spiritual vibrations and essences of everyone on the whole planet is raised and made pure in the process.''

"Does that mean that if one has a spiritual guide said to have lived long ago that they're actually experiencing them in contact from that point of history, not from the Beyond?'' I asked.

"It could be an energy essence or a thought pattern that person actually had of positive worth, and they're using that or sharing that as part of their personal spiritual awareness and essence and it shows up as a guide who appears as that person. [It's a matter of] reaching into the past or other realms and sharing a worthwhile energy or thought concept.''

I asked Dennis if his guides had anything to say. Dennis nodded, noting he was getting goose bumps on his arms as he felt their communications with him. With his eyes wide open he relaxed and relayed the spirit's message.

'' 'We acknowledge you and give you greetings,' '' Dennis said. '' 'We work with your guides and band members as you come forward to learn and share of spiritual nature and essence of things. So, as we say in group acknowledgment, thank you for the opportunity. There is much we can share with you and learn from you and with your guides and helpers as well, this being generally true of any person. This is especially true for you because we find you delightful and enjoyable and of a high nature.'

"That's the end of a quote,'' Dennis said with a smile.

I asked if the entities had any special message for the readers of this book. Dennis was quiet for a moment, listening to the inner voice of his guides before responding. '' 'Let them know if you can that we are real, that we desire to grow ourselves and help our fellow entities grow. And this growth in the spiritual realms is the essence of all existence.' ''

The next morning we headed to Cassadaga. We parked by the Andrew Jackson Davis Building, the meeting hall at the entrance to the camp. The Cassadaga camp was as quiet and placid as an early Sunday morning. There were no other cars on the narrow road that passed the homes with their trimmed lawns and white picket fences. By the main gate of each house was a little sign inscribed with the resident's names, and underneath was the legend, MEDIUM.

We walked past a grassy knoll over Spirit Pond. A gazebo by the pond had benches for gazing over the placid pond to the forested hills beyond. Generations of Cassadaga camp residents had experienced wonderful reveries there. There were legends about that place, too, that sometimes at night spectral lights flashed over the waters, or deceased residents would return for a spectral stroll.

We met up with some of the local mediums on our Cassadaga walk. Harry Fogel, a soft-spoken spiritualist minister, invited us into his office to show us his spirit photographs. He took photographic developing paper, held a sheet near his navel, and then watched an image form. He showed us well-defined images of Indian chiefs that had come through, as well as some shadowy wraiths who had supposedly shown their face from the Other Side.

Some of the camp residents were relative newcomers. Medium Marie Lilla and her husband had moved into the community in 1984. She had retired after thirty-five years of executive-level work for a large orthodontic firm in Orlando. Her house was off the road, the driveway curving around a thicket of trees. Their home was bigger than the normal camp house. We met her at the door and she led us to her office. On the wall were a number of framed photographs, including departed yogic master Paramahansa Yogananda, whom she claimed to be in spiritual contact with. Like many mediums, she had an entire host of spirit beings around her.

''Oh, it's beautiful,'' she said, describing her spiritual communications. "It's a flow. There's no thinking, there's just a flow. I receive [their messages] in various ways. I sense it. I also have clairaudience. It sounds like the whole world hears what I'm hearing and they're not. And sometimes I have clairvoyance."

Like many who called Cassadaga home, she felt the special magic of the place. "You have to remember that this community was established almost one hundred years ago. You've had people living and working here of like mind, so naturally there's an energy. It's peaceful here. You can tune in anywhere. You can tune in on a New York City subway, because I have. But on a daily basis this kind of community is optimum."

Fred and June Bowermaster are two camp mediums who also sing praises of the place. Ted and I met up with them while Dennis went back to the car for a nap. The Bowermasters were sipping tea and smoking cigarettes at a table on the grassy front yard in front of their house when we met them. They were both big-boned people physically. Fred in particular made a formidable appearance with his thick torso, brawny arms, broad shoulders, and glistening pate.

The two of them were naturally convivial. June, looking at us through dark glasses, stubbed her cigarette out in the ashtray and told us they had recently moved into the house. It had been vacated when the former tenant moved to another part of the country. The place had originally belonged to founder Colby's daughter. When they got the place it was overrun with trees and brush. Fred, with a herculean effort, had managed to clear away the forest a few weeks before.

It was getting near noon and the Bowermasters had not yet breakfasted. Ted and I piled into the backseat of their Lincoln Continental to drive to a nearby breakfast place outside town.

Cassadaga was a place where people hung together, they told us while lighting up a couple more cigarettes. There were a lot of unfounded fears about the place held by outsiders, they said. June remarked that the other day she had received an unmarked envelope with a tract proclaiming, "Why You Need a Personal Savior."

"Ignorance is bliss and there's an awful lot of happy people out there," Fred said in his native West Virginian drawl. "They'll stand there and thump their Bible at you—but they won't read it."

"You know, a few years ago some college kids found the Lake Helen-Cassadaga Cemetery and desecrated it—turned over gravestones, dug up graves. A baby's skull was found at a fraternity house," June interjected.

"Our leaders of tomorrow." Fred frowned. With an easy hand at the wheel he drove out of the tree-shaded rural road and out onto the main highway.

"But Daddy had enough money to keep the boy out of jail." Fred shrugged. "But I think Spirit had their way of handling that."

It seemed the young man who had instigated the desecration was blackballed from his fraternity, which promised to see him stripped of any future success he might seek.

"Spirit influenced the fire department volunteers to man the woods with baseball bats every year [during Halloween]," Fred observed. "Anybody that asks where the graveyard is—we tell 'em! But we also say, 'Son, you're gonna hate it.' 'What do you mean?' 'Well, don't be surprised if a bunch of fellows fall out of the woods with baseball bats and you go home with both legs and both arms broken!' You know, they don't like that."

Fred steered the big Lincoln into the parking lot of a shopping center. We found a table at the crowded restaurant they favored. They were regular customers at the place, which was done up with a country kitchen motif. I was impressed by Fred's repast—a tall stack of plate-filling pancakes topped with eggs over easy and drowned in maple syrup.

The Bowermasters said that most of their clients were professional career people, including one famous lawyer. They noted that some people seeking their services thought they were fortune-tellers or prophets. But they felt their mediumship was really about providing guidance.

"You always have free will, that's the bad part of this whole thing," Fred said between bites of his huge breakfast. "I could sit here and see the way the vibrations are set now, that's all you can see. You can't see any variations."

He did say that sometimes a future course, event, or decision was preordained. No matter what twists and turns resulted from an individual's actions along the way, they would still at some point arrive at that prophesied junction. The mediums also had to take into account the perspective of their guides when providing psychic guidance.

"If Uncle Harry was a fool on the Earth plane and he goes to Spirit, it does not automatically make him a genius," Ted interjected, warming up to the conversation. Fred and June both nodded.

"Unless a person has been taken over by an entity and is channeling through the crown chakra, you have to use your conscious mind to interpret," June said. "I tell people Spirit's never wrong, but I may be."

June said that the guides often didn't make it easy to interpret the data. "Isn't that aggravating when they give you an idea but no words to go with it?" June said. Fred and Ted nodded in knowing agreement.

"So how do you keep yourself clear to be a pure channel?" I asked. "Do you have to be in a meditative state, be educated in the ways of mediumship?"

"A little bit of all that," June replied. "I've heard it likened to being a gunfighter, where everything is reflex. Now, they didn't stop and think, 'Can I outdraw this person?' They just did. So they put themselves on automatic. But there are things you need to learn. You may be born with the greatest talent in the world but you still need to polish it up."

Fred and June were also proud of the fact that they were the only ones in the camp who did past-life regressions. And there was that occasional deep-trance channeling state. "Some channels have allowed their entire body and consciousness to be taken over, and they don't remember anything about it," June said. "I've gone into that deep channeling. It's happened to me five times. And not because I've asked for it. It's just happened. I find myself sitting outside my body watching it happen. I'm conscious to a certain extent. Tessa [the entity] comes in through the crown chakra when I'm in a channeling state like that.

"It's scary when it happens. I was doing a reading once and began trembling all over. I held the hand of the client and asked that only the best and highest good come in. The next thing I knew I was sitting on the edge of the sofa watching my body and all those words coming out. So it's a very strange thing to happen to you."

"I don't always see my guides," said Fred. "But I recognize where [the information] is coming from. As I understand it, I ask my guide to contact your guide. The information your guide gives my guide is pure. Through my subconscious, from me to you, is the only loss in credibility. My interpretation of what I'm seeing and what I say to you, therein lies the only loss of information, as I understand it."

When the breakfast was completed and we were back in the Lincoln tooling back to Cassadaga, I asked Fred and June what it was like living in the camp. "We live in Granola City—fruits, flakes, and nuts—and I'm the head flake!" June laughed. "No, it's wonderful. And I'm not sure I could live in the real world. It makes it better."

"The level of intelligence and positiveness is so far superior to any neighborhood you could live in," Fred said. "You know, there's that joke, but it's not a joke, where two mediums meet at the post office and say, 'You're fine, how am I?' "

"But it's also bad because you know what your neighbor's thinking about you," June added. "If they're having bad thoughts, without a word being said [you'll know it]."

June said it was a sight to see a Trivial Pursuit game in the camp. Fred laughed, remembering some recent sessions. When mediums got together to play a board game, the action was often spiced with the players trying to read each other's minds for the answers, or telepathically planting wrong answers into the opponent's mind. And, of course, dice games were a mismatch if you played with a psychic who could automatically turn up any needed roll.

The conversation turned serious again when I asked the Bowermasters their opinion of the public visibility of New Age channeling. "I think there's a reason for all the renewed interest with channeling," June said. "I think Spirit's coming through with a message for mankind. And it has to do with the fact that we've let things get out of hand with what we're doing to our planet. I think we're being told to back up and take another look, to straighten out conditions that are here. I personally believe that the Earth shift will occur. We'll be helped by people from other planets, as we're now being helped by people from other planes of existence. It seems that in times of greatest need is when Spirit speaks to us the most."

Fred mused that the coming evolvement would see people reach higher planes of spiritual wisdom and even lead to people graduating from the Earth plane.

"I don't agree with you, Fred," June replied. "I think the Earth will always be inhabited, but it will be by choice."

"I don't perceive it as ending," Fred replied. "But others may graduate and a whole new set come in, like a tank where water flows in and it flows out."

"You must have interesting dinnertime conversations," I interjected.

"We never run out of things, we just never do." June laughed. "We tell dirty jokes or tell spiritual things, depending on what kind of day we've had."

"It's serious [their mediumistic activities], but it's in an extremely light tune, with no pressure," Fred said.

"Like, reincarnation is not a main tenet of spiritualism, but with us it's a matter of choice," June said. "We discuss and disagree with different points of view."

"If there were no disagreements how dull things would be!" Ted said.

"Good grief, isn't that the truth," June answered.

Back in Cassadaga we said good-bye to the Bowermasters. Ted thought they were good people and next time he would be back with Jan. We met up with Dennis, who was in the driver's seat of the car, the seat in a reclined position, his radio headset on. He smiled as we came up to him and filled him in.

Back at the Robles' trailer, Jan and Ted gave me their psychic perspective, which had begun with supernatural encounters in youth. Ted as a youngster had a vision in which his favorite grandfather appeared to him at the moment of his death to say good-bye to him. As a young girl Jan had experiences where she saw strange earthbound entities and heard strange voices.

Ted's father, a psychic himself, introduced Ted to the art of trance channeling in 1950. Ted brought through an entity called King La, who he says is still a part of his circle of spirit guides. Jan was also taught how to trance.

In the attic of their home in California, in any one of dozens of boxes that fill the room, are the old reel-to-reel tapes of the conversations they channeled from those entities. "Then we both outgrew trance mediumship," Ted said. "As the entities themselves express it, 'Once you can accept the truth that we do exist, it is no longer necessary to render you unconscious. It is a lot simpler to put an idea into your head than it is to operate your speaking apparatus.'

"One of the important things that came through was what King La said: 'You do not believe anything. Belief implies doubt. You either know something or you do no know it.'

"Then other entities began coming through, including King James I of England and Jeb Stuart of Civil War fame. But the really interesting guides are Jan's."

Jan explained that one of her guides was Hsii, a Tibetan in a former incarnation. "If we ask to see these people, now that we don't have to trance, all we have to do is ask and we get them. You can feel the difference in their personalities in your mind."

I asked if their guides were present.

"Teddy's full circle is here and I have four of my guides here now," Jan replied. She explained that in this life she had to work out some past-life traumas before she could channel. A major emotional past-life block was the loss of Jesus Christ, who had been very dear to her in that lifetime.

"Jesus was not known to me as Jesus," she said. "He always spoke to me telepathically. To me he was the dearly beloved one.' I was only about fifteen when I knew him. I was a Greek girl. The loss of Jesus in that lifetime had piled up so much grief it almost didn't matter what I lost in this lifetime, there was just a sense of grief I couldn't handle."

"I'm being told by King La that I'd better tell you this," Ted interjected. " 'We are not all-knowing as some would have us be. We are in relation to you, as people standing on a hill to people in the valley. We can see farther than you but we can't see over the mountains, either.' "

"Are there others above them who can see over the mountains?" I asked.

"Yes," Ted answered.

"Do your guides communicate with them?" I asked.

"The Akashic Records, which is apparently the sum total of knowledge gained by the huge network of consciousness of everything, rocks, trees, sky, other planets—on some level it's all connected," Jan said. "Now, if you can reach into that, if you can allow yourself to become totally one with that, you can reach whatever knowledge you want. There were many times when I reached for an answer and felt that it was going a long, long way before the answer came back. It was like it was galaxies even.

"I never know where my answers are going to come from, but I always say to the universe at large, 'Whatever it is I'm getting, let it be for the best and highest good for the person for whom I'm getting the answer,' then I trust in God."

"Are one's personal guides separate from the entities that you channel?" I asked.

"Yes and no," Ted replied. "It's a very, very loose terminology—guides, guardians, angels. King La did clarify once the notion of angels. He said angels, so called, are celestial robots, special constructions made to oversee the development of the universe. Now they're just part of the supernumeraries. They just hang around. They have lots of intelligence and lots of initiative, and if their program went wrong there was all hell to pay.

"But they are not spirits in the sense that they go into the physical and come out of it. They always remain the same. They're unchangeable. King La didn't think much of them, actually. But I detected a note of envy there, though."

"Shii is telling me to tell you that the most important thing to realize is that everything is connected," Jan said. "Nothing stands by itself. Everything is part of God, or whatever you want to call it. There is always reasons for things, there is always cause and effect. Karma is cause and effect.

"Shii also says: 'The most important thing we have heard recently is that one should concentrate on being a part of the Oneness. Now, one should not think about differences. The minute you think about differences you are no longer being part of everything, the Oneness of everything. You are separating and you get out of tune.' "

Then Ted began channeling comments from one of his own entities. " 'There are guardians for individuals, there are guardians for groups, for races, for nations, for entire planets, and each member of the hierarchy has their own function. But all is One.

" 'Since your planet is designed to separate people, it is difficult for you to achieve the Oneness. It does not mean you should not try, you should try.'

"That was King La." Ted smiled.

"I'm interested in getting a glimpse beyond those mountains," I said.

"Yes, I think King La gave you a small glimpse there," Ted said. "There are guides for the planet. I'm asking if it's possible to contact the planetary guides and I'm getting a sort of 'Well, they're kind of busy at the moment.' " He laughed.

The Robles had a sweat lodge planned for me, and the connection for that would be Earth Star, an Indian woman they had been introduced to by Ellen, a mutual friend.

Prior to the sweat lodge we arranged a meeting with Earth Star. It seemed she knew of a channel who lived out in the countryside that we all should meet.

Ellen met us that morning at the trailer for the drive out to meet Earth Star. Ellen was an attractive blonde whose husband worked in St. Petersburg. They had an expensive second-story condo overlooking a prime stretch of Florida beachfront. Ellen was a student of metaphysics and concerned about all the Earth change talk she'd been hearing lately. One prediction foresaw tidal waves hitting the Florida coast. The killer waves would nicely crest over the roof of her condo.

"Ted, I'm happy here, I don't want to move away from Florida," Ellen said in her Southern drawl. Ted and Jan tried to assuage her worries, pointing out that such predictions were only the shade of what could be.

We met Earth Star at the friend's home, where she was staying for a brief period. Her own home was a van, which was undergoing repair work. For our day trip we would have the use of her friend's van.

Ted, Jan, and Ellen all piled into the back of the

van, while I took the passenger side next to Earth Star. Everyone in the back instantly fell into conversation as we headed for the countryside to see Earth Star's channeler friend.

Earth Star was a Delaware Indian with healthy doses of German and English ancestry. Slim and attractive, she looked half of her forty-eight years. Her real name was Joyce Elaine Hubbard. She claimed a spectral voice and a follow-up dream had given her the name Earth Star.

She had been married, had once been wealthy—she recalled spending $100,000 in one year—but now she looked at things ''energetically.'' She preferred living out of her van, touching bases with her friends in Florida and around the country, living close to the earth, and asking the universe to provide whatever she needed.

''But if you don't believe [the universe will provide], it won't work,'' she said. ''You can create a thought image, send out that vibration, and that's why intent is so important, because your thought is what manifests physically. Your thought is a vibration that is moving out there.

''But it works both ways—if you can send out good vibes you can also send out bad vibes. We do that real well. We think nasty of our boss and we forget that what we send out we're going to get back tenfold.''

She mentioned that famed medicine man Wallace Black Elk had given her many secret ceremonies, including tribal ways for healing physically or mentally handicapped people. But without pure intent, the power of the Great Spirit would not come during even the most sacred of rituals.

''You know, the in thing now around white society is the vision quest and the sweat lodge,'' Earth Star explained as we drove. ''There are also crystal ceremonies which have been made up by people who are going among white people to make money. The thing is, anything you want to do can be a ritual or ceremony and it'll work, if that's what you want to do.

"If you set up the sweat lodge and you didn't have the tobacco line going in a certain way, it's the intention that the person has doing the ceremony, that's what counts."

This was a realm of energetics largely unknown, or forgotten, in Anglo society, she said. There was the power of sacred objects to even kill if used incorrectly, or with the wrong intent. (During this trip I heard a true story about a medicine man who had been empowered by the thunder beings, but was misusing the power. One night a bolt of lightning came crashing into his house, hit a nail that tacked up a painting, shot through the wall, and killed him as he lay in his bed.)

"Society loved to categorize things, seeking to control them," Earth Star said, frowning. Once she was performing a healing on someone, with eight people gathered around to observe. Each person had a different reaction to the healing. Some called it "polarity balance," "combing the aura," or "laying on of hands."

"I'm hearing all this, but I'm doing *one* thing. Everyone had a different label for it. That's why labels are really difficult to speak, particularly in the English language. But the essence of what you're doing is love. Because love is light which is energy which is God and everything."

She slowed down and stopped to let a wayward dog walk across the country road we were driving. It reminded her of the time she had been driving to a party at night along a rural road in Iowa. Suddenly a deer leaped in front of her and she hit it. Scrambling out of the car in her fancy dress, she held the deer and watched it die in her arms. The only thing she could do was hold it and send it love. She showed up to the party with blood all over her dress, tears streaming down her face.

When we arrived at the home of psychic Cecilia Hoffman, she came out to greet us. She was a tall, handsome woman, who wore an amulet, rings, and bracelets of precious stones. After greeting us, she explained the jewelry she had on were energy stones that helped center and focus her psychic powers.

She invited our little band in to talk metaphysics. As we were settling down in her living room she asked if anyone wanted coffee. A few earnest hands went up, so she excused herself to go to prepare it. While the group plunged into the discussion I followed Cecilia into the kitchen. She prepared the coffee with a care I thought was reserved only for a Japanese tea ceremony.

Cecilia picked up a bag of fresh beans from Mexico and Peru. The Mexican beans paid homage to the ancient Mayan influence, and the Peruvian beans suggested to her the mountains in which many Tibetans had settled. She roasted the beans, then put them on a plate so we could smell the aromatic release of their energy. She then ground them and set a pot of spring water to boil. Once the coffee was prepared and served to the group she sat down for talk.

"I basically ask for the spiritual guides that work with all of us," Cecilia said. She pointed out that to be an effective channel required getting the psychic body in shape. "There has to be something taking place in the person's physical and in other bodies," Cecilia said. "And until that takes place, it [channeling or other psychic feats] could be of a depletion nature, or an unbalancing for that person. You have to bring up the vibratory rate of your body and get it more in alignment with the other bodies that you occupy. Your soul is like a life force, it's a nonmaterial thing."

"The vibratory level of the body is like a buzzing," Earth Star said.

"It can be something like that," Cecilia agreed. "Different people seem to have different sensations, depending on their backgrounds and lifetimes they've had and the way they do their own tuning. But there will be that inner knowing and a lack of fear. I think that's the biggest point.

"The Bible says, 'Many are called but few are chosen.' Well, we're all called but few choose to go, because the responsibility [of spiritual practice and daily meditations] is not convenient and comfortable for a culture that teaches convenience and comfort."

"The truly spiritual person wakes up and says, 'Good morning, God!' " Ted smiled. "The twentieth century hedonist says, 'Good god, morning!' "

Ellen mentioned her Earth change concerns. The doomsday talk went around the circle.

"The vibratory level of the planet is moving up, and unless the physical vibratory rate in people's bodies is up, too, then they'll find it extremely difficult to stay in the body during the onset of the New Age," Cecilia observed.

There was an acknowledgment that a strict practice of regular meditation would help raise the vibratory rates of the spiritual and physical bodies. It would also raise the level of awareness needed for the onset of the New Age and help eliminate, postpone, or diminish the feared Earth changes.

"The Earth changes will come to the degree that we call them forth because of our own spirituality," Cecilia concluded.

"It's like, okay, there's going to be this change, but the timing of it and the intensity of it, we have control over it," Earth Star said.

Then we repaired to another room. One by one we returned to the living room to have Cecilia give us an individual channeling session. During the sessions she sat upright, holding her power stones. She would go into a deep but conscious trance during the session. (She did not demand recompense, but accepted any gifts offered in thanks for her channeling. Jan had a necklace of precious stones she gave to an appreciative Cecilia.)

At the end of the visit I thanked her for her reading. She gave me a copy of a special morning meditation prayer that she said had come from an ancient Atlantean tradition. She told me she would mail me a tape of the meditation recording and the Indian chants that accompanied it.

We drove on to the home of John Standing Eagle, the medicine man leader of the sweat lodge ceremony I would be attending in a few days. Earth Star was going to pick up her pet wolf that she had left with him for a few days while she waited on her van repairs.

She sung the praises of John Standing Eagle for his work as the lodge leader and water pourer. The intensity of the sweat lodge experience made it important to have a strong leader and water pourer. "People hear and see things in the sweat lodge," Earth Star explained. "Little spirits, little energies, little balls of light that bounce around. But the basic idea of the sweat is a unification of spirit and body. You pray for what you came for, so you don't feel the heat. The more you pray, the less you feel the heat."

She described a personal sweat lodge experience in which she saw a vision of two pyramids placed sideways and outlined in gold that became two golden eagles that flew out and touched her. In another sweat lodge vision a beautiful white wolf that had a gold eye and a blue eye appeared to her. When she was in New England sometime later she was presented with the gift of a wolf puppy with a gold and blue eye—the wolf she had dreamed. That dream wolf was the animal we were on our way to pick up.

She mentioned that John Standing Eagle had also been gifted with the power of the sacred pipe by the Great Spirit. He had moved to the countryside to be away from crowds, to live life at a slow pace, to be at one with nature. But trouble had followed him—a waste-burning plant was being scheduled to move in near him.

"It just shows you can't escape," Earth Star said. She hoped that John Standing Eagle would use the power of the pipe to stop the plant from being built.

We arrived at John Standing Eagle's house, nestled in the middle of a forest. Out back, Earth Star's pet wolf was happily bouncing around on the end of a leash tied to a tree. The wolf grinned at us, a twinkle of light shining off the multicolored eyes. As she put the wolf in the van, John Standing Eagle sauntered out of his house.

He was a lean, light-colored man with a moustache. I shook his hand and his eyes looked away from me. He talked awhile before his eyes came up to me. It was as if he circled around things, feeling their energy before opening himself up. I told him I was planning on being at his sweat lodge as few days hence. He nodded and smiled.

After the exchange of a few pleasantries we all waved good-bye to him and drove off.

As we drove I was sorting out in my mind all the talk of energy and guides, power stones and vibratory rates. But most of the anticipation revolved around the ushering in of the New Age. From all the talk it seemed that the near future was a good/bad proposition. The good news was an era of peace and happiness was coming. The bad news was apocalyptic, planet-cleansing disasters would have to be hurdled to get there.

It is time to ponder the end of the world.

15

The End of the World

I was eight or nine years old when I had my first inkling about the end of the world.

I was with my family on a summer vacation trip to Jack London's old estate, now a state park, in the famed Valley of the Moon in Sonoma County, California. It was fun hiking around the ruins of the great writer and adventurer's beloved Wolf House, a dream abode fashioned from lava rock and redwood. The place was legendary: Weeks before London and his wife were to have moved in, the house was destroyed in a mysterious fire. (London himself would pass away three years and three months to the day that his Wolf House burned down.)

Sometime during the trip, I came across a biblical tract tacked to a hotel bulletin board. It was full of Book of Revelation prophecies describing the conquest of the planet by the beast, an evil leader who would put the saints to the sword. A servant of the beast would bring fire from the sky and perform other miracles that would awe the world. The beast would blaspheme God and Jesus Christ, kill anyone who refused to worship him, and brand everyone on the right hand or forehead with the infamous number 666.

God would allow the Antichrist to have his evil ways for a time before retaliating with global plagues and earthquakes. Then God's army would descend from the heavens and utterly destroy the Antichrist and his works.

The rest of the tract, all about the heavenly city being set up on Earth and ushering in the millennium of peace and prosperity, held no solace. It seemed that everyone, and everything good and beautiful, would have long since been destroyed by the time the good guys arrived.

The Second Coming had been promised in the Old Testament:

> For by fire will Yahweh execute judgment, and by his sword, against all mankind. The victims of Yahweh will be many. . . .
>
> "From New Moon to New Moon, from sabbath to sabbath, all mankind will come to bow down in my presence," says Yahweh.
>
> "And on their way out they will see the corpses of men who have rebelled against me. Their worms will not die nor their fire go out; they will be loathsome to all mankind." [Isaiah 66:15–24]

The Judaic/Christian tradition does not have a monopoly on end-of-the-world visions. Tibetans have ancient prophecies that speak of drought, famine, disease, and war sweeping the planet in the end times. Materialism will be rampant and people will have turned away from religion. An evil king will emerge (much as the Antichrist of the Bible) and rule the world. It is then that the hidden land of Shambhala will be revealed, and Rudra Cakrin, the future king of that mystic land, will lead a spiritual army into battle and defeat the evil king.[1]

Of course, one needs not look to ancient spiritual texts to get an inkling that we may indeed be living in the prophesied time of the end. The atmospheric ozone layer is being depleted. It is believed that this damage is already resulting in potentially catastrophic changes in global weather patterns.

The general destruction of the planet by man includes the alarming depletion of such global oxygen sources as the rain forests; the extinction of entire species of plants and animals; continuing pollution of air and water sources; and of course, that old favorite, the possibility of nuclear war.

Some of the most controversial Ramtha communications channeled by JZ Knight concern such so-called Earth changes. During my first meeting with Knight in San Francisco I asked her about the criticisms that Ramtha's doomsday prophecies were not only causing panic in Ramtha circles, but were completely inaccurate. I left feeling Knight had not satisfactorily answered the charges that the Ramtha Earth change talk was bogus.

Some months later Knight sent me a letter with a nineteen-page attachment documenting Ramtha's Earth change predictions. Although Ramtha had discussed acid rain and other problems which have been known for years, there were also predictions made in 1986 that a long drought cycle would deplete America's abundance and even result in ". . . murderers on the street who will rob your cupboards and slay you for only a sliver of bread." (1988 marked the second straight year of hot weather and low rainfall in the Western states, resulting in water rationing in California.)

"I feel a truly enlightened person could not help but be aware of the environment and the changes that are taking place all around us," Knight wrote. "Ramtha perceives us as evolving souls and evolution means change. It would be a duality to say that we are expanding our consciousness without making any changes. Ramtha provided a window at that historical event for us to see what was coming regarding changes in the environment that would affect our social order. He addressed this, Mark, not to create fear but to give us options to make changes in our life. He does not simply pat us on the head and tell us everything is going to be all right. Perhaps what saddens me most is that people are shocked that our world could change even though most of our scientists recognize this and these changes are taking place all around us every single day."

Many spiritual traditions believe the planet itself will restore environmental vitality. The Hopi call the resulting period of volcanic eruptions, earthquakes, and other natural disasters, the ''Day of Purification.''

''I've had visions of the coming planetary cleansing, and it's truly a horrible thing,'' Rolling Thunder has told the *Mother Earth News*.

> Unlike the natural disasters of the past—which involved fire or water—this upheaval will involve both fire *and* water. Cities will be reduced to rubble, and most of the survivors will turn on each other violently. The whole thing will take some time, though: There'll actually be *forty years* of purification, four decades of the earth's vengeance upon those who have harmed it . . . with much destruction and much terror, many storms and many wars.''[2]

Sun Bear explained to me his view of the coming Earth changes. ''The Earth is a powerful living entity itself,'' he observes. ''There's a great intelligence in the Earth and in the powers that are around it, and they are making the necessary changes now in order for the planet to ultimately survive. Man has to be brought down into an understanding of that.

''It's called a cleansing of the Earth Mother. It'll change major areas and a lot of the places that are population centers at this time will no longer be, because people won't be able to survive there anymore.

''I think the cities probably won't be around after a while. The cities are not necessarily natural in their present form. And too much of it is built on man's arrogance, that he can do anything he wants to nature and it's okay.

''[The Earth changes] will be for a period of time, particularly up to the year 2000. You'll see a lot of changes happening, very powerful changes. A lot of the people who've been the smiling heroes of the day will be looked at as deeper and deeper villains for their stupidity and the things they've brought about upon humanity for not making a conscious effort to help humanity, but rather just sucking them dry and running.''

But Sun Bear noted that this time will also have within it the seeds of renewed possibilities. ''Particularly at this time in the Earth, major changes are coming about. As a result the spirits are very open about working with us, and if we're willing to respond to them, that's what their responsibility has been for thousands of years. Right now they're very much working with us because they are seeing that these powerful changes are supposed to happen. Those who are aware of the changes and are in harmony with the spirits, the spirits help them.''

Writer and psychic Ruth Montgomery also agrees that a period of cleansing and chaos will precede the ''new age of enlightenment.'' She shared her perspective with the *New Age Journal* in a 1987 interview. Citing the information given her by spirit guides, Montgomery said,

> The Christ spirit will enter a perfected person within some twenty to thirty years after the earth has restabilized. People's eyes will then be opened to the reality that it is all one world, in different vibratory levels. And as their minds are also opened to contact between those differing vibrations, it will be a wondrous time on earth.
>
> [The guides say] the shift is a very necessary process to cleanse the earth of all pollution and evil people. I have interviewed geologists and scientists who believe they have firm evidence that this happened a number of times in prehistoric days. It's a normal process. That's why the guides say the shift is inevitable. It's a universal law; it happens on other planets, too. . . .
>
> The guides say that millions and millions will survive, and it's going to be a very exciting, wonderful time.[3]

During Sun Bear's Malibu medicine-wheel gathering, there was a point during the consecration of the wheel when individuals placed the sacred stones in the circle. Seneca medicine woman Twylah Nitsch was in the circle, seated in a chair during the consecration. As the ceremony ended and the participants left the circle, she remained seated, nodding as if asleep. Later she reported to the gathering that her spirit guides had come to her in a vision. They had told her that the Earth changes could be prevented or diluted if people began manifesting love and appreciation and sharing those emotions with others.

That is the other side of all the rumblings of destruction of Earth changes: A spiritual renewal could yet reverse the prophecies of future disaster.

After I returned from Florida, I received a letter from Ted Robles, who had some choice comments to make about the Earth change controversy: "For the past several years, otherwise respectable and reputable psychics, sensitives, and seers have been predicting, prognosticating—nay, *demanding* so-called Earth changes, ranging from the relatively minor cracking off and sinking of California west of the San Andreas Fault, to a monumental pole shift with concomitant three-thousand-foot tsunamis and total vulcanism and fault slippage leading to the scouring of the Earth and the extinction of all terrestrial life of a higher degree than that of the cockroach.

"Well, as Sportin' Life sang, 'It Ain't Necessarily So.'

"If one spends all his time worrying about the manner of his death, he will accomplish little in life.

"So, first of all, granted that Earth changes will come. The Earth, not being static, is subject to, and does, change. Second, it is quite likely that in ten thousand years San Francisco will be at the latitude of Seattle. Hopefully people will have become a trifle more intelligent about the choice of their domiciles by that time, if indeed mankind is to remain a dominant life-form on this planet. Even so, it is not necessary that the Earth change be in a catastrophic or overly violent manner; evolution is preferable to revolution any time.

"Therefore, I would admonish everyone that they cease dwelling on the likelihood of calamitous Earth changes; that they live their lives in a manner consonant with soul development as they visualize that at this time. That they recognize God's will, being the sum total of all the wills on this and other planets, *will* be done, and that by asking for calamity they aid in causing it. Therefore, by not asking for it they are at the very least postponing it. Finally, that they give this order to the universe, in exactly these words:

"If there is no reason why any necessary planetary alterations cannot be done without undue damage to the inhabitants thereof, let it be so.

"And let it go. Then, go about your own life, doing what is right as you conceive it to be right, doing no harm to yourself or others, and in general, living as Nature intends you to."

Others are of similar opinion that fears and prophecies of cataclysmic events can be self-defeating as well as self-fulfilling. Publisher Hank Hine remembers that during the global catastrophe talk that preceded the Harmonic Convergence, his friend Frank LePena, a California Indian leader, received many concerned inquiries.

"[LePena] was asked, 'If the world was going to end, would you do anything different?' He said, 'You can't do anything different, don't even concern yourself with the world ending, do what you're supposed to do. What would have happened if our ancestors had stopped doing what they were doing because they thought the world was going to end? Where would you be? There's a certain amount of equanimity—cool it.' "

Psychic Patricia Diegel is certain there will be no calamities. She has already journeyed into the future and seen a future incarnation living and prospering in Sedona. By her calculations, the Harmonic Conver-

gence started in 1981. She notes that just as a recording tape has a clear leader you can't record on but
which brings up the tape, so too will the years 1981 to
2001 be a clear-leader period getting the New Age on
track.

"Whatever we do in this twenty years is going to
set the pattern for the next two thousand years," Diegel says. "That's for us individually and also for the
human race."

Determined to get some final word on all the Earth
change prophecies, I decided to obtain the viewpoint
of some friendly entity. Donna Hale, a young hypnotherapist and channel from San Anselmo, California, came by my home to let the being Methusa speak
on those points.

Donna told me her great dream was to someday scientifically prove the validity of channeling. She described being at a seance in which apparitions had
appeared and responded to her mental commands.
That would be difficult to prove, she admitted.

Another time she was having a series of Kirlian photographs made of her fingerprints when she mentally
asked that Methusa send through an image of herself.
She showed me the sequence of color slides documenting the Kirlian photo session. In the middle of a
succession of colored aura prints was a murky image
she claimed was the spectral face of Methusa.

"Methusa is connected to the angelic forces and
is one of the female deities," Donna observed.
"Methusa says the Goddess energy is coming back,
which is our source of creativity. It started going
underground at the time of Plato as the more male-
dominated Earth religions began coming through.
Methusa is channeling through to inspire, to be part
of the transition to the reawakening of our connection to the Goddess.

"We're all being pointed to our own sense of truth.
This is a big shift. We can't depend on anything outside of us as the Truth, not the president, the pope, or

Ramtha. That is a web of illusion. The illusion has been fantastic, like a fire-breathing dragon.''

Donna then settled in to channel. She described Methusa as projecting the form of an old grandmother. As Donna closed her eyes and began to make the transition to the channeling state her body hunched over, and the Methusa voice began to come through in a soft, slow hiss.

"Good evening, this is Methusa. It is my great pleasure to make of you my acquaintance.''

"Methusa, why are so many beings channeling through to Earth at this time?'' I asked.

"Many of us are clamoring at this time to be heard,'' the entity said. "There is, shall we say, a great need, a receptivity to be assisted, to be given spiritual leadership in the great transition that is taking place on Earth at this time. For those who have desired to evolve there are changes occurring, not only in the mental bodies, but in the perceptive bodies as well. There is an escalation in the energy system of the human being so that it may function and perceive more subtle levels of fields of light, fields of sound, and fields of direct knowing. All of these senses are being heightened so that we may open up our doors of perception to include an awareness of realities and dimensions that exist way beyond this three-dimensional reality.''

"Is this shift unusual, or are such shifts common in human history?'' I inquired.

"We are at a particularly, shall we say, pregnant point in the Earth-generation cycle,'' Methusa responded. "There are cycles occurring for each planet within this galaxy as well as others.

"Now, at this point in time, there are tensions and forces that are building and have been building for perhaps twenty thousand years. There are other cycles of energy that have been building for two thousand years to propel us into a tremendous level of expansion. We are now moving into another phase that will bring the planet into more of a harmonic vibration with other planets. There will be greater lines of communication open to other intelligences. The planet itself is coming to a healing crisis.

"In order for the masses to open to greater capacity it must be forced to let go. The bowels of the Earth contain within it forces that are pushing upon it. We are experiencing unique disasters, distractions, accidents all over the globe. There will be more.

"But we are not to be harbingers of doom and gloom, as we are more so here present considered to be part of the legions of light—illumination to inspire and to remind all those who bide here that the changes that are taking place are for the betterment of mankind. There is nothing truly to be afraid of, if one keeps in mind what we are truly moving toward.

"All of us, spirit and human, have built within us all that we need to know. We have within us a guiding system, shall we say, that will immediately go into action during a time of crisis, during a time when we need to know.

"Some of the guidance that [is] coming is to prepare people by giving them possibilities of probable realities. You see, those that speak more of doom and gloom offer to those that are listening to choose that reality or not. If you notice, some of the predictions that have been made have not taken place. Deep within each of us is the ability to choose yes or no at any moment in time. The collective society of mankind has the ability to alter its course. There is always omnipresent free will."

"But will the predicted disasters come?"

"They are things that can be changed. Within the larger scope, the destiny of this planet, there are certain major probabilities of Earth changes that will take place. The populations of certain areas has its own will to choose whether or not it will be of a certain magnitude, whether it will be in a certain location, but these decisions are made on a very deep soul level.

"There is a battle going on, shall we say, between the forces of darkness and the forces of light.

"The nature of the darkness is the desire to control, simply to have power over, to suppress, to restrict, to limit, the forces of light. For those of limitless harmony and expansion the light seems a bit dim these days and will appear at times to grow dimmer. It will not though, it will not. The Phoenix effect is taking place. The great rebirth.

"The forces of light shall assist and will come to bear, moving people to a whole new level of being, beyond fear. Therefore, we are brought by those of you who are frightened, concerned, need assistance to go through this great period of confusion and chaos, to remind you of the truth of what is truly happening.

"Do not be afraid. Each of you individually have wondrous things occurring in your life, new feelings, new perceptions, new openings. Do not become overwhelmed by what you see on the outside, but stay kindling that wonderful flame within you. Bring to yourself love, good will, friends, good cheer. Stay happy, listen to the forces within you that propel you to one direction or the other, and you will ride this great change out with ease."

"There are so many descriptions of the culmination of these changes," I mentioned. "For example, is Christ physically coming back?"

"The coming of Christ is really a statement of the return to remembering that you are Christ, that you are total understanding, acceptance," Methusa replied. "It is not a being. It is not time for people to hinge all their faith on a particular being and make that being into a deity. That time has passed. You are the deity!"

"Is there a specific year when you see all this coming to pass?"

"It is again, you see, in this dimension of time and space that humanity decides when is the appropriate time, much like a child decides when it is going to give birth. The child will release a hormone within its mother's system initiating the contractions. We as humanity are doing the same.

"Now, we do see a time frame. We see it as being after the year 2000. Perhaps around the first decade or so. It is a probability. It is up to the humanity to decide when it is ready to live without fear, without outside leadership, without illness, without limitation."

"And, assuming these realities in the future do exist and are choices, what will the Earth look like in the year 2020, for example?"

"It will be a place of great respect and harmony. Communication will be more telepathic, more conscious. There will be little, if any, conflict. There will be no disease. If people become ill, or out of balance truly, there will be very select technologies to regain that balance. Surgery as you know it will not exist. There will be no need for it. There will be no need for a monetary system. The planet will be restored to healthful agriculture. The water tables will be cleansed."

"That sounds like drastic change in a very short time."

"It does, indeed."

"How can each of us help bring about that vision?"

"One must look to how they individually envision the perfect planet. That is all. You see, thought is creating reality. Reality can change very, very quickly.

"Perhaps it is best left to the reader to think how they would envision the perfect planet, and to realize that this is a possibility. If you were to give them a specific vision, that, too, would limit subjective reality. No, go for the feeling. It is the feeling. That is the magic that will transform this place. What kind of feeling do you want to experience here on this planet?"

Methusa then mentioned that it was nearing the time to depart. For a moment I remembered Charles Dickens's *Christmas Carol* account in which the visiting spirits could only manifest on Earth for a short time before being inexorably drawn back to their spiritual realm. I asked if the entity had any final words.

"Know that what is occurring is constantly changing," Methusa said. "Listen to yourself more than any outside source for your own truth. The outer form is only a reflection of what we create on a mental plane.''

"I appreciate your coming down and talking to me—I guess you didn't come down, you came through!''

"Oh no, I only came through. I don't go anywhere, you see. I just walk sideways into dimensions. We shall bide you farewell.''

A short time after I had returned from my Florida trip, I received the meditation tape Cecilia Hoffman had promised me. It detailed the prayers and practice for a Diamond Body Meditation Practice. On the tape was the voice of Dhgani Ywallo, a Cherokee woman who described the practice as an invoking of "the guardians of the directions, those angelic beings that guide all people to realizing the mystery as it is.''

The meditation had been passed down through twenty-seven generations, Ywallo explained. The practice had originally been given to the people of Atlantis 100,000 years ago during a visitation by the people from the stars.

Cecilia had told me the meditation was to be performed every morning. Through the practice the vibratory rate of the spiritual and physical layers of the body would be brought into right alignment.

"By calling upon the power of chant, the power of affirmation, the energy of visualization, the mind is brought to stability,'' the voice of Ywallo explained. "One is able to perceive the stream of thought and be in good relation.''

The visualizations involved an opening of chakra and energy points, culminating in imagining seven stars above one's head, "each a gateway to a realm of knowledge, ever more subtle and more refined.'' From the seventh star a radiant beam of light was to be visualized going out to the fifth star, making a stitch through the sixth, and back to the seventh star, repeating three times the elaborate mental embroidery. The stitching continued in the same weaving pattern, moving from the fifth to the third star, then from the third to the first star. Once the tapestry of light had been completed and the force mentally linked with the other already opened energy systems, the seven stars could then descend into the body "till you yourself are the vastness of the open sky," Ywallo concluded.

"One can always come again to that pure mind within, to awakening the heart to the spirit of generosity, through acting in consideration for how it will be for the people seven generations from now," Ywallo noted. "So, you see, your thinking is a sacred trust. Your actions, your deeds, let them be deeds of future good relations with the Earth and the people. Let what you do now bring forth what is good for people."

In one of her dream channelings Marcia Lauck heard a voice speaking to all humanity about the coming Earth changes. The voice proclaimed that the millennium, which had been in preparation for ages, was at hand. It would be an opportunity for humanity to "lift up the light together, and in doing so, transform the Earth." Do not fear, the mysterious voice said, this coming age had been invoked by humanity itself through time. The dreaming was over, the reality was about to begin.

"There is no turning back," said the voice. "Yet who of you knew the full implications of what it meant to cry for wholeness? To know truth? And yet all of you knew it was unalterably your true path, and chose it willingly and surely, however blindly. So it is for humanity now, and those of you who can must sing the song of peace, and light the way home."

16

My Heart Was Made
Glad I Come

It was a warm late afternoon when Ted Robles, Dennis Dort, and I walked across a college campus in St. Petersburg to the sweat lodge ceremony of John Standing Eagle. The lodge was being held in a secluded greenbelt area on the fringe of the campus.

Beyond a forest of trees and tall grasses, we saw an old battered Chevy parked by the edge of a clearing. Once in the clearing itself we saw that the grounds were being prepared for the sundown sweat. Two young men were hard at work putting the final touches on the assembled lodge and cutting branches for the sacred fire. John Standing Eagle was sitting on an old tree stump, whittling some short, thin sticks.

We greeted John Standing Eagle. As was his way, his eyes barely looked up, but he nodded as we sat down in a circle on the grass around him. He was wearing a white cap and soiled white tennis shoes. Suspenders were pulled up over his blue T-shirt across which "old fart" was written in small letters. From one of the front pockets of his jeans a packet of Marlboros were trying to escape.

I had my tape recorder and notebook ready to interview him about his water-pouring talents and his use of the sacred pipe. I asked him if it was a good time to talk. He continued his whittling, but his eyes looked up and met mine. He smiled for a moment before turning his attention back to his whittling. He reached over and picked up another freshly cut stick and began tying the two together in the form of a cross. Ted, Dennis, and I watched in silence. The air had a soft, drowsy feel to it. The two other workers were going about their preparations in silence. Standing Eagle slowly looked up at me again as he laid down the cross and picked up his knife to shave wood scrapings off another thin stick.

"No, don't use your tape recorder," he said.

I asked if it would be all right to take notes. He shook his head and smiled again. "You know, the sweat lodge came to us from the Plains Indian tradition, as a gift to all nations," he said. "The Great Spirit in a vision allowed this.

"Sure, I could talk to you about the sweat lodge. I could talk to you about the sacred pipe. I could tell you stories. But they would be for you, not for anyone else. I'm not a spiritual showman.

"This is sacred. Like going out on a vision quest, where you're in the wilderness without food and water, praying to the Great Spirit. You can die.

"So, sure, I can tell you some things. But they're not to go out of this circle."

So Standing Eagle whittled and tied his sticks together and told us stories about how to approach the Great Spirit, about the pure heart that was needed to make the sacred quest. As he talked, the fire for the sweat stones began flaming and crackling. The sun was dropping lower in the sky, and other sweat lodge people were starting to come down the dirt trail and assemble for the ceremony.

Standing Eagle then took a white, blue, red, and a yellow cloth and affixed one to each of four crosses he had made. He told us the figures would stand for the four directions and all the people of the Earth. They would be placed on the altar mound outside the sweat lodge. That task finished, Standing Eagle excused himself to tend to the sacred fire.

Ted, Dennis, and I were quiet for a few moments. It was relaxing just sitting back and smelling the sweet twilight air coming off the grass. Ted and Dennis both decided to forgo the evening's sweat, but would wait for me and watch for signs of energy from outside the lodge.

Then we heard our names called out. Earth Star had arrived. We all stood up and hugged her in greeting. She had her hair pulled back and was wearing a loose-fitting dress in preparation for the sweating.

A table was set up to hold the food people were bringing for the thanksgiving meal after the ritual.

I thought about the nature of ritual, of ceremony. These rituals had been used for ages to channel through the power of the spiritual forces, to touch the spirit in the land. That urge to shake off the restrictions of flesh and experience realms beyond time and space was the reason for such ceremony.

I thought of my own ritual spot in Chrysalis Canyon. Months before I had come to this spot in Florida, months before traveling the Southwest in search of hand tremblers and medicine men, months before conversations with channels, exorcists, and metaphysicians I had gone to the canyon for my tenth annual trip.

The year had almost slipped away before I made my arrangements with Mike Doran to head out to the canyon. Spring had passed and the heat of summer was on. Although Brian, our usual canyon companion, couldn't join us, Mike's friend Jim Taylor was going to come along. Jim, who had introduced Mike to the spot, had not been to the canyon for almost ten years and was looking forward to his return.

I had decided to make this trip a vision-quest experience. For several days beforehand I had not eaten food, hoping it would make me clear to channel through positive energy.

On the appointed day we made the long drive to the canyon country, drove down the rural road we had driven so often, and parked by the old cattle guard.

We pulled out our backpacks for the long hike in. Mike and Jim had brought bread, meat, cheese, and beer, but I was determined to continue fasting in preparation to pray in the canyon.

We dropped our packs over the first barbed-wire fence and then slid under. After rising and slapping the dust off our jeans, we picked up our packs and slung them on our backs.

"Hey, Vaz, check this out," Mike said.

I walked over and he pointed out a sign advertising acreage for sale. "I tell you, they're getting closer," Mike said with a frown.

Jim and I shrugged. All three of us headed off for the first hill. As we walked, Jim wondered if the waterfall would be happening. Mike shook his head. This far into the summer the whole creek was probably dry as a bleached bone.

As we climbed the hill, Mike pointed out a new dirt road below that hadn't been there before.

At the top of the hill we surveyed the tableland out to the horizon. In the distance was the faithful guide tree and we began hiking in earnest for it. As we came to the next barbed-wire fence Mike pointed out surveyor's sticks that had sprouted since the previous year's canyon trip.

"They're planning on building right up to the canyon's edge," Mike said, pointing to the planted stick as the final, irrefutable proof that the sanctuary of the canyon was being violated.

We were sweating under the hot sun as we continued on. My mouth and throat felt parched, but I thought it would be good for the soul to continue without swigging any of the water we were packing in. I picked up the pace, and was a ways ahead of my friends when I heard an unmistakable sound and turned to see a truck rumbling over a dirt road that crossed in front of me.

About eight young men were sitting in the flatbed, looking at me with passive expressions. I waved and the truck came to a stop. In the cab two other men were seated next to the driver.

"Just what are you doing?" the driver asked me as I peered in.

"We're just hiking into the canyon."

"I know where you're going, I asked what you're doing."

I noticed the rifles in the rifle rack at the back of the cab.

"We're just hiking in to camp for the weekend."

"Well, you can just turn around and hike on out of here."

"But we've come a long way. We've camped out here a lot of times. We'll be no problem."

"Listen, this is private property. We're with a gun club and we've been allowed to go shooting down there. So it's not going to be very pleasant. I'm telling you for the first and last time, turn around and just keep going. Get out of here."

That said, he drove down the dusty road. Mike and Jim came up to me just as they were driving away. They asked me what the conversation had been about and I told them. Jim dropped his heavy pack off his back and made a weary exhalation.

In the distance the truck had stopped. They were watching us and waiting for us to turn around. The three of us stood in the early afternoon stillness, wiping the sweat from our foreheads, making longing looks at the guide tree that was so close.

Mike mentioned that in all his years of hiking to the canyon he had never been turned away. A time or two he had met a few of the cowboys that worked the cattle grazing areas of the table mountain plain, but they had always let him pass. (Much later Mike would come to the conclusion that the supposed gun club members were marijuana farmers who were heading in to harvest a crop they had hidden in the canyon forest.)

We finally turned to head back. I looked out across the guide tree and watched the flight of birds over the canyon. In my mind I could almost hear the explosions of rifle fire. The waste and stupid cruelty of the thought chilled me. I turned back and caught up with Mike and Jim as they made it over the barbed-wire fence and stopped to rest by the spot of the surveyor's sticks.

They were grumbling as Mike reached into one of the packs and pulled out a still cold six-pack. He tossed one to Jim and then offered me one. I shrugged and accepted it.

"Fast—over," I said, popping the top and taking a refreshing gulp. But I didn't feel troubled or disappointed at being turned away. I realized that the pure experience of the canyon was an intrinsic part of me that nobody could touch or violate. In that moment I realized that sacred truth doesn't come solely from a ritual or a special place—it can only be found in the heart. And in my heart the canyon was enshrined as a sacred resource for the spirit.

I remembered that realization as I prepared for Standing Eagle's sweat. The stars were filling the sky as I walked outside the light from the sacred fire and stripped down to my swimming trunks. Over a dozen people were seated around the firelight as Standing Eagle, a towel wrapped around at his waist, stood up, leaned on a shovel, and began telling us about the sacred truth of the sweat lodge.

As he talked, I thought about all the people I would bring into the lodge with me, that I would think about in my prayers. There was my mother and father, brothers and sisters, my cousin Clementina, family, friends, and associates.

I'd also be thinking of Leroy Curtis, praying that he receive the ceremonies the hand trembler had prescribed for him. The seer Ted Silverhand came to mind, as did Grandfather David and the Hopi elders of the Southwest. I thought of Maria Lauck, wondering what incredible dream world she was entering on the other side of the country. Kevin Ryerson, JZ Knight, Loretta Ferrier, the Bowermasters, and some of the other channels I had met were in my thoughts. Chris Griscom and Dr. Bill Baldwin were two brave explorers of the psychic frontier—I mentally invited them to join me as well. I thought of Sun Bear, Cecilia Hoffman, Dennis Dort and the Robles, Patricia and Jon Diegel, and all the other seekers who had shared with me their vision of the spirit in the land. I remembered all the spectral voices that had spoken to me, the voices claiming to have manifest from beyond time and space.

I thought as well of the final, painful vision Black Elk had given John Neihardt when they talked in the 1930s. The great medicine man had seen the death of the sacred tree and the circle of the nation broken and scattered.

But then I recalled Bear Heart's talk at the medicine wheel gathering at Malibu. He had talked of miracles not in the sense of extraordinary physical and spiritual feats, but in terms of the gentle power of the inner smile to forgive the seemingly unforgivable, to bear gratefully the heaviest burden. That was the real, and true, manifestation of the power of the spirit.

Bear Heart had greeted us that day by saying he was happy to be with us, happy to share the ancient ways of his people with other races and religions. "My heart was made glad I come," he had told us.

And then he had told us of his dream. In it the peoples of the world began to live together. They decided to renew and honor the Earth Mother. They began to live lives of such strength and truth that generations after would walk proudly in their footsteps. It is a beautiful dream.

After Standing Eagle had finished talking, he told us to line up by the lodge entrance. He kneeled on the ground and held the flap open for each of us. He told us to get down on all fours and crawl inside, honoring our kinship and brotherhood with the animal world.

I looked over at Ted and Dennis to wave good-bye to them. They were standing in front of the sacred fire, gazing into it, lost in their own thoughts. They didn't see me wave.

I turned my attention back to the lodge and saw Earth Star crawling in. Soon we had all crawled inside.

Standing Eagle had one final thought for us as we entered the lodge.

''Remember, there's no such thing as a mistake in here.''

The sacred stones, the bringers of wisdom from beyond time and space, were brought to the lodge pit, the flap was pulled down, and we were plunged into darkness. . . .

NOTES

Introduction

1. Arrian, *The Campaigns of Alexander* (New York: Penguin, 1971), p. 153.

2. John F. Avedon, *In Exile from the Land of Snows* (New York: Alfred A. Knopf, 1984), Ch. 8.

3. Jerry Stahl, "Channel Hopping," *Playboy,* December 1987, p. 136.

4. John Tierney, "Fleecing the Flock," *Discover,* November 1987, p. 54.

Chapter 1

1. Katherine Martin, "The Voice of Lazaris," *New Realities,* July/August 1987, p. 28.

Chapter 2

1. Joseph Epes Brown, ed., *The Sacred Pipe: Black Elk's Account of the Seven Rites of the Oglala Sioux* (New York: Penguin, 1971), Ch. 3.

2. John Lame Deer and Richard Erdoes, *Lame Deer Seeker of Visions: The Life of a Sioux Medicine Man* (New York: Pocket, 1972), p. 172.

3. John C. Neihardt, *Black Elk Speaks* (New York: Pocket, 1972), p. 230. For more on Wounded Knee: Dee Brown, *Bury My Heart at Wounded Knee* (New York: Bantam, 1972).

4. *Ibid.*, pp. 1-5.

5. Sally Springmeyer, "The Astral Kid and the Spirit Mine," *American West*, March/April 1982, pp. 31-32.

6. Hans Holzer, *Window to the Past: Exploring History Through ESP* (Garden City, N.Y.: Doubleday, 1969), pp. 13-14.

Chapter 3

1. Frank Waters, *Book of the Hopi* (New York: Penquin, 1986), p. 168.

2. *Ibid.*, p. 21.

Chapter 4

1. Richard Colgan, Plowboy Interview, "Rolling Thunder: A Native American Medicine Man," *Mother Earth News*, July/August 1981, p. 18.

Chapter 5

1. Jim Swan, "Sacred Spots," *Yoga Journal*, May/June 1985, p. 38.

2. Dale Champion, "Logging Road Banned from Indian Land," *San Francisco Chronicle*, May 26, 1983, p. 1.

3. Gayle Johansen and Shinan Naom Barclay, *The Sedona Vortex Experience* (Sedona, Ariz.: Sunlight Productions, 1987), p. 5.

Chapter 6

1. Kenneth Grant, "Atavism," in *Man, Myth & Magic* (England: BPC Publishing, 1970), p. 163.

2. R. Crumb, "Jelly Roll Morton's Voodoo Curse," *Raw*, issue 7, 1985, pp. 5-10.

3. Carol McGraw, "Bewitching: Covens of the '80s

Don't Match Lore Stirred by Tales of Halloweens Past,'' *Los Angeles Times*, October 31, 1987, Part 2, p. 1.

4. Dennis Oliver, ''Satanists Suspected in Calf Sacrifices,'' *Daily Review*, November 25, 1987, p. 11.

5. D. Scott Rogo, ''Satanic Abuse?'' *Omni*, October 1987, p. 142.

6. *Mysteries of the Unexplained* (New York: Reader's Digest, 1982), pp. 174-175.

7. Doug Boyd, *Rolling Thunder* (New York: Dell, 1974), p. 197.

8. William J. Baldwin, Clinical depossession material used with the permission of the Center for Human Relations.

Chapter 7

1. Paramahansa Yogananda, *Autobiography of a Yogi* (Lost Angeles: Self-Realization, 1979), pp. 402-404.

2. Pupul Jayakar, *Krishnamurti* (New York: Harper & Row, 1986), p. 46.

3. Jacob Needleman, *The New Religions* (New York: Crossroad, 1984), p. 4.

4. Carl Jung, *Psychology and the East* (Princeton, N.J.: Princeton University Press, 1978), p. 108.

5. Peter Payne, *Martial Arts: The Spiritual Dimension* (New York: Crossroad, 1981), p. 46.

6. Buddhist Text Translation Society, *The Shurangama Sutra, Volume 8* (Talmage; Cal.: Buddhist Text, 1988), p. 10.

7. Ibid., p. 161.

8. *Ibid.*, pp. 84–89.

9. John F. Avedon, *Interview with the Dalai Lama* (New York: Littlebird, 1979), p. 52.

10. Lewis M. Hopfe, *Religions of the World*, 4th ed., (New York: MacMillan, 1983), p. 144.

11. Edwin Bernbaum, *Way to Shambhala* (Garden City, N.Y.: Doubleday Anchor, 1980), p. 123.

12. His Holiness the Dalai Lama, *Concerning the Kalachakra Initiation in America* (Madison, Wis.: Deer Park, 1981), p. 9.

Chapter 8

1. Marcia S. Lauck and Deborah Koff-Chapin, *"At the Pool of Wonder: Dreams and Visions of an Awakening Humanity,"* Unpublished manuscript, (copyright © 1987, selections used with permission.)

Chapter 9

1. Jon D. Miller, "Ignoramus Americanus," *American Demographics;* reprinted in *This World*, magazine of the *San Francisco Examiner/Chronicle*, September 27, 1987, p. 7.

2. Katy Butler, "Sex, Fear Broke Guru's Spell," *San Francisco Chronicle*, November 27, 1987, p. 1.

3. Tierney, *op. cit.*, pp. 50-58.

4. Ronald A. Schwartz, "Sleight of Tongue," in *Paranormal Borderlands of Science*, Kendrick Frazier, ed. (Buffalo, N.Y.: Prometheus, 1981), p. 104.

5. Harry Houdini, *Houdini: A Magician Among the Spirits* (New York: Arno Press, 1972), p. xii. For additional information on the master magician: Melbourne Christopher, *Houdini: A Pictorial Life* (New York: Crowell, 1976).

6. Swami Bhakta Vishita, *Genuine Mediumship of the Invisible Powers* (Jacksonville, Fla.: Yoga Publication Society, 1919), p. 194.

Chapter 10

1. Katherine Lowry, "Channelers," *Omni,* October 1987, p. 50.

2. Joshua Hammer, "On the Trail of the Brain Builders," *California,* December 1987, pp. 58, 63.

3. Marlys Harris, "Shirley's Best Performance," *Money,* September 1987, pp. 169-171.

Chapter 11

1. Edgar D. Mitchell, "Introduction: From Outer Space to Inner Space," in *Psychic Exploration,* John White, ed. (New York: Capricorn, 1976), pp. 25-49.

2. "Signals from Inner Space," *Life,* July 2, 1971, p. 68.

3. Martin Ebon, "A History of Parapsychology," in *Psychic Exploration,* John White, ed., p. 69.

4. *Encyclopaedia Britannica,* ed., s. v. "Pythagoras," p. 802, Volume 18.

5. Robin E. Rider, *The Show of Science* (University of California, Berkeley: The Friends of the Bancroft Library, 1983). Printed at the Arion Press, San Francisco, pp. 9–11.

6. Johann Wolfgang von Goethe, *Faust* (Garden City, N.Y.: Doubleday Anchor, 1963), p. 97.

7. Robert Louis Stevenson, *Dr. Jekyll and Mr. Hyde* (New York: Pocket, 1972), p. 90.

8. Mary Shelley, *Frankenstein* (New York: Bantam, 1977), p. 23.

9. Nandor Fodor, *An Encyclopaedia of Psychic Science* (Secaucus, N.J.: Citadel, 1966), p. 69.

10. *Ibid,* p. 70.

11. Arthur Hastings, "Investigating the Phenomenon

of Channeling," *Noetic Science Review,* Winter 1986, pp. 25-26.

12. William H. Kautz, "Science, Creativity and You," *New Eyes: The Quarterly Newsletter of the Center for Applied Intuition,* Fall 1987, pp. 1-3.

13. Lawrence LeShan, *The Medium, the Mystic, and the Physicist* (New York: Ballantine, 1975), pp. 34-40.

14. R. W. Sperry, "Structure and Significance of the Consciousness Revolution," *The Journal of Mind and Behavior,* Winter 1987, pp. 37-65.

15. Fritjof Capra, *The Tao of Physics* (New York: Bantam, 1977), p. 296.

16. Gary Zukav, *The Dancing Wu Li Masters: An Overview of the New Physics* (New York: Bantam, 1980), p. 280.

17. Findhorn Community, *The Findhorn Garden* (New York: Harper Colophon, 1975), p. 82.

18. *Ibid.,* p. x.

19. Harold Gilliam, "Talking With the Universe," *This World,* November 8, 1987, p. 17.

20. Willis Harman, "Societal Transformation," *Noetic Sciences Review,* Winter 1986, pp. 13-14.

Chapter 12

1. A.R.E. Field Program, *You Can Be Your Own Psychic* (Virginia Beach, Va.: A.R.E. Press, 1987), p. 11.

2. Vishita, *op. cit.,* pp. 180-199.

3. "Spirit Teachings—Intuitive Reality," Taped material, copyright © 1986 Lin David Martin.

Chapter 13

1. Zora Neale Hurston, *The Sanctified Church* (Berkeley, Cal.: Turtle Island Press, 1981), p. 91.

2. Dean Anderson, "Optimal Performers," (Unpublished manuscript, copyright © 1986), Optimal Performance Institute, reprinted with permission, p. 6.

3. Michael Murphy and Rhea A. White, *The Psychic Side of Sports* (Reading, Mass.: Addison-Wesley, 1978), p. 130.

4. Mark Vaz, "On the Psychic Frontier With Michael Murphy," *Yoga Journal*, January/February 1983, p. 20.

5. Franz Lidz, "Duel of Two Minds," *Sports Illustrated*, December 7, 1987, p. 61.

6. New Dimensions Foundation, *World's Beyond: The Everlasting Frontier* (Larry Geis and Fabrice Florin eds., with Peter Beren and Aidan Kelly (Berkeley, Cal.: And/Or Press, 1978), p. 13.

7. Otto Friedrich, "New Age Harmonies," *Time*, December 7, 1987, p. 69.

Chapter 15

1. Bernbaum, *op. cit.*, Ch. 10.

2. Plowboy interview, *op. cit.*, p. 22.

3. Florence Graves, "Searching for the Truth," *New Age Journal*, January/February 1987.

MIND POWER

☐ **THE POWER OF ALPHA THINKING: Miracle of the Mind by Jess Stearn.**
Through his own experiences and the documented accounts of others,
Jess Stearn describes the technique used to control alpha brain waves.
Introduction by Dr. John Balos, Medical Director, Mental Health Unit,
Glendale Adventist Hospital.   (156935—$4.50)

☐ **SELF-MASTERY THROUGH SELF-HYPNOSIS by Dr. Roger Bernhardt and
David Martin.** A practicing psychoanalyst and hypnotherapist clears up
many misconceptions about hypnosis (it is not a form of sleep, but
actually is a state of heightened awareness), and shows how to put it to
use as a therapeutic tool in everyday life.   (159039—$4.50)

☐ **SELF HYPNOTISM: The Technique and Its Use in Daily Living by Leslie
M. LeCron.** Using simple, scientifically proven methods, this guidebook
provides step-by-step solutions to such problems as fears and phobias,
overcoming bad habits, pain and common ailments, and difficulty with
dieting—all through the use of self-suggestion therapy.

(159055—$4.50)

☐ **DAVID ST. CLAIR'S LESSONS IN INSTANT ESP by David St. Clair.** Through
astoundingly simple techniques, discovered and perfected by a recognized
authority on ESP, you can learn how incredibly gifted you are—and put
your gifts to practical and permanent use to enrich and expand your life.
(153782—$3.95)

*Prices slightly higher in Canada

Buy them at your local bookstore or use this convenient coupon for ordering.

NEW AMERICAN LIBRARY
P.O. Box 999, Bergenfield, New Jersey 07621

Please send me the books I have checked above. I am enclosing $_____
(please add $1.00 to this order to cover postage and handling). Send check
or money order—no cash or C.O.D.'s. Prices and numbers are subject to change
without notice.

Name_____

Address_____

City _____ State _____ Zip Code _____

Allow 4-6 weeks for delivery.
This offer is subject to withdrawal without notice.

CREATE YOUR OWN REALITY WITH NEW AGE BOOKS FROM SIGNET!

Enter a world of greater awareness and spiritual growth, and learn all about the fascinating New Age!

Let Signet New Age Books open up a new world of spirituality and wonderment, as they show you how to master the secrets of the Tarot . . . discover the healing powers of crystals . . . uncover the mysteries of the great pyramids . . . experience out-of-body travel and clairvoyance . . . channeling and much more. Look for these exciting New Age titles:

ALIEN ABDUCTIONS, by D. Scott Rogo

SIDNEY OMARR'S DAY-BY-DAY GUIDE FOR 1988, by Sidney Omarr

SIDNEY OMARR'S ASTROLOGICAL GUIDE FOR YOU IN 1988, by Sidney Omarr

THE CRYSTAL HANDBOOK, by Kevin Sullivan

MANY MANSIONS, by Gina Ceramina

TRANSCENDENTAL MEDITATION: *Science of Being and Art of Living,* by Maharishi Mahesh Yogi

MASTERING THE TAROT, by Eden Gray

YOUR MYSTERIOUS POWERS OF ESP, by Harold Sherman

THE SIGNET HANDBOOK OF PARAPSYCHOLOGY, edited by Martin Ebon

MYSTERIOUS PYRAMID POWER, edited by Martin Ebon

THE ALIEN AGENDA, by Clifford Wilson

THE TAROT REVEALED, by Eden Gray

SPIRIT IN THE LAND, by Mark Cotta Vaz

HEALING FROM THE INSIDE OUT, by Sheri Perl

THE TIJUNGA CANYON CONTACTS, by Ann Druffel and D. Scott Rogo